SO MANY LIES

PAUL J. TEAGUE

ALSO BY PAUL J. TEAGUE

No More Secrets

Two Years After

Friends Who Lie

Now You See Her

INVITATION

Join us in celebrating the seventieth birthday of
Tony Harrington
Saturday 2nd – Sunday 10th June
Gather at Singapore Changi Airport (at Toastbox, Terminal
2) 2pm Saturday 2nd June for transfers by boat
Book your own flight (we'll pay you back!)
We've taken care of all transfers and expenses
Prepare for a week of sun, sand, sea and relaxation
See you there,
Tony & Susan
PS It will be lovely to have all the family back together again!

CHAPTER ONE

June 2018: The Island

Ben was shaken out of sleep by the sound of a bird which seemed intent on making the most grating sound possible. According to Mauricio it was a koel. To Ben it was an irritating nuisance. His eyes were stuck shut, gritty and sore from the sand that had lodged in them. He had to force them open. Where the hell was he? This wasn't his house. It wasn't his bed either. In fact, it was more of a mattress than a bed.

His head was aching. It was persistent and painful. He closed his eyes again and tried to work through the events of the previous evening. As it all started to come back to him, so too did the sick feeling deep in his stomach. And the desire to sleep – forever if possible – to avoid the inevitable hellish aftermath.

The koel let out its grating call once again.

'Get lost!' he half shouted, half groaned.

He could hear the sea too, it was close – really close. And voices in the distance. Concerned voices.

He looked around him. He saw that he was in a wooden hut. It seemed familiar – he knew he'd been there before. Beyond the open window he could see lush green foliage gently swaying in the morning breeze, behind it the bright blue sky.

Where was the baby? Was the baby safe?

She has a name, you know. She's called Harper.

Ben heard Laura's chiding voice in his head. He knew he should call his daughter by her name, but a part of him – the part that had thought he'd be retiring in a couple of years and living a life of relative leisure – that part of him still couldn't accept that he'd be saddled with a third child until he was in his mid-sixties. He'd be 66 years old when Harper left home. He'd only just got there with Ted and Alice. He should have been jettisoning responsibilities, not adding to them. Yet, there he was, with a young wife and new baby. Not a wife – a girlfriend or partner? He still wasn't sure how to refer to Laura. When he and Diana became a couple, they'd done things the good old-fashioned way – albeit they had moved in together at first, much to the disapproval of their parents. They lived together for a couple of years before getting married then having the kids. That's how they did it in the old days. Not quite the way the Bible intended, but close enough.

With Laura ... Well, he wasn't even officially separated from Diana when she dropped the bombshell on him. Maybe the headache Ben was experiencing was just another day in his screwed-up life, the throbbing in his head simply a symptom of the mess he'd got himself into.

The koel squawked one more time, tilting its head to

one side as if to make sure that it had had the desired effect, then flew away to perch on a distant palm tree.

'Thank God for that!' Ben said aloud. His voice was hoarse and weak. He could hear voices again, they were drifting in and out, he wasn't certain they were even real. He was fully clothed, he hadn't realised that when he woke. He still had his shoes on. Too exhausted to move, he lay on his back gazing out of the window.

He tried to re-trace the events of the night before. It had begun politely enough. In fact, it had looked like they might get through the evening without it all becoming a mess. But that was too much to hope for. When the Harringtons got together, nothing was ever simple. It was coming back to him now. Steve and Kiki – what a couple of stuck-up, pompous pricks. And Mina, fancy waiting until your grandad's seventieth birthday to make that announcement. The little cow. It could have waited. She must have known the impact it would have.

Then there was Gaby. God, Ben wanted to love Gaby, she was his kid sister after all. But she was so self-righteous and whenever the wine began to flow she'd glide into ferocious rants about the husband who'd abandoned her with her spoiled horror of a child or, even worse, she'd start singing. Ben cared for Gaby and he felt sorry for her. He of all people knew what the impact was when a feckless man left the family home and abandoned some poor woman to cope with the kids on their own. He was that man. It was his gift to his own children – Ted and Alice would forever have their view of what a father is shaped by his treacherous abandonment of their mother. Nice one, Ben. What a legacy.

And he'd forgotten the cherry on the cake. Richard. Richard's presence had been a problem from the start. And that punch from Tony. No wonder it had all gone to pot so fast. Their get-together had been doomed right from the start.

Ben could only piece together snippets of the night before, his mind was so hazy. He remembered Alice leaving. She'd had to wear her callipers that night, he could have cried for her. She looked stunning, he was so proud of his young daughter. She'd worn the most beautiful floral dress and pushed her hair up.

'It's only from a charity shop,' she'd smiled when he complimented her on how wonderful she looked.

She'd always have to wear those callipers, the shackles which prevented her from living the life he'd always dreamed of for his kids. He loved Alice with every bit of his heart. Even after all these years, he still blamed himself for the life they'd given her.

Ben was coming round now. His senses were kicking into life. Outside the air was fresh and invigorating. The morning sun was shining. The birds were chattering in the distance as if they'd just arrived for work and were catching up with the latest gossip.

His clothes were soaked with sweat. Cautiously he turned over, peeling his top away from his skin as he did so. He turned around awkwardly, he was sore all over. Resting his weight on his elbow, he twisted round to get a better view of the other side of the hut. On the bed was some wet clothing. It was drenched with sea water, he could smell it now. That was Alice's dress, the one she'd been wearing the night before. There was no sign of Alice, his beautiful Alice. But there on the floor, as if discarded in a fight, a kitchen knife sat in a pool of blood. He jumped up, ignoring the sharp pain in his groin.

He could picture it clearly now. They hadn't been able

to find the knife at the party. Tony had never got as far as cutting the cake.

Ben dropped back down on the bed, drifting out of consciousness.

As his world grew dark once again, all he could think of were the horrors of the night before.

'Oh my God. What have we done? What the hell have we done?'

CHAPTER TWO

April 2018: Six Weeks Before The Party

'Oh, for heaven's sake, not again!'

Laura wasn't the only one who'd had enough of Harper's colicky cries. Ben was at his wits' end. Alice and Ted had never been this much trouble. Or maybe he'd just left it to Diana. Men could get away with much more back then.

'It's your turn,' she mumbled, turning over, her back to him. He was no body language expert, but using his finely tuned skills of intuition, he interpreted that as a *Bugger off, I'm going back to sleep. You deal with the baby.*

That was another thing that had changed since he was a young man. The midwife had taunted them with a seemingly endless stream of 'breast is best' reminders when Ted was born. Diana was recovering from an emergency caesarean and an infected wound. They'd been struggling helplessly with latching on and she'd become increasingly frustrated. It had all been too much for her, and they eventually ordered the man out of the house and tried the baby on bottled milk. Like a spiteful brat who'd relished taunting his poor old mum for two whole weeks after the birth, Ted had guzzled a full bottle of artificial milk as if it was what nature had intended for babies all along.

'He's a male midwife. What the hell could he possibly know about what I'm going through?'

She'd been angry. Ben had just wanted some semblance of peace back. The baby was unhappy and barely feeding. The midwife was a nuisance, forcing the breast-feeding issue without, it seemed, a care for the mental wellbeing of the mother. And the baby was just plain stubborn. Ted would not feed from the breast, it was as if he was repulsed by the very thought of it.

In an act of desperation, Ben had taken a secret drive out to the supermarket to buy a box of baby milk and a pack of three small bottles, along with some sterilising tablets. He remembered it well. The supermarket had only just started late opening at the time – when it had been reported in the news, he'd scoffed at the idea.

'Who the heck wants to go shopping at ten o' clock on a Saturday night?'

He'd answered his own question. Tired fathers with babies who show no appreciation for the 'breast is best' mantra, that's who.

He'd scurried off in the car, leaving Diana upstairs pleading with the baby to feed. He'd gone out on the pretence of going to buy more cabbage leaves to stuff down her maternity bra. They'd heard about it at their childbirth class. It was supposed to help with engorgement, brought on by an awkward baby who wouldn't feed.

When Ben got home, he shouted upstairs to let Diana know he was back. He went directly into the kitchen, boiled up a saucepan of water, dropped in a sterilising tablet and cleaned the three bottles. Carefully measuring out the powdered milk, like a scientist in a laboratory, he mixed what would be the first of hundreds of bottles of baby milk that he would prepare for his first two children.

Guiltily, he read the list of ingredients on the box. He tried to ignore the adenosine-5-monophosphate, inosine-5-monophosphate sodium salt, nicotinamide and numerous other chemistry lesson ingredients, focusing instead on the vegetable oils, lactose, vitamin C and fish oil. Fish oil increases intelligence, he reassured himself as he ran the newly prepared bottle of milk under the cold tap to bring it down to a temperature that would be safe for the baby.

When he walked into the bedroom, Diana was exactly where he'd left her. Her eyes were red, she'd been crying and was trying to conceal it from him.

'Any luck?' he asked, knowing what the answer would be.

'He's just not interested,' she replied, the tears starting again. She looked exhausted – she'd found the caesarean challenging to say the least.

'Look, I know you didn't want to do this but I got some bottled milk. Why don't we try it? If he rejects it, we'll go back to what the midwife said. If he likes it ... well, he's made his own choice.'

Diana didn't look keen.

'I know I can do this. If we keep working at it I'm sure we'll get the hang of it.'

Ben knew she was desperate to breastfeed, but with his privileged position of male detachment, he could see they needed to try something else. It was as much motivated by his own desire to create some sense of normality as it was concern for Diana's welfare.

'Let's try it just this once. If he takes it, it'll give you both a break.'

Diana nodded. She needed the decision for this to come from him.

Ben carefully took Ted in his arms and gently moved the teat of the bottle over his lips. His eyes were closed, he'd worn himself out fussing about with Diana's sore nipples. Without even bothering to open his eyes, he pulled the synthetic teat deep into his mouth and proceeded to drink the lot. He announced that he'd had enough with a loud burp, sicking half of it up on Ben's shirt.

'I think he just told us what he wants,' Diana sighed.

You awkward little devil, Ben had said to himself. He wasn't having to cope with the cocktail of hormones, self-doubt and physical pain that his wife was enduring.

Eighteen years later, Laura had experienced no such problems with Harper. The baby had latched straight on to her breast and had been happy to take the bottle too. That meant there was no hiding for Ben. He had to take his turn with the night-time feeds. He didn't mind that too much – he'd done the same with Ted after that first night with the bottled milk. When Alice came along Diana had another quick try on the breast but soon decided that what had worked for Ted would work for his little sister. After all, whatever the midwife's warnings, Ted had grown into a healthy toddler who seemed none the worse for being fed from a bottle.

Another thing that had changed since Ben had the first two kids was the fact that you could now entertain yourself while feeding the baby. He sat up in bed next to Laura, holding his phone in his left hand while nestling tiny Harper in the crook of his elbow; in his right hand he positioned the bottle. It was the very picture of the modern father, simultaneously bonding with his child and checking out the latest Facebook updates. At least Harper got to keep her eyes closed while she lazily sucked at the milk. Ben had to stay awake so he could return her to her crib after the feed. Looking at his phone kept him alert.

He dimmed the screen so as not to disturb Laura. The next day was Saturday. If he was lucky Harper would oblige them by sleeping through until nine o' clock.

There were two Facebook notifications and five new emails. Ben went for the emails first. Four of them were trying to sell him junk that he didn't need or want. The other caught his attention immediately. It was the distinctive capital letters announcing the senders' names and the rare sighting of a Hotmail address that made him sit up.

Laura sensed it and stirred in bed.

'Everything alright?'

'Yes, she's fine. Go back to sleep.'

The message was from his mum and dad. TONY AND SUSAN HARRINGTON the email header announced. Ben and Steve had told them a hundred times to lose the capital letters. It's like shouting on the internet, Dad. It's bad practice to use all capital letters in emails, they'd said. Ted and Alice found it hilarious. It was just one more thing that made the skills of the older generation feel a million miles apart from those of the youngsters. The kids simply didn't get why Nanny and Grandad hadn't got a clue about this stuff. It counted for nothing that they'd lived through the Cold War and several incompetent British governments.

Ben clicked on the email. He hadn't heard from his mum and dad for ages. Things had been a bit tense since he left Diana and the kids. Steve said they were touring in the States to promote her new book. Lucky things, they always seemed to be somewhere hotter than the UK.

It would be terrible if he forgot his dad's seventieth birthday. Gaby was usually the one who reminded them about these things, but even she seemed to have missed it. Or maybe she was still doing her bitter and twisted thing about him getting together with Laura. Perhaps she was going to drop him in it with his mum and dad.

'Well I'm blowed!' he said out loud, forgetting that he was supposed to be in stealth mode.

Harper, jolted out of her sleeping state, pushed the teat of the bottle out of her mouth and began crying. Laura was immediately alert and turned around grumpily, looking at Ben with no attempt to hide how she was feeling about being woken up.

'It's an email from my mum and dad. They're having a seventieth birthday party for my dad in June.'

'Is that what you woke me up for? Well, at least I'll get to meet them at last. Perhaps I can convince them I'm not the marriage-wrecking whore they all think I am.'

'They don't think that,' Ben tried to reassure her once again. 'It's just that we haven't been together that long and ... well, it was a bit of a surprise for everybody at the time.'

'So, what's the big deal?' Laura snapped at him. 'Here, give her to me!'

Ben did as he was told. Even though he was quite capable of settling Harper, he bowed to Laura's territorial rights. At least it freed up his hand so he could read the email properly.

'Damn, this is going to be a problem.'

'What is?'

'We're supposed to fly out to Malaysia – they're putting us all up on some island for the week. Mum must be making a fortune from those books of hers.'

'Sounds good to me,' Laura snapped again. 'What's to worry about?'

She did that a lot. Sometimes he wasn't sure why they were together. She appeared to find him perpetually annoying.

'We've got to pay for the flights upfront. The credit cards are up to their limit and I have a maintenance payment to make by the end of this month. They're promising to reimburse us later, but how on earth are we going to manage in the meantime?'

'For heaven's sake, Ben. Man up and tell that wife of yours to get a job. That way you can spend your money on your new child and pay your way properly. Now, take Harper off me and put her back to bed, will you? I'm knack- ered. I want to go back to sleep.'

He took the baby from her and she rolled over, her back to him like an impregnable fortress. He put all thoughts of a Saturday morning sleep-in out of his mind and started trying to figure out how they could attend the seventieth birthday without having to admit the truth to his family.

CHAPTER THREE

April 2018: Six Weeks Before The Party

Ben skipped the filter coffee out of laziness, heading instead for the instant. He heaped three teaspoons of coffee into the cup and poured out the water from the kettle. He'd drink it black. As he'd predicted, Laura was playing dead upstairs in bed. Harper had honoured her part of the deal by staying asleep, but when he'd foolishly attempted to slip his hand up Laura's nightshirt to run it up her leg, she'd brushed him away and mumbled that she was tired and just wanted to sleep. Harper wouldn't stay asleep forever and he wasn't so stupid that he was going to waste this precious free time dozing in bed.

The post slammed through the letterbox. Before taking his first sip of coffee, Ben walked over to the front door to see what they'd been sent. He'd thought his days of living in a small terraced house were over. It was twenty years since his front door had opened into his living room, but that was how life was now. He and Laura had rented this place just before the baby came, leaving Diana and the kids in their spacious detached house. The one with a garden. The one with a hallway, which meant your front room didn't open directly into the street. What had he been thinking of? And now here he was, in the outer orbit of his fiftieth birthday and living like a newly-wed again. Only there had been no heady days of falling in love, courting and getting married. Instead, he'd been frustrated with Diana, angry about Alice's hunt for a place at university, and annoyed with Ted. And he'd done the most stupid thing a middle-aged man can possibly do. He'd got a young fling pregnant and now he was damned if he left her to it and damned if he left his family. He was almost fifty and screwed. He was out of options. It would have helped if he'd been madly in love with his new and younger partner. Instead, he was still in love with a wife who despised him, while his children resented him and his girlfriend only tolerated him because he could just about manage to support them all.

And now, here was Steve on Facebook wanting to message him. Ben blew on his coffee to cool it down. He decided to check the post first. He'd get agitated if he spoke to Steve. Super Steve. Successful Steve. Sanctimonious Steve. He loved his older sibling, but he also resented him: his effortless life, perfect marriage and high-achieving kids. They were like the adverts you see on TV, all of them perfect. He'd got a lot of crap going on in his life. Sometimes he wished he could have a taste of Steve's world. A tiny bit of his money would help.

The post was mainly rubbish. Ten percent off pizzas at the local takeaway. Twenty-five percent off double-glazing. Ben hadn't seen a double-glazing ad for some time. He was surprised they were still at it. There was a red letter from the mortgage company and the latest credit card bill. Two weeks until payday, £10.27 credit remaining on the Mastercard and £300 still to pay on Diana's mortgage. Then it would all start over again, with the rent on the terraced house due on the first of the month. And now this airfare to pay. It was his dad's seventieth birthday – there was no getting out of it.

Ben decided to see what Steve wanted. He was always offering to help. But how could he take handouts from his elder, slimmer and infinitely more successful sibling? Ben was too busy trying to paper over the cracks in his life. He would never admit to Steve just how desperate things were getting.

Hey bruv, how's things?

Jesus, he thinks he's a rapper now.

Got your invite yet? I take it you're going?

Ben saw the green icon indicating that Steve was online. He decided to bite the bullet.

You there, Steve? Yes, bit of a surprise getting the invitation. I didn't realise it was Dad's seventieth. Guess we can't say no.

Ben was reaching a bit with his last sentence. He knew that Gaby was struggling financially too. Maybe they'd be able to convince their mum and dad to hold it in the UK. He could blame it on Harper being so young.

Steve began typing his reply straightaway, and then Ben noticed that he'd stopped. The distinctive call tone of Skype began to sound through his laptop. Ben had a quick look around, seeking the best angle to do a video call. Steve hadn't seen the terraced house yet. He didn't need to know that Ben had fallen on hard times. Not yet, anyway.

'Hey Ben, how are you doing?'

'All good, Steve. How about you and the kids?'

Steve looked perfectly groomed, toned and handsome. Even his hair had retained its colour, though he was almost two years older than Ben. Ben's hair had gone greyer since the baby had arrived.

'It's all going great.'

Of course it is. Sometimes Ben hated how bitter he was becoming.

'Mina just passed her Grade 7 in piano and Henry was accepted on the county rugby team. A couple of stars, both of them. How about you?'

My life has turned to shit. My wife hates me, my daughter is having a terrible time with her disability and my son is playing up at home because his dad is a piece of trash who left him just when a young lad needs a stable father figure in his life. Oh, and I've got a baby who I love but never really wanted and a girlfriend – partner – lover – whatever she is – who doesn't seem to like me very much. And I forgot to tell you, I'm about to go under financially too. Bruv.

'All fine at this end.'

'So, what do you think about the family gathering? That should be quite an occasion. Will you bring Lara along?'

'It's Laura,' Ben corrected him. Not for the first time either. 'Yes, it seems a bit ambitious asking us all to head out to Singapore, don't you think?'

'Not at all. It's a great idea. It's Dad's seventieth. You've got to push the boat out a bit when you get to that age. Kiki and I are already planning our fiftieth birthdays – we thought we'd get everybody together in New York for our celebration. It's our 25th anniversary year too. And it's—'

He stopped short. He was going to say, 'And it's your and Diana's 25th wedding anniversary too. We could have had a joint celebration.' Ben filled in the pieces of the unfinished sentence for himself. He and Diana had done so well. When they'd found out why Alice was having problems as a toddler it had put them under a lot of pressure, but they'd worked through all that and they'd been strong for a long time. Then he'd screwed it all up.

Steve changed the subject. He was always on safe ground when he discussed money.

'You okay with the airfare? I'm happy to help if you need cash flow. I know how things must be with the baby and all that.'

Ben wished he could accept a sincere offer graciously. He honestly believed that Steve meant nothing by it, yet the offers of money always stuck in his craw.

'No, it's fine thanks, Steve. I'm good. Besides, they're footing the bill for everybody and you can't say fairer than that.'

'Yes, it'll be great. It's ages since we were all together. Is Gaby going?'

'Gaby doesn't talk to me much these days. You know how it is. I think she uses what I did to Diana to vent her spleen about Nigel leaving her. I'm the fall guy for Gaby's hang-ups. So, in a word, no. I don't know if she's going. I see no reason why not though, do you? If Mum and Dad are paying.'

There was a moment of silence. Both men were taking a breath before proceeding with the next step. It was always the same with the family. You started at the top with the eldest, Steve, and down to the bottom – the youngest – via Ben and Gaby.

Steve broke the silence first.

'And what about Richard. Do you think he'll dare show his face?'

Ben pictured their younger brother as he'd looked the

last time he'd seen him. He was the black sheep of the family, his presence always created tension.

'Yes, Steve. I'd put money on Richard being there, even though things will be difficult. You know Richard. If there's an opportunity to protest his innocence, he'll turn up, just like a bad penny.'

CHAPTER FOUR

1979: The First Lie

'Dammit Tony, this is the last thing we need right now.'

'I know, I'm sorry. But they're kids, they're bound to get into trouble from time to time.'

'But this, Tony, this! This isn't scrumping apples or playing knock and run. This is burglary! There are just too many things at stake here. It feels like everything we've worked towards is on a knife edge.'

She turned her attention to the child standing in front of her.

'For God's sake, Steve. You're nine years old. You should be able to do up your own tie.'

'I don't want to go, Mum. I want to stay at St Cuthbert's with Jed.'

'This school will be much better for you. And the sooner you're rid of Jed the better. He's a bad influence on you. We'd never be in this trouble if it wasn't for that boy.'

Steve moved his tie around as if it was some alien object

he'd never seen before. Tony reached over to straighten it for him, then adjusted his jacket.

'You look good, Steve. You'll blow them away!'

He mumbled something and was saved from having to say anything more by Ben stepping into the room.

'Dad, I can't manage this tie. It won't clip on. Can you help?'

'What's that in your hair?' Susan said sharply. 'What have you been doing up there?'

'It's just talcum powder. Gaby said we should put it on to make us smell nice—'

'Jesus, Ben. Do you have to make this mess every time we're in a hurry? Sort out these two, Tony. I'm going to see what Gaby's been doing upstairs.'

Tony winked at the boys.

'Don't worry, she's just stressed out because her book is about to be published. She's not mad at you.'

'She seemed pretty cross after those policemen came to the house, Dad.'

'Well, can you blame either of us? I mean, really boys, you know better than that, don't you? You could land yourselves in serious trouble.'

Ben and Steve looked chastened.

'It was Jed who suggested it,' said Steve. 'He said they always leave the top window open when they're away during the week and we could climb up that drainpipe and have a look around. He said they had dirty magazines under the bed. We didn't mean to steal anything.'

'I know, I know. Don't worry about it. Dad's got a plan. Look, get your hair combed, your shoes on and wait by the door. Let's try and get Mum calmed down.'

There was shouting from the top of the stairs.

'Bloody hell, Gaby. Look at the mess you've made! Get

the boys in the car, Tony – I'm going to have to give her a quick shower. She'll have to go in her old dress. This one is ruined.'

They were in the headmaster's office within the half hour. Susan could still smell the talcum powder in Gaby's hair as she held her tightly on her lap and smiled sweetly at Mr Hodges B.Ed. (Hons).

'All you've got to do is sit quietly while Steve, Dad and I talk to the man,' she'd warned them. 'If you behave, we'll go out for a Wimpy burger afterwards. Deal?'

'Deal!' they'd all shouted, excited at the prospect of eating some food which didn't come with peas and carrots.

The kids were as good as their word. Gaby's only offence was picking her nose, but Mr Hodges was quick to correct her. Tony and Susan had expected nothing less from the headmaster of the most prestigious private school in the area. If they could just get Steve his place there, they'd be on their way: influential local businessman and his wife, a soon-to-be published author. Tony and Susan Harrington were on their way up in the world and nothing could stop them now.

'Well, everything looks to be present and correct, Mr and Mrs Harrington, and just to confirm, you did say that you'd be able to leave your generous donation with the school today, didn't you?'

Tony reached for his inner pocket, but Mr Hodges held up his hand to indicate that he could not preside over anything as distasteful as accepting a cheque in his own grubby little hands.

'Miss Avery will be happy to assist with that matter on your way out, but thank you very much for your support.'

He looked uncomfortable for a moment, and it was clear that he was about to address the topic that had been lingering in the room like a foul stench. Not even Gaby's talcum powder could conceal it.

'There is the small matter of ... of the police. You understand that it wouldn't be possible for us to admit a new pupil with an ... er ... a record of criminality. You do understand, I hope. Is it in hand?'

Tony and Susan exchanged glances. They'd prepped for this. Tony took the cheque out of his pocket, as if he was preparing to leave the room and drop it off with Miss Avery as instructed. However, he made sure the amount was clearly in view of Mr Hodges. Five thousand pounds. Tony had been creative in finding the money – he didn't want it to show up in the accounts. It had the desired effect on the headmaster, who darted his eyes to the side to peek at it. His face flushed. He'd already worked out that it would pay a teaching salary for a whole year. Suddenly he felt compelled to overlook the matter with the police, if the Harringtons were somehow able to deal with it.

'Don't worry,' Tony reassured him. 'Ben and Steve are good lads, they wouldn't steal anything from a neighbour's house. It was that other boy from the local estate who was to blame. It's only a matter of time. The police will drop the case well before the new term begins.'

Hands were shaken, the Harringtons were dismissed, and Mr Hodges removed himself from the outer office before Miss Avery did his dirty work for him and snatched the cheque from their hands. He closed the heavy oak door of his office, no doubt to attend to the school budget and factor in an extra teacher in next term's staffing. It never ceased to amaze him just how generous some parents could be.

The Harrington children were rewarded with their Wimpy meal, as promised, and it was agreed by all that they'd done an excellent job of passing as the type of family any headmaster with a B.Ed. (Hons) after his name would want in his private school.

As they arrived home, tired but pleased with themselves, they saw a police car waiting on the drive.

'Oh, for heaven's sake!' Susan cursed as she saw the officer step out of the car.

Tony was on to it immediately, welcoming the man into the house and offering him a cup of coffee.

'Kids, go upstairs and get ready for baths. Steve, help your sister ... and keep her away from that talcum powder!'

'Can I stay, Mum?' Steve asked, his face white.

'No, go upstairs. I think the officer wants to speak to us alone.'

Steve did as he was told.

'So, officer,' Tony said. 'Where are we up to?'

'It's good news, I'm pleased to say.'

'Really?' Susan sounded surprised.

'Yes, it's a complete turnaround. Your neighbour came into the police station this afternoon and told us that he'd been mistaken. He'd only seen the one boy running away from his property. He identified that child as Jed Staples, your son's friend.'

'What did the Staples family say?' Tony asked.

'Well, after an anonymous tip-off this afternoon, Jed Staples' teacher found silverware matching the description of the items stolen wrapped in a cloth in his desk drawer. Staples has been caught red-handed and your boys are completely in the clear. The owner of the property has confirmed that all stolen items have now been returned to him.'

Susan released a long breath, as if she'd been holding

the air in ever since it had first been revealed that her boys were implicated in the amateur burglary.

'Thank goodness for that.'

'I do apologise for the discomfort this will have caused you and I wish you and your family well.'

He stood up to shake hands with Tony and Susan. As he did so, Tony saw Ben peeping around the side of the door frame. He waved him away and Ben ducked into the kitchen while the police officer was shown out of the front door.

'What a relief!' Susan cried as soon as the door closed behind him. 'The nightmare's over. I *thought* Jed would be to blame and look how it's all come right in the end. What a day! And that will be Steve's place assured at the school, too.'

'Dad—'

'Just one moment, Ben. Let your mum finish speaking.'

'It's okay. I'll go and make sure that Gaby hasn't got into any trouble upstairs. I'll tell Steve too. He'll be delighted.'

'Dad—'

'Just a second, Ben.'

Tony looked at him, as if ordering a dog to stay put until he gave the command to move.

'What is it?' he asked, once Susan was safely up the stairs and talking to the other two children.

Ben took two silver spoons from his pocket.

'I thought I'd better tell you the truth, Dad. We did steal that stuff. It was Steve who told us to. Jed had nothing to do with it. He didn't even climb into the house. We just don't like the man who lives there and we wanted to teach him a lesson.'

CHAPTER FIVE

April 2018: Six Weeks Before The Party

It wasn't quite the morning that Ben would have wanted, but it was long overdue, and it had to be done: doctor, solicitor and bank – in that order, each one a torment. He knew Laura suspected that he was up to something – and he was – but he couldn't find the will to tell her. As he nursed his coffee, he thought about why that was. And he was surprised at the conclusion. He was embarrassed, that was the emotion he felt. At the age of 47 he was humiliated to be in such a financial fix and he was ashamed that he'd let his marriage and family slip away like that, too.

Ben looked around the coffee shop and surveyed its early morning occupants. Most were on their way to work, as he would have been if he hadn't taken a day off to sort out his life. He had a choice of five coffee shops to choose from in the city centre and he'd gone for the one that paid its taxes. He tried to be ethical like that whenever he could. He wondered what had caused humanity to require that a coffee outlet is placed at half mile intervals wherever you happen to be in the country. Petrol stations, newsagents, libraries – they all had the branded coffee outlets. If only having a doctor's surgery that could fit you in for a convenient appointment was so available, he might have held out more hope for society.

The coffee was just what he needed. He'd had to take an 8.50 a.m. appointment with a doctor he didn't even know. It was that or wait another two weeks to see somebody. It had got to the stage that he was grateful when the surgery could fit him in within the next ten days.

'Is it urgent?' the receptionist had barked.

He'd mumbled something, aware that he was surrounded by coughing and ill-looking people. The chances of his getting out of that surgery reception without some deadly infection had seemed minimal.

'So, is it?'

It wasn't urgent in the scheme of things, but it was important to him. And he didn't really want to say it out loud to a woman who was not medically qualified. Sure, she'd probably applied a few sticking plasters to the knees of her kids, perhaps administered baby medicine on some occasions, but she hardly seemed to be in a position to deliver triage services. And he didn't want to announce to everybody that he wanted to ask about a vasectomy – not in an open surgery.

He wished he'd had it done after Alice was born. Steve had had one. He'd gone private, of course – no embarrassing appointments for Steve – and it had gone like a dream.

'Nothing to it, Ben,' he'd boasted. 'I was back on the squash court in no time. Kiki says she barely noticed an interruption in service. You should have one. Men of our age are done with babies.'

Ben had thought he was done with babies too. He should have listened to Steve. Diana had had a hysterectomy after Alice was born, so he'd managed to cheat the mid-life snip, but it seemed there wasn't a man over 45 who hadn't had it done. He'd never thought he might end up in a different relationship – that's what came of working through his unhappiness with a woman who was so much younger than him. Their biological clocks were misaligned and while everything in his middle-aged body was telling him it was time to wind down, everything in her body was screaming that if she didn't have a baby now, she probably never would.

Ben wondered what had brought his fellow coffee drinkers there so early in the morning. He had left home at the normal time so as not to arouse suspicion, a lurker killing time before an appointment. Several people were postponing the inevitable and hanging out a hot drink until the last moment when they would have to go in to work. A couple carrying sports bags had just come back from the gym. Others were in and out in as short a time as possible, rushing to get a decent coffee to take into the office. Perhaps there was only instant in the staff kitchen. He looked at his phone. It was almost time. He took faster swigs of his drink – it had cost so much, he didn't want any of it to go to waste.

Steve had unsettled him on their Skype call the previous day. Ben had stopped thinking about Richard some time ago, preoccupied by his own baggage in life. It had been so long since he'd seen his youngest sibling. The poor guy, he'd always had a hard time of it with their mum and dad. He felt a pang of guilt. Richard had always been on the margins. He, Steve and Gaby had been such a strong unit when Richard had arrived – a surprise to all of them. He'd never quite fitted in. He wondered if Tony and Susan would even want their youngest son at the birthday. Surely they wouldn't exclude him – in spite of what he'd done?

It was time to go. He didn't want to miss this precious appointment. There would be queues of sick people ready to take his place. Besides, if he missed it he might have a second child with Laura by the time they managed to offer him a new slot at the surgery.

He entered the packed waiting room feeling like an extra on the set of *The Walking Dead*. He shuddered to think he might ever be afflicted with anything serious, anything life-changing. Then he felt a surge of heat through his body. Alice. He scolded himself for not thinking of her. Once again he was overwhelmed by the guilt of having abandoned her. Sometimes he despised himself.

'What can I do for you?' the doctor asked, remarkably chirpy since it was still before nine o' clock.

Ben walked him through it.

'Normally, Ben, we prefer to see you with your wife to make sure that this is the right decision for you—'

'I'll stop you there. I'm separated from my wife – soon to be divorced.'

The word *divorce* stuck in his throat like a blockage he couldn't clear. He hated the word. It said failure to him. He was a failure, he'd let his marriage and family slip away from him.

He didn't mention Laura. She used a different medical practice to him; the entire baby experience had remained below the radar as far as his medical records were concerned.

'So, you're done with babies then. Can't say I blame you. I've got five of them myself – I'll be working here until I'm an old man paying for them all. Get the snip as fast as you can, I say. If I'd known then what I know now, I'd have had it done when I was 15.

Ben wondered if this was the kind of thing a doctor should be saying, but he warmed to the man.

'Everything seems to be in order. We can get you in quickly if you want. It doesn't take long.'

'How quickly?'

Ben was keen to hide it from Laura if he could. There had been no talk of more babies. He'd put it down to old age if she did decide she wanted another child and somehow didn't manage to get pregnant. He was certain he could get the snip without her knowing.

'By the end of next month. No need to hang around – you'll be in and out in no time. Does that work for you?'

'Any pain or discomfort afterwards?' Ben asked.

'Not usually. Just don't go climbing any mountains or swinging from any trees. Wait one week before intimate activity resumes. You work in an office, I think you said, so you'll have no problems. They'll talk you through it at the clinic.'

'That sounds great!'

Ben was relieved that it was all so simple. It might mean telling a white lie to Laura, but he was pretty sure she wouldn't want any more children after Harper. And, after all, what was one more lie when he'd already cheated on Diana and done the most despicable thing he could think of?

CHAPTER SIX

April 2018: Six Weeks Before The Party

Ben hadn't anticipated feeling quite so depressed about how the day was going to pan out. At first it had seemed routine – just a series of appointments. But walking out of the surgery, he realised that it was more of a funeral. He'd set in a motion an operation which would mean no more kids. He was closing something off, something that had once been wonderful – the births of Ted and Alice, their childhoods, everything had been magical.

Of course, he loved Harper as any father would love a child. But he hadn't wanted a child at that time in his life. He was struggling to reconcile the two things. Not only was he ending something that had once been special – his ability to bring children into the world with the woman he loved – but he was also about to trigger the process that would end his marriage to Diana. Twenty-three years of marriage, most of it great, only punctuated with the occasional episodes of tension. That was par for the course, nobody gets through life completely free of problems.

Ben was sitting on a bench outside the solicitor's office. It was late April and before him a cherry tree was in full blossom, boldly banishing the last of winter. As its pink petals drifted to the ground, he saw that everything that had been precious to him would soon be like that tree. By the end of May its proud colour would be blown away. He'd be stuck with a new family that he didn't particularly want and rid of an existing family he should never have abandoned in the first place. However he ran it in his head, there seemed to be no way it could end well. He'd have to take it on the chin and do what he had to, a Kamikaze pilot roaring towards his target.

'Ben Harrington. I have a 9.45 appointment.'

He'd found the cherry tree too depressing and decided to wait out his time in the solicitor's office. He still had fifteen minutes to kill, but if he got lucky, they might even start early. He checked his phone. Financial necessity had forced him to revert to a pay-as-you-go contract after he'd moved out of the family home. He was able to pick up an open Wi-Fi signal sitting in the reception area, so he checked his emails and Facebook messages.

Steve had been on – again – wondering what they should buy their parents as a gift. More expense. Ben tried to figure how low he could go with a seventieth birthday present. He reckoned £75, maybe £100. He'd have to leave the annual service on the car as late as possible, until another salary had gone through. If the bank played ball later, he'd just about make it.

He had an email from Gaby. That was unusual. She was on the ever-growing list of people who resented him. And she was reluctant to use her Facebook account like everybody else because she was convinced that the Russians were tracking her every move.

'Who the hell cares what you're up to?' her loving former husband would scowl at her. '*I can barely maintain interest in your daily life, let alone Vladimir from Moscow.*'

He was nice like that, her ex. It was probably a good thing that he'd disappeared. Ben was not a violent man, but he'd spent his life wanting to punch Nigel in the face.

It was the forwarded seventieth birthday invitation.

Hi Ben, hope you're well. You know I'm still angry with you for messing things up with Diana, but it looks like I'm going to have to get over it. What do you think of this? I don't even know where Mum and Dad are now, do you? Haven't heard from them. What are we doing for a prezzie? Gaby x

She'd put one kiss at the end of her message. Before he left the family home she used to type a couple of lines of them. A single kiss on an email was like the thawing of relations with North Korea. It was a great start, and there might even be a Nobel Peace Prize in the offing.

'Mr Harrington? Ann White, pleased to meet you.'

Ben hastily pushed his phone into his pocket, stood up and reached out to shake her hand. She gave a quick smile, but her expression was serious. From the moment their hands made contact, everything would be on the clock. More money he didn't have.

He followed her into her office and took a seat. It was old-fashioned, the chairs upholstered in leather, the walls lined with books which would never have got read anywhere but in a legal setting. Ann's desk was covered in cardboard wallets, but she was discreet enough to hide anything which might give away a name or an identity.

She ran through her routine spiel about the initial free consultation. He let it wash over him as he considered her life. She was probably about the same age as him, maybe slightly older. She was in that difficult zone for women where her hair wasn't yet grey enough to force the *Should I dye it or not?* decision, but it was on the turn. He imagined that she had been diligent and consistent in her life, working hard, raising a family, and nurturing her marriage. In ten years' time she'd have her pension paid up, her house paid off and it would be an easy cruise through from retirement to Alzheimer's or whatever joy awaited her in old age. Everybody he met seemed to be goading him about his own life. At his age he should have been like Ann, not stuck in a tiny house with a small baby and deep in debt.

'Have you had time to think about which of the five facts applies in your own marriage?'

Ben knew he should have come to this meeting with Diana. She hadn't pushed for a divorce and he didn't really want it either, but Laura had been talking about Harper's future security. He'd felt duty-bound to at least find out what the options were, even though he would postpone them as long as possible. Just like the annual service on the car.

Twenty-three years of marriage had come down to this. Five options, that was it. Cheating, unreasonable behaviour, desertion, and living apart. Living apart offered two options, contested and uncontested. Five choices and not one of them acknowledged the grey areas that exist in any relationship.

Strictly speaking, they were probably limited to facts one and three. Yes, he had cheated – technically – and yes, he had deserted them – technically. They'd barely been apart for a year. Laura fell pregnant very quickly, so the two-year rule didn't apply. Yet facts one and three seemed so cold. He'd cheated because he'd been unhappy – they both were. The outcome was cheating, but they were both responsible for the cause. And desertion? Well, yes, he'd left the house. But only because it was the best thing to do for the kids. They were so angry with each other they could barely speak. He'd left the house, but Diana had wanted him to go.

Ann worked through the options, explaining that adultery has its own set of rules. It was all news to Ben and a world he'd never expected to be familiar with. He and Diana had had their problems, who hadn't?

'You seem very uncertain about this, Ben,' she said, after becoming fully acquainted with the details of this particular marriage breakdown. 'I wonder if seeking a divorce is the right direction in which to take this? Perhaps you need to spend more time speaking to your wife? I do feel in this case that the next step might be a legal separation rather than a divorce. And you may find that family mediation would help.'

Family mediation. To Ben, it was a passive-aggressive way to work through marital problems – taking turns to have your say while really wanting to scream at each other like the couples do on the telly. But it was true that he didn't feel ready to go straight for a divorce. Mediation might keep Laura off his back and improve things with Diana and the kids.

'When my first husband and I separated, we found family mediation very helpful, particularly as far as the children were concerned.'

Even Ann was divorced. He hadn't expected that. Was nobody safe? Did anybody stay together anymore? He wondered how his parents had managed it for so long. That generation seemed to make it look so easy. They must have had their fair share of crap too, right?

'Ted is an adult now, but with Alice needing care throughout her life, perhaps you need to sit down and talk. I understand that your wife and family are angry with you, but do you think that could be the best course of action here?'

Ann was right. And she should know, she'd been through it herself already. What had he been thinking, coming here without talking to Diana first? It was Laura who'd pushed him into it – she couldn't wait for him to offload his old family and commit to his new one. But that wasn't how Ben felt. He had never intended to wind up with Laura, it had a been a fling, an expression of anger and frustration. It was stupid, he knew that, even as they were making love together in her bed. And then she'd become pregnant and he'd been instantly cornered. Just like a gullible animal wandering stupidly into a trap, he'd made the classic middle-aged man error. And just like that animal, all he could do was struggle pointlessly until he became worn out by the effort of it all and finally resigned himself to the inevitable.

CHAPTER SEVEN

1980: The Second Lie

'Can I take the kids in now?' Tony asked the nurse.

'Yes, she's tired out, but she's desperate to see them. Send them in.'

Tony opened the door to let the three children into the private room. The meat business was going well, Susan's debut book was making decent sales, they could afford it. Gaby rushed directly to the baby, who was asleep in a small cot placed close to the bed. Steve tried to be cool and aloof, Ben ran up to the other side of the bed and gave Susan a hug.

Tony could see that she was exhausted. He sighed. It wasn't all joy. This was a difficult time for them and their relationship.

'What are you going to call him, Mum?' Gaby asked.

Susan forced a smile.

'We think he's going to be called Richard,' she said at last, beckoning Steve over to her.

'Richard!' Gaby exclaimed. 'Like Grandad Richard?'

'Yes, like Grandad Richard. I thought it would be nice to remember him like that – as if he was still here with us.'

Grandad Richard made him sound old and frail, as if the life he'd lived counted for nothing. But he was the strong, visionary man who'd helped create this amazing life for them, the founder of Harrington Meats, suppliers to shops, restaurants and supermarkets throughout the north of England. Besides, the name choice would appease Tony. He needed some kind of stake in this child.

'How are you doing, Susan?'

Tony was distant and aloof. They had to keep up the charade for the sake of the kids. Neither of them had anticipated a fourth child. Yet here he was, the newest member of the family.

For Steve it was a complete nuisance. He'd resisted the idea since Susan and Tony first mentioned that they were getting a new sibling. They had told their other children late in the pregnancy – one minute it was just the three of them and the next there was a baby due in a matter of weeks.

Steve had other things on his mind, like the constant bullying he was the victim of at his new school. He didn't fit in, but Tony and Susan couldn't see it.

'So, you come from a family of butchers?' they'd say.

'Well no, not really, we—'

Then they'd flush his head down the toilet before he got a chance to explain. They were the sons of stockbrokers, bank managers and investors. His dad ran a big butcher's shop. They were right, he didn't fit in.

The thought of a baby screaming in the house while he was trying to do his homework horrified him. And he wished Tony could be something more than he was – the son of a butcher who'd done a good job of growing his business.

Gaby, meanwhile, was ecstatic at the thought of having somebody younger than her in the family. She was excluded from Ben and Steve's world, they treated her like she was a perpetual nuisance and would barely give her the time of day. All she wanted was their approval, but it never came. She stroked the baby gently and held its tiny clenched hands. She danced around the crib and spoke excitedly to Susan and Tony. She was too young to see it then, but she appeared to be the only person in the room who was excited by the arrival of this new buddy. She'd understand many years later, as an adult with a child of her own. In time she'd come to see that scene very differently. It would always be better viewed through a child's eyes.

For Ben, this was a chance to catch up with his mother. The announcement that a new baby was on its way had surprised him briefly and later in life he'd reflect on the irony of his reaction when he was told about it.

'But you're far too old to have a baby!' he'd said.

He missed Susan when she was out of the house; he could always sense the change of gear when Tony was in charge and he didn't like it. It wasn't that Tony wasn't great with the kids, it was just that since the episode with Jed, Ben hadn't known quite what to make of his father.

'You must be mistaken, son. The policeman told us Jed was responsible.'

'But I've got the spoons here, Dad.'

'Do you have any more of those, Ben? Can you bring them to me, so I can take a closer look?'

Ben did as he was told and Tony feigned a close inspection.

'You're wrong, Ben. These are your mum's spoons – we

bought them before any of you kids were even born. I'll take them and put them back where they belong. You've done well bringing these to me.'

Ben didn't know what to do. By the time he'd finished the conversation with his father he genuinely believed that he must have got it all mixed up. He never mentioned it again, but a feeling lingered for some time afterwards that he was missing something, things weren't quite right. Susan remained consistent in his life, so he was pleased to see her again. Only, she seemed tense now, as if something had changed since they'd last seen her. He was too young to even guess at what it might be.

The baby woke up. Gaby became excited at the prospect of finally getting to hold him and Susan signalled to Tony that he should bring him over to the bed.

'Go on,' she said. 'You'll need to get used to handling him. The best time to start is now.'

Slowly, reluctantly, Tony moved towards the tiny infant and gently picked him up. Richard might just as well have been a vase in a shop, his father was so on edge. Tony handed the baby back to Susan, who patted the bed to encourage Gaby to her side. Gaby made herself comfortable on the bed and took Richard on her lap, as if she'd just been handed the crown jewels.

'I'm going outside to look for a chocolate machine,' Steve announced. 'Can I have some money, Dad?'

Tony felt in his pocket and handed over some loose change.

'Get something for the others,' he said. 'And don't wander off. I don't want to have to come looking for you.'

Steve left the room. He was pleased to get out of there. He attempted to get a fix on where the room was located. The signs throughout the hospital were largely meaningless to him, just a load of big words that he didn't understand: oncology, gynaecology, anaesthetics, A&E. They were in maternity – he understood that word. He also understood canteen, and that seemed to be the best direction to head in.

It wasn't long before Steve was completely lost in the labyrinth of sterile corridors. He decided to get to the canteen, buy the chocolate, then try to figure out where he was. Sure enough, he found the machines, bought the snacks and decided to consume his in peace before heading back to the mayhem of his mum's hospital room. Babies were not really his thing.

Eventually, looking at the clock on the wall and noticing a group of three nurses getting up to continue their shift after a break, he decided to head back.

'Excuse me, where are the babies kept?' he asked one of them.

She smiled at him.

'I think you mean the maternity wing. Follow Moira here, she'll take you. That's where she works.'

Before long, he was relieved to find himself back in the entrance area.

'Thank you,' he said to Moira. 'I'm just going to the toilet before I go back to see Mum and Dad.'

As he entered the toilets, he could hear voices. He looked around, trying to figure out where they were coming from. It was two men, they were in the cubicles, talking quietly and conspiratorially. He placed the chocolate bars by the sinks, then moved towards the urinals.

Suddenly he realised that one of the voices was his father.

'So, it's done? You're sure there'll be no fallout?'

'It's all taken care of.'

'You're certain this is all watertight?'

'It's good, Tony. Believe me. I've got it sorted. I'll need to use the factory tonight. Is the alarm code still the same?'

For a moment, Steve was going to whisper *Dad* through the wooden door of the cubicle, but something warned him not to. He zipped up quickly as one of the cubicle doors opened. It wasn't Tony, but another man who barely even looked at him, striding out of the toilet as if he had some urgent matter to attend to. Steve didn't want to get caught by his dad, so he grabbed the chocolate bars, forgot all about washing his hands, and dashed back into his mother's room.

Ben was now holding the baby, with Gaby looking on jealously. It was only a minute or so later that Tony followed Steve into the room. Susan looked up at him, a small frown on her face.

'You took your time. Where have you been?'

'Oh, nowhere in particular. I needed to step out for a moment. It's so stuffy in here.'

'Are you sure that's all you've been doing?'

Steve looked at his father, waiting for him to mention the man he'd been talking to in the cubicles. He said nothing, just repeated his story that he'd been taking the fresh air outside.

His father had told a lie, and it wasn't the first time. They'd never spoken about Jed after the visit from the police, but Steve knew he was off the hook as far as the burglary was concerned. He'd never given it any more thought. He'd just assumed they'd got lucky. But perhaps there was more it than that. And now here was his father lying to his mother about speaking to the man in the toilets, a man he'd never seen before.

CHAPTER EIGHT

April 2018: Six Weeks Before The Party

'I'm sorry, Mr Harrington, but we're going to struggle to extend your existing credit. If you look at the numbers, you're beginning to stray into very dangerous territory.'

Ben wanted to cry. He'd felt like that a lot recently. A grown man who just wanted to hang his head in his hands and have a good sob about what his life had come to. Was this his mid-life crisis? Did all men of his age go through similar experiences? He had nowhere to go, yet he had to keep moving, he had to keep earning. What would happen if he stopped? The entire house of cards would come tumbling down.

'Is there really nothing you can do? My parents have assured me that they'll be picking up the tab for this trip, so it really is a temporary loan – one to two months at the most. Couldn't you extend my credit card limit for three months?'

The banking adviser tapped a few keys on his

computer, running the numbers once again. His name was displayed on a badge pinned to his jacket: he was called Peter. Ben wondered if it would have been any better if he'd had a bank manager. He remembered his dad talking about meetings with the bank manager, but by the time he'd gone to university and got his first bank account they didn't seem to exist.

'I'll tell you what we can do for you,' Peter answered.

Ben might as well have been talking to a loan shark. As far as he could see, the only difference between them was that one would break your legs to get their money back while the other would claim your whole life. Not in a life and death sense, but in a 'we'll take your house, your car and your future' kind of way.

'If you switch your credit card to our Platinum Account Plus option, we can extend your credit by a little more than you need.'

'What's the catch?'

'There isn't one really. You'll need to pay an initial set-up admin fee, plus there's 1% on your balance transfer at an APR of 18%, which is a very competitive deal.'

All Ben heard was blah, blah, blah. He simply needed to know if he could afford the monthly payments until some future event might arise to miraculously dig him out of his current hole. He wondered what it must be like for people who genuinely had nothing. Ben was middle-class broke. His entire life was underwritten by a monthly salary, which was as stable an income source as anybody had in the 21st century. With it he could buy a car, a house, get credit cards and pay for anything he needed in convenient instalments. There was always somebody who would offer a little more, so long as that monthly salary continued to come in, regular as clockwork. The only question for Ben was could he afford to pay what he owed each month and put food on the table? If the answer was yes, then he collected the cash and took on the debt.

'If Harper travels on our laps, we're up for two seats to Singapore. British Airways reckons it's £500-plus per ticket, so let's say £750 per ticket. If we can add on £2000 to my limit, what will my minimum payment be each month?'

Ben held his breath. He needed the answer to be something he could afford.

Peter tapped into the computer once again.

'That makes your total amount of credit £10,000. At 18%, your minimum payment will be less than £250 per month. Plus, you'll have the 1% to pay on the £8000 you're carrying over. How does that feel?'

It felt excruciating.

Ben tried to keep his poker face on while running the figures in his head. At school they'd taught them about logarithms, statistical analysis and trigonometry. It had been a waste of time. The teachers would have been better off showing them how to calculate how much of a financial mess they were in at any given point in their lives. It would have been a lot more useful.

He totted up the numbers – rent, mortgage, bills for both houses, credit card and car. He was £50 short per month. When he got the money back from his parents for the flights, he could use the extra £2000 that he'd borrowed to make up that £50 monthly deficit. That would buy him another forty months. Harper would be in an assisted nursery place then and Laura would be able to go back to work.

'At that rate of payment, you'd have the balance paid off in sixty-one months or thereabouts,' Peter smiled at him. 'Shall I proceed? If you want to go ahead, I'll just need to go through some paperwork to explain your consumer rights to you.'

Ben wanted to laugh out loud at that. Consumer rights, what a joke. He had no choice. Harper would be five years old by the time he paid off the cash and that was assuming that nothing else happened in the meantime. It didn't allow for car repairs, roof leaks, work clothes or new shoes. It assumed that life would be completely predictable for the next sixty months. It was fine telling him all about his right to cancel the agreement, but if he didn't go ahead he was completely done for. The thought of the timescales horrified him. It seemed so far off into the future, a future which he felt completely uncertain about.

Laura's voice sounded in his head.

It doesn't matter, you'll get your mum and dad's money eventually. Borrow what you need. It's all underwritten by your dad's business. I know there are four of you to inherit, but even split between all of you, you'll be doing alright, won't you? Enough to pay off Diana's house and get us somewhere decent to live. And Alice won't be your dependent forever.

It was so easy for Laura to speak like that. She was so much younger than he was. She didn't understand that kids don't magically disappear from your life at the age of eighteen.

'You get them for life,' he'd told her. 'Like it or not, they're your kids. And besides, Alice is a special case. She's always going to need more care.'

'It says on the government website, as soon as they're out of school you don't have to pay for them anymore. How old is Alice? Sixteen? Seventeen? She'll have to fend for herself when she leaves school. Or perhaps Diana could get off her backside and get a job.'

It always seemed to come down to this. It was fine for Laura to give up work and stay at home to look after Harper. She hated her job and couldn't wait to get away from it. She'd take the maternity pay, which was not very much, then resign as soon as she could do so legally without any financial loss. Leaving Ben to pay the bills. He and Diana had done the same but somehow it had never been right for Diana to go back to work. She'd tried, but Alice needed the support. Diana wanted to be there if she ever had a fit at school, and Ben wanted her to be there too.

Laura didn't seem to get that. She simply didn't see why Ben couldn't wash his hands of his disabled daughter the minute she was officially an adult. But Ben was tied to his daughter until the day he died and he wouldn't have it any other way.

'So, shall I proceed?' Peter asked.

Ben had been distracted, thinking about Alice. He'd try to contact her, reach out again, see if she would at least tolerate him now. Maybe she'd go to the birthday party with them, if Laura would agree to it. The four of them could travel together – they'd have a row of seats on the plane. Once Alice had got used to the situation, she'd love caring for Harper. But that would be even more money. The £2000 credit card top-up wouldn't stretch to another ticket. That could sink him.

'How soon will the funds be available to me? I need to buy the tickets as soon as possible, in the next week if I can.'

'No problem,' Peter replied.

Ben wondered how much commission he'd be making on the upsell of a more expensive credit card.

'Once we get these forms completed, the account will be set up and authorised by the end of the week. You'll get your new card by the weekend, so you'll be able to buy your tickets as soon as Saturday. Shall I go ahead?'

Ben considered the options once again. He'd known a guy at work who'd gone bankrupt. It seemed surprisingly straightforward. Nobody had died, his marriage had remained intact, life had gone on. He'd been subject to a few restrictions about what he could spend his money on and limitations on accessing credit. But it hadn't seemed at all bad. He'd weathered the storm and they'd even let him have a mortgage again after a couple of years. If the worst came to the worst, he'd have to declare himself bankrupt. He'd never live down the shame of it, particularly not with Steve – his brother would be merciless in his disapproval. But it was heading that way; things were getting so precarious, he wasn't sure how much longer he could hang on. He promised himself there and then that he would talk to his mum and dad at the birthday visit. When he could see them face to face, he'd have a serious talk about money.

'Okay, let's go for it!'

Even as the words came out, he knew he was making a terrible mistake. He had just signed his own pact with the devil.

CHAPTER NINE

April 2018: Six Weeks Before The Party

'We've been robbed ... someone broke into the house ... I don't know what to do!'

Laura was sobbing on the phone, Harper screaming in the background. Ben had been nursing another coffee in a different coffee shop, working through the sinking feeling in his stomach. The papers were signed, the new credit card was on its way. And now here was another crisis. His first thought was that he hadn't bothered taking out contents insurance on the rented house. He and Laura hadn't got that much stuff between them, and certainly nothing worth stealing. In his former life with Diana he'd paid premiums for almost a quarter of a century. He'd made the decision to take a risk on the insurance. It seemed to be a reasonable gamble. And now, like everything else, it had all gone sour.

'Try to calm down, Laura. Are you sure it's a break-in? Has anything been damaged?'

'The door was open when we came home from Harper's

check-up. I know I can be careless sometimes, but I'm certain I locked up. And besides, things have been moved.'

'What things?'

'I don't know. I can just tell that somebody's been in here.'

'Were we due a house inspection by the letting agents today? We haven't got the dates wrong, have we?'

'Look Ben, I just know we've been broken into. Come home from work, will you?'

Ben was grateful for the small deceits that mobile phones facilitated. When he and Diana had been a young couple, his wife would have had to phone the work switchboard to pass on a message. Laura's generation had never known a life like that. It was serving him very well that morning, because if she had phoned him at work he'd have been rumbled.

Why weren't you at work?

Oh, no big reason. Just booking in a vasectomy I'm going to keep secret from you, getting another loan that we can't afford, and trying to avoid the divorce proceedings that you're so keen for me to get underway. How's your day going?

As it was, he was able to get a takeaway cup for the rest of his coffee and be back at their rented property in a suitable amount of time so as not to arouse any suspicion.

'Thank God you're here. I suddenly thought they might still be in the house.'

Laura rushed up to Ben to give him a hug. At least he still served some purpose in the relationship other than as a financial workhorse.

'Talk me through what happened. It doesn't look like anybody's been in the house. The TV is still there. Your tablet hasn't been taken.'

'Would you take that old TV if you broke in? Personally,

I'd be tempted to leave a small cash donation and a polite suggestion that you might like to buy something decent.'

Ben looked at the TV set which had been bought at a bargain price from one of the charity shops which now specialised in home furnishings. It was the opposite of flat screen. Their house was furnished in the style of The British Heart Foundation. It had supplied the sofa, the bed and the kitchen table. Ben hoped it would at least give him some credit in the good karma department when he finally keeled over with a heart attack as a consequence of the stress he was suffering.

'How was the door when you came home?'

Laura walked up to the front door which opened directly from the street into the lounge. She grasped the handle and placed it slightly ajar.

'It was like that, maybe closed a bit more.'

'You're sure you didn't forget to lock it? There's a lot to do when you're moving the pram out onto the street.'

He could tell by the look on Laura's face that he'd ventured into dangerous territory.

'Look Ben, I'm telling you. I locked up.'

'Okay, okay. Have you been upstairs yet?'

'No, I waited by the door and left it open, so I could scream if anybody was in the house. I'm not going to get beaten up in my own house.'

'That's probably a good strategy. Has anything been moved downstairs?'

'I'm not certain, but take a look at that cupboard drawer. It hasn't been closed properly. You know what I'm like. I'd never leave it open.'

She was right about that. Laura could be scatty and untidy in so many other ways, but she was fanatical about shutting drawers and borderline obsessive when it came to having straight cutlery at the dinner table. The crumbs underneath it and the food debris plastered all over the oven didn't appear to concern her.

'I'm going upstairs. You stay with Harper.'

Ben walked cautiously into the dining room then peered into the kitchen. It looked like a house that had been left in a rush that morning. His laptop was still sitting on the dining room table.

'Did you use my laptop?' he shouted through to the next room.

'No, why?'

'The lid is up. I know I shut it when I left the house. It's a recent habit after Harper vomited her milk up all over it.'

Ben walked slowly up the stairs. He didn't believe anybody was up there. The floorboards hadn't creaked at all other than as a result of his own movements. The bathroom door was open. On the floor was the changing mat along with all the paraphernalia Laura required just to exit the house for a routine baby check-up. Ben pushed open the door of the main bedroom and scanned the room. The quilt had been hurriedly pulled over the bed. There were some discarded clothes on the floor from the day before. They each had a rail on casters on which to hang their clothing. Ben had never expected to be living like a student again at his stage in life.

He'd taken Laura a cup of tea before he left the house and the cup was still on her side of the bed. It looked just like it should do. If somebody had been in the house, they might have taken the trouble to tidy up a bit.

'Can you see anything?' Laura shouted up from the bottom of the staircase. 'Is anybody up there?'

There was certainly nobody in the main bedroom.

There were two more rooms to check. Harper's was

closest to the main bedroom. They hadn't moved her in there yet. She was still in the carrycot at night. But the room was ready, packed with cuddly toys and sleeper suits. There was nothing in that room to steal, unless you were a thief desperate for newborn disposable nappies.

The door to the study was shut and Ben had to give it a firm push to get it open. Some folders had fallen out of an open box onto the bare floorboards. They called it a study, but really it was a room in which to store all their junk.

'Have you been in the study?' he called down to Laura.

'No, why?' she said, stepping up onto the landing.

'Did you shut the front door?'

'Jesus, Ben. Yes, of course I shut the front door. Harper's asleep now, I wouldn't leave her down there with the door wide open.'

'Sorry, Laura. I'm just feeling a bit jittery. I think someone has been looking at my laptop. And look at these folders, I didn't leave them on the floor, did you?'

He could tell by the look on Laura's face that she hadn't touched them. There was no reason why she would. Most of the stuff in there belonged to him, the remnants of a former life. Ben lowered himself to a squatting position to sort through them.

'These are some old photos and other bits and pieces that I took from the house, the ones Diana let me hang on to.'

'Can you see if anything's missing, Ben? Why would anybody be interested in all this old stuff?'

That old stuff was his life. He looked through some of the images: school photos of him on his own, school photos with Steve and Gaby, then later with Gaby when Steve had moved on to the private school. A picture of him in his graduation robes. A couple of old Polaroids with a very young-looking Diana. His heart ached for those days, but he moved on, it was best not to dwell on the past.

'I think there's a newspaper clipping missing. I don't think I'm being paranoid. It's that one I was hanging on to because I was certain I knew the bloke. You know which one I mean, don't you?'

'Yes, it's the cutting you showed me a couple of weeks back – you were convinced the guy was connected with the meat business in some way and you wanted to ask your dad about it. He'd been fined for speeding, something like that.'

'Yes, that's the one,' Ben replied. 'It's not here. You're right. Somebody must have been in the house while we were out.'

CHAPTER TEN

1988: The Third Lie

It was the lowered voices that alerted Ben and Gaby to the gravity of the situation.

'Shh, let's wait on the stairs and listen in,' Gaby whispered.

Ben sat next to her on the bottom step.

Richard was in bed, out of the way. Homework was done and it was time to raid the kitchen for supper. Steve was in some kind of trouble and it was taking the full attention of both Tony and Susan to resolve it.

'He's been weird since after his eighteenth birthday. Something happened that night. Did you see anything?' Gaby asked.

Ben didn't answer. He'd been there at the party having just scraped sixteen and had been delighted to find out there were no reasonable grounds to stop him joining in.

'Just make sure he stays away from the drink, Steve. And any damage to the house, you know where the money comes from – you pay it yourself if your friends wreck anything.'

Tony and Susan were courageous parents, and they knew that if Steve was to be trusted with the business one day, he had to be given the responsibility that would come with it. This would be the perfect test of maturity: the family home cleared of all under-sixteen siblings and parents plus a decent budget to arrange a house party that would be the envy of his friends.

Ben was jealous of Steve's entrepreneurial abilities even then. His brother had retained one third of the budget to pay a cleaning company who were booked in at nine o'clock the next day. That was how he had his back covered. And he'd charged what he called his Tier 2 friends to attend the event, hence making a small profit, even after factoring in the cleaners. He was happy for Ben to join in.

'You might finally get lucky. And in your own bed!'

Ben wasn't so sure. It was all his friends seemed to talk about, as if being a teenager had switched on a heat-seeking missile below their waists which wouldn't rest until reaching its destination. He didn't feel ready to move on to the next step, although his hormone-fuelled body often suggested otherwise.

Tony and Susan should have been awarded a medal. They left the house with Richard and Gaby by six o'clock, leaving Steve and Ben to make the final arrangements in readiness for the first guests to arrive two hours later.

'Any problems, call the hotel switchboard,' Tony said. 'We'll be back at midday tomorrow. You have until then to make sure that everything looks the way we left it. I don't care how you do it, just make sure it's all straight by the time we get back.'

Steve watched them drive off. He turned to Ben and

smiled.

'Great, they've gone! Eighteen hours on our own. The countdown starts now. Look, I got these from the chemist. Do you want one?'

Ben's face turned red. Steve was holding two large packs of condoms in his hand.

'I'll leave these in the kitchen in case anyone needs them. Got to be responsible and all that!'

For the next hour, the two brothers executed a carefully drawn plan of Steve's making.

'Take anything that might get broken or stolen and put it on a blanket in the garage,' he instructed. 'Place a sticky note on everything saying where it belongs. I know we look at this junk every day, but when we have to rush round putting it all back tomorrow morning, we'll forget where it goes.'

Ben was grateful that he had Steve to guide him – he'd never have thought of such meticulous planning on his own. He knew that even if he had it in him to arrange such an evening of debauchery, he'd inevitably be facing up to the consequences the next day. He wouldn't be capable of formulating an advance strategy the way his brother had. Steve had thought it through like a military operation.

'Right, I want all our sheets off the beds, folded neatly and placed in this suitcase. No embarrassing stains on bedding.'

Steve had bought cheap sets of bed linen, which he planned to dispose of the next day. It was all factored in to his profit-and-loss planning. He claimed he'd be a hundred pounds up on the event, all in.

'Even Gaby's?' Ben asked. He was wondering if it would have been better to spend a night in the hotel with his parents.

'Even Gaby's!' Steve grinned. 'Love doesn't care where it expresses itself. Besides, I'm renting out the bedrooms to couples. Gaby's bedroom is an essential profit centre.'

There was a knock at the door. Steve opened it to find a woman standing on the doorstep with a couple of large cardboard boxes.

'Delivery for Mr S. Harrington?'

'Yes, that's me.'

It was his delivery of booze and plastic glasses from the off-licence. Steve had even had the foresight to order from the next town, to cover his tracks.

'Are you sure about this?' Ben asked.

He was beginning to lose his nerve. Steve had briefly outlined his plans for the evening, but it was a little too much for Ben. It had the potential to go terribly wrong and he didn't want to be involved if it did.

Soon after the alcohol supplies arrived, they went off for showers and to get changed. Guests started to arrive soon afterwards, and it took no time at all before the evening was in full swing. Ben had invited a couple of friends over, but they had to leave at ten o' clock, so he was always going to end up a bit of a spare part.

He reckoned there were about thirty people there in all. He didn't know most of them, they were all from Steve's school and seemed a bit full of themselves for his liking. They were loud, confident and boorish, not like the kids that Ben mixed with at the local comprehensive school. He wondered if passing entrance exams made you cocky. Failing them had certainly knocked his confidence.

He spent most of the evening chatting away with Tessa and Penny, keeping out of things and staying away from the booze. Every now and then there would be roars of laughter and cheering, and these got louder as more drink was consumed. With his friends there, Ben didn't take much notice of what was going on. He was aware that everything was getting louder around them, but it seemed good-natured enough and Steve appeared to be enjoying himself on the few occasions he saw him. It changed when Tess and Penny left. Their parents dutifully turned up at the appointed time, expressed concern about the boisterousness in the house, then offered Ben a sofa and a sleeping bag for the night if he wanted to extricate himself. He thought for a moment but decided he'd just head for his own room, place a chair against the door, listen to music on his headphones and go to sleep. It seemed like a decent plan, but things didn't quite work out that way.

'Have a drink!' Steve urged, his arm around an attractive girl whose name was Jenny or Janine. Ben didn't quite catch it.

He tried to refuse, but Steve thrust a glass into his hand. A couple of his friends, sensing this was a first-blood scenario, started chanting.

'Drink it! Drink it!'

Ben relented, took too big a gulp and ended up coughing it out.

'Here, add some cola,' Steve laughed. 'It'll taste better like that.'

Before Ben knew it, he'd been pulled in to the party. He sipped his drink, which Steve had now topped up, and joined one of the groups. He couldn't get away. He was becoming more and more woozy. He assumed it must be a consequence of the noise and atmosphere as the drink itself tasted like cola. Eventually, when the group to which he'd become reluctantly attached began to disperse into kissing couples, he decided it was time to take refuge in his bedroom. His head spinning, he climbed the stairs and opened the door, only to hear giggling from the darkness inside.

'Oh, sorry!'

He shut the door and moved on to Steve's room. Again, the door was closed. He knocked gently. He couldn't hear anything, so he walked in and turned on the light. Steve was in bed with the girl he'd been with earlier. They were naked.

'Jesus, Ben. Piss off!' Steve shouted. 'And turn off the light!'

Ben gave up trying to find a bed for the night and made his way out to the garage. His eyes screaming at him to rest, he crashed out on the edge of the blanket they'd used to protect his parents' valuables on the hard floor.

He was startled out of his sleep by the sound of a door banging. It was the cleaners entering the garage to begin moving items back into the house. He felt terrible.

'Morning, Ben!' Steve greeted him, bright and cheerful. 'Great party last night, but it's time to get moving. Mum and Dad are back in just over two hours.'

Steve's plan was well executed and by the time Tony and Susan returned to the house it was spotless. Temporary sheets had been disposed of, items replaced in their proper locations, all signs of alcohol removed and everything exactly as it had been left. Ben felt wretched and was sick twice before they got back. He kept out the way, relieved that the weekend gave him a recovery day before having to turn up at school again.

And that's the last he'd thought about it until about six weeks afterwards Steve's mood suddenly began to change. He'd been arrogant and sure of himself up to that point, particularly as he'd made a profit of £150 on the event. Then phone calls started being made at unusual times. The girl that Steve had been with that night visited the house with her parents. Ben kept out of the way, assuming it was parents meeting parents. Then, one night there was shouting from downstairs and he looked out of his bedroom window to see the girl being taken back to their car in tears, her mother's arm around her, comforting her. He heard Steve storming up the stairs to his bedroom, slamming the door behind him.

Something was wrong. The atmosphere in the house had changed, and it had to do with this girl and her family. Usually Ben didn't give Steve's life much thought. They got on well, but they ran on parallel tracks, Steve at his private school, Ben at the comp.

As Ben sat on the stairs with Gaby, listening intently to the hushed conversation in the kitchen, he finally managed to figure it out.

'And that's the end of it. They've agreed that she'll go to the clinic?'

It was Susan who was leading this conversation.

'Yes, her father gave me his assurance. It'll be taken care of by the end of the week.'

Tony's voice this time, sounding in control.

'And then it's all over?' said Steve.

'Yes, and you should consider yourself very lucky. That might have screwed up your life. Think about things before you act. Don't be an idiot!'

Steve emerged from the kitchen and Ben and Gaby quickly got to their feet, trying – and failing – to make it look as if they'd been on their way to supper.

'Everything alright, Steve?' Ben asked, doing his best to sound casual.

'Yeah, great. Me and Jenny just split up, that's all.'

CHAPTER ELEVEN

April 2018: Six Weeks Before The Party

'Are they even real coppers?' asked Laura.

'They're community officers,' Ben replied. 'We should be thankful they bothered to send anybody around at all. They don't even deal with lost property these days.'

'So, sir, you say that only a newspaper cutting has been taken?' the policewoman asked, carefully making notes on the pad in her hand.

'Yes, that's right. As far as we can tell.'

Ben hadn't warmed to her. He couldn't help wondering what she did as a day job. Whatever it was, it was clear that the role of Police Community Support Officer was giving her a fix in her life that she wasn't getting elsewhere. It was like an amateur dramatic version of *CSI: Crime Scene Investigation.*

Her hapless young colleague was examining the locking mechanism for the third time.

'There's no damage to this door. Are you sure you didn't leave it unlocked?'

Ben could see that Laura was tiring of the lady-with-new-born-baby-whose-brain-has-turned-to-mush insinuations. So what if she'd put her knickers in the fridge instead of the washing basket the day before? Everybody did it, she'd told him, when he found them next to the margarine. She still maintained that she'd closed that front door.

'So, is there anything you can do? Fingerprints perhaps?' Ben suggested, sensing Laura's growing impatience.

'With no evidence of a break-in and no property damaged, there's very little we can do, sir. It would help if something valuable had been stolen, or if somebody had been hurt.'

The officer was obviously letting her imagination get the better of her. Perhaps if Laura had been hit with a cosh, Harper snatched and then abandoned in a ditch, and their little terraced house ram-raided, they might have got a little more action from the police. As it was, they could barely feign interest.

'If you genuinely believe that this was a break-in, sir, we suggest changing the locks straightaway and reviewing your security measures. It's lucky we were in your neighbourhood today – we have been experiencing several break-ins in this area. But this is not the normal modus operando. If you *were* broken into, it's not by the gang we're looking for.'

Laura was getting increasingly agitated.

'It's modus operandi.'

'Exactly, madam, and this modus operando is completely different.'

Ben moved fast to head off a storm.

'Well, thank you for coming round, officers. We really

appreciate it. Will we get a crime number in case we decide to report it to the insurance company?'

Ben almost laughed out loud at his own nerve. Insurance? That was a joke.

'I'm not sure what you'd report here, sir. There isn't actually any damage or evidence.'

Ben gave it up as a bad job. However grating it was to have this amateur detective in the house, she was probably right. He wouldn't dream of pushing Laura, but she'd been scatty since the baby arrived. On more than one occasion he'd had to retrieve the shopping from the back of the car several hours after she'd returned from the supermarket. And empty baby-milk bottles were becoming like an alcoholic's secret stash, he was finding them in the unlikeliest of places. Only the previous week he'd discovered one in his briefcase. When push came to shove, that newspaper clipping could be anywhere. Perhaps he'd left it at the house – Diana's house. He'd ask her about it if they ever spoke in a civil manner again.

'Thanks once again for coming. I know you must be busy.'

'Yes, the work of a PCSO is never done,' the woman said. 'We've barely time for lunch and then we're heading off to the local primary school to do a presentation on cycle security. Unfortunately, crime never sleeps.'

Ben wouldn't have been at all surprised if she'd broken into a smile, but she didn't, she was dead earnest. And to top it all, her colleague was nodding in confirmation, as if she'd just said something incredibly profound.

They left the house and Ben closed the door, making sure it was locked behind him.

'Don't even say it!' Laura said.

'I wasn't going to. I believe you, honestly. It's myself I'm doubting. I may have left that newspaper clipping at Diana's. It's possible I threw it away. I'm questioning my own memory.'

Ben's phone vibrated in his pocket.

'Damn, that's Gaby again. She's been chasing me all morning.'

'Do you want a cup of tea? I take it you'll go back to work after lunch? By the way, you didn't take your briefcase with you this morning.'

Ben's face turned red and he pretended to busy himself with his phone. He was useless at deception. In telling his white lie to Laura about his whereabouts, he'd forgotten to cover his tracks by sticking completely to routine. She didn't push the issue and he volunteered no further information.

'What does Gaby want? She's not still chiding you for leaving Diana, is she?'

Ben read the stream of messages on Facebook.

Hey Ben, you around?

Need to chat when you've got a mo, Gaby x

WTF? Are you ignoring me? Please let me know when you're online!

'Well, she's been able to write three messages without calling me a feckless husband and father, so things look like they're improving. And she must be keen to talk, she usually gives Facebook a wide berth.'

Ben typed a quick message and sat down with Laura at the small table in the kitchen.

'So, are we going to this party? It's high time I met your family and we got all this out in the open. I'm the mother of your third child. They need to get over it and move on.'

'Yes, we're going. I can't miss my dad's seventieth birthday. Imagine how that would play out. We'll need to get Harper a passport. Is yours up to date?'

'We need to get a passport for a baby? You're kidding me?'

Ben looked at his phone. Gaby had replied.

Have you thought about a present for Dad? Where are you flying from – Newcastle or Manchester?

'Yes, it's a bit tight on the dates. I wish they'd given us more notice.'

'Well, it's no surprise that your dad's 70.'

'Yes, but I assumed ... well, what with them travelling, I assumed we'd be doing it later. Or in the UK at least. It just all feels a bit sudden.'

Ben was typing, running the two conversations alongside each other.

No thoughts about present, ask Steve, he's good at that stuff. Prices are similar from Newcastle and Manchester. How about we meet you at Newcastle and fly out together? You taking Jaxon?

'I can't believe we have to get a passport for Harper. What are they going to do, have a line-up parade of infants? How will they tell them apart? "We're looking for a suspect with no hair, a nappy that smells disgusting and milky sick down their sleepsuit. Oh, that seems to be every baby on earth!"'

Laura laughed at her own joke and picked up her tablet to figure out what was going to be involved in securing a passport for Harper within the next fortnight.

Yes, Jaxon coming with me. Newcastle is good. Spoke to Mum and Dad. We have to overnight at Kuala Lumpur, it's all very cloak and dagger. We get taken to some secret island. It's very swanky, Mum says. How exciting!

'We'll have to use the fast-track service for Harper's passport ... Oh, and we might have to go private for any injections that we need.'

Can you book the hotels and Mum and Dad will pay you back when they settle up with us? I'm a bit strapped for cash at the moment.

Ben hadn't even had time to take his first sip from the cup of hot tea before he'd got landed with two extra bills. What with changing the locks, a fast-track passport, travel injections at a private clinic and now hotels for an overnight stay, he could already see the extra money he'd secured at the bank only that morning was woefully inadequate.

He was beginning to sweat. Recently he'd been experiencing what he'd concluded from internet research must be panic attacks. Until he'd started having them, Ben thought these were reserved only for teenage girls. His chest tightened, and he wondered if this was his heart telling him that something had to change. He had to do something to resolve his current situation. Ben Harrington was cornered by his own life and he was going to have to do something radical to escape.

CHAPTER TWELVE

May 2018: Three Weeks Before The Party

Ben usually resented his ageing bladder for forcing him to get up early in the morning but on this day he was grateful to it. The appointment for his vasectomy had arrived in the mail and it had NHS and clinic details plastered all over. Hardly subtle. Had Laura intercepted it, the game might have been over.

He quickly checked the date. Wednesday 2nd June. Of course it was, immediately before the seventieth birthday trip. But the feedback he'd read on the clinic's website made it sound very routine. He wouldn't be doing anything strenuous on the holiday break – he reckoned he'd be fine.

His new credit card had arrived too. It seemed it was all coming together. Laura had agreed to skip getting the locks changed, so that was an immediate cost-saving. The hotels at Kuala Lumpur airport were cheap and they didn't take payment until check-in. What with his end of month payday just before the trip, Ben calculated that the influx of salary at the beginning of June, combined with swift repayment by his mum and dad, would mean that things should just about work out. He wished that he shared Steve's money-making abilities. Some people made cash generation look so easy.

They had a busy day ahead of them. Passport photos and vaccinations.

'It's a lot of fuss for a seventieth birthday,' Laura sighed.

'Yes, but when you reach that age, it's good to mark the milestones. Your parents are still young – come to think of it, they're not much older than me. I'd never thought about that before. You're not with me because of some father–daughter thing, are you?'

'No, you fool. It's because I like a man with a middle-aged paunch and greying hair. What's not to love?'

But Ben did wonder what was in the deal for Laura. They'd met at work. He was middle management, she was in the office. They'd always talked and got along well, but he'd never thought about her as a girlfriend. Well, perhaps he had, but he was married. He would never have done anything about it.

It was Alice's test results that had shaken things. And the restructuring thing. Ben could never recall a time in his entire working life when there had been so much uncertainty. That was a shock.

'Alice's eyesight is getting worse. She's going to have to start using a stick when she's out and about,' the doctor had said.

The diagnosis of cerebral palsy several years before hadn't come as a surprise to Diana. She'd been researching her daughter's symptoms in the library. Ben had rejected her theories all along, so when it was finally confirmed it was a huge blow. He blamed himself, that was the problem in a nutshell. On the other hand, Diana seemed to take it in her stride. His reaction had been to take himself off to the pub. Diana let him get away with it for a week or so before telling him to get his act together.

'She's your daughter, nothing's changed just because she has CP. So, get on with it and stop feeling sorry for yourself. Alice is going to have a lot more challenges to contend with than we are, believe me.'

He knew she was right. But it wasn't self-pity that had driven him to the pub. It was precisely what Diana had said. He was sorry, not for himself, but for the life they'd given their child. She'd have all sorts of problems to deal with, and not just the physical struggles of everyday life. It would be other people – more specifically, other kids – who would make Alice's life much harder.

When the sight diagnosis had come at age fifteen, his life had been rocked for a second time. Alice's vision would slowly deteriorate. And now, as if her existing struggles weren't enough, she'd have to navigate life with a stick. Once again, Ben blamed himself while Diana was able to accept it and move forward.

'We just need to make some small changes,' she said. 'We've managed this far, we'll manage again.'

It didn't feel quite so simple to Ben. He feared for Alice's future. What would she do when he and Diana got old? Would she ever be able to live independently? His concerns about the future ate away at him.

Laura became a refuge from real life. It started with lunch breaks taken together and it continued with drinks after work – at first with colleagues, later on their own. It all came to a head on a work weekend away. It was a moment of weakness. They were all staying overnight at a hotel in Scarborough. The idea was to mix up the staff members and get them thinking about how the company could be improved. As soon as he got there, Ben received a photo message from Diana showing Alice with her new stick. She'd gone for a blue one in a small act of defiance.

'I'm not blind, Dad. I'll get a blue stick, it's way cooler than a white one. And I don't need it most of the time, only when I'm in crowded locations.'

Ben could have cried. The rational side of his brain told him this was just nature doing its thing. The emotional side – the father – despised himself for letting down his child. They'd given her a crappy deal in life and she made it worse by just getting on with it without making a fuss.

That day Ben ended up in a working group with Laura. After a day spent blue-sky thinking and an evening in the bar, it was bound to happen. He'd been brooding over the photograph of Alice with her stick instead of coming up with inspirational new ideas. Laura had had a little too much to drink and her guard was down. It was a convergence of events. Had any one factor been excluded, perhaps things would have turned out differently.

Now, fewer than eleven months on, they were trying to figure out how to get a decent passport photo for Harper, and the daughter that Ben had been so desperate to protect had been abandoned by her father. He simply didn't know what to do for the best. New daughter, original daughter? New partner, original partner? He'd jumped ship in a moment of panic and now he got to live through his terrible choices every day.

The photographer knew what she was doing. Had they gone for the budget option and tried their hand at a photo booth or a smart-phone image, it would all have gone wrong. As it was, after a few tries Harper obliged by keeping her eyes open and they got their passport photos.

The injections also went well, and for a moment Ben felt that everything was just a little too easy. He wasn't used to that, bumps in the road were the norm these days. Granted, Harper was screaming away in a coffee shop and people around them were tutting at their seeming lack of parental intervention. But, for Ben, this was what passed as a good day.

Laura was assembling the express passport paperwork and cutting out the photos of Harper right there at the table.

'If we get this done now, we can get it checked at the post office and send it off today. At least that's another thing out of the way.'

Laura was right, and Ben was grateful that she was taking a lead with the paperwork. Anything to do with forms and he would run a mile.

His phone vibrated in his pocket. He struggled to recollect the days before mobile phones. It wasn't that long ago, but there was a time when he'd have sat in that coffee shop chatting or reading a book. Of the people around him who weren't tutting at Harper's shrill cries, he reckoned over half of them had phones in their hands or in front of them on the table.

'It's Gaby again,' Ben said, as much to himself as to Laura. 'Wow, and Steve too. Something must be kicking off.'

He opened his Facebook messages.

Steve and Gaby were clearly excited about something or other.

Richard is coming!!! But stay quiet, only Mum knows!!!

Gaby loved using exclamation marks.

Guess who's coming to Dad's party?

Steve was a little more restrained, but still keen to share the news.

They hadn't seen Richard for a long time. But Susan had thought it best to invite him. It was anybody's guess how Tony would feel about that.

CHAPTER THIRTEEN

1992: The Fourth Lie

It was the summer vacation job that turned Ben into a vegetarian, much to the horror of his father. Tony never forgave him for turning his back on the family business.

Purveyors of the finest meats throughout the north of England the sign boasted. Harrington was a name synonymous with meat products. They supplied butchers, restaurants, caterers and supermarkets throughout the entire region. The business had been established by Tony's father who'd handed it over to his son. All Tony had to do was not to screw everything up and it would generate a decent income for the family for generations to come.

Ben had never really taken much interest in the business. It had always been there in the background. If he visited the industrial unit on the outskirts of the city, he never went further than the admin offices. He knew what they did, but he'd never got his hands dirty. Until the age of eighteen he'd been happy to enjoy all the advantages it brought in terms of wealth and privilege but had no interest in following in Steve's footsteps and getting weekend work there.

Tony seemed particularly keen on his eldest son taking over the reins when he'd had enough and decided to retire. Ben was not the kind of youngster to hold grudges, but from time to time he'd remark that it seemed that Steve was being groomed to become Tony's successor. He knew it wasn't just because his brother was the eldest of the siblings, it was more that his nature was better suited to the work.

Ever since he and Steve started to deliver GCSE and A level success, Ben realised that Tony had always felt inferior to his business colleagues in the local community. Their father would remind them that he was disinfecting the factory floor when he was their age and had never had the opportunity to study and earn the prestige that academic success brought with it. It was why, Ben assumed, Steve had been pushed towards private school. It was a badge of honour for Tony, a means of gaining status through his child rather than through his own achievements.

Steve had worked in the factory since he was fourteen. Like Tony, he began by cleaning the floors and helping to dispose of the carcasses. Soon it became obvious that he had a flair for the business side of things and Tony would spend many hours deep in conversation with his eldest son, almost to the exclusion of the other siblings. That didn't particularly bother Ben. In fact he was pleased he'd managed to avoid having to get weekend work until now. His needs were modest. So long as he could afford to buy second-hand books and CDs from the local charity shops, that was enough for him.

But Tony was on the warpath. For a man who'd had to do physical work from such a young age, he struggled to reconcile the sedentary life of his sons with his own experience of hard, physical graft. It annoyed him that Ben spent his days reading, listening to music or studying. With Ben's A levels completed and a long summer holiday in front of him, Tony dealt him a body blow.

'Your brother paid half the cost of his driving lessons with money earned in the factory. If you want to pass your test, you'll have to do the same. All you have to do is put on a pair of blue wellington boots, a mob cap and a white coat and get the brush and disinfectant out, just like I did and just like Steve did.'

'But come on, Dad. You know I'm not cut out for that kind of work. You said it yourself. I take after Mum. I'm not built for grafting.'

'An honest day's work will do you good. What are you going to do all summer – lie in bed all day wasting your life away? That's the deal, Ben. If you want driving lessons, I expect you to put 50 percent upfront. Take it or leave it. You have a bicycle in the garage and you can take that to university if you're not interested.'

Tony's offer helped to focus Ben's mind. It was the last thing he wanted to do – his plans were to spend his summer holiday at home, getting up at midday, going to bed as late as possible, and spending as much time with Maisie as he could before he moved on to university and they went through the inevitable break-up.

Ben had it all worked out. If he could pass his driving test first time, like Steve had, he would get away with working for three weeks at the factory and then he could leave. The only trouble was, Ben wasn't a natural behind the wheel. He simply couldn't get the hang of the reversing around a corner manoeuvre and as for reverse parking in a supermarket car park, that was a no-go area for him.

Anything that involved going forward was in, anything backward was out.

From the day of his induction, Ben knew he was going to hate working at the factory. The heady idealism of being eighteen years of age made every bone in his body resent what his family were doing to make their money, although he managed to contain his outrage until the driving test was passed, on the third try.

'How many animals are our family responsible for slaughtering since Grandad set up the business?' he'd challenge Tony at the dinner table.

'Enough to keep two generations and counting of the Harrington family in comfort,' Tony would answer, visibly annoyed at his son's naivety. 'Enough to pay for this lovely house and the holidays we enjoy every year. Enough to pay for you to have plenty of money when you go to university. It's a business, Ben. If people didn't eat meat, there would be no business. As long as people eat meat, it'll keep a roof over our heads.'

Vegetarianism and veganism hadn't been an issue for Tony's dad and it had only recently been an issue for Tony. The world was changing, things weren't quite as black and white as they'd been in the 'meat and two veg' days of his childhood. And now here was his own son calling him to account over the business which put the shirt on his own back.

The sight of the blood and the carcasses would turn Ben's stomach. He had always been a meat-eater, but there was nothing quite like working in the factory to rethink his life choices. He thanked his lucky stars that they weren't slaughtering. At least the Harringtons were at the processing end of the food chain.

Every day trucks filled with the headless carcasses of

sheep and pigs, as well as sides of beef, would arrive in refrigerated vans at the back of the factory. Ben and the other young workers would have to unload the meat and take it through to the factory where it would be chopped, sawn and minced. Every day they would be responsible for swilling away the blood that coated the floors, throwing discarded bones and fat into massive bins and disinfecting the work areas, for it all to begin again the next day. The meats would then be processed and finessed in the other half of the factory. Sprigs of herbs would be added, stuffing injected, pats of butter applied, and then it was wrapped up in attractive packaging. By the time the products were moved into different refrigerated vans at the front of the building, they were the socially acceptable face of eating animals: beautifully packaged meat products which allowed the people buying them to completely disassociate themselves from the death and distress that had led to the creation of that mouth-watering product.

Ben had never even thought about it before, but the factory reminded him of a death camp, all neatly packaged with condiments. He hadn't even completed his first day at work before he decided he was going veggie as soon as he left the family home and was able to cook for himself. His idealistic eighteen-year-old self found the whole thing distasteful, but he'd tolerate it a few more weeks while his mum was cooking the meals.

It was on his last day at the factory that Ben finally confirmed his decision never to work in the family business again. He'd leave that to Steve – he was much better suited to the work. Ben had checked out with his supervisor, said a farewell to his colleagues and driven back home in the old banger which he'd managed to fund in addition to his driving lessons. As he liberally applied his aftershave in eager anticipation of a night out with Maisie, he realised that he'd forgotten to drop off his locker keys at the factory unit.

The detour past the factory wasn't too far out of his way, and with the freedom of driving himself still a novelty, Ben decided to drop them through the office door. If there was one thing his dad had been right about, it was that he needed to act more responsibly. He got that now.

Pulling up at the front of the building, the car park lit up as Ben's car triggered the light sensor. He stepped out, feeling in his pocket for the locker keys. He walked over to the letterbox mounted on the wall beside the office door and pushed them through the opening, making sure they'd dropped inside properly.

He was returning to the car, thinking about Maisie, when he heard a heavy door slamming at the rear of the building. The factory was supposed to be shut until seven o' clock the next morning, so Ben decided to do the responsible thing and check it out. Stealthily he walked around the edge of the unit. He could hear voices – two or three of them, he couldn't be sure, they were keeping the noise down. There was a large industrial bin to the side of the building which allowed Ben to get a good view of what was going on without being seen.

There were two of them working out of a small van – it wasn't refrigerated. One of the loading bay hatches was opened up and the lights were on. They were moving something in, rather than stealing equipment. Was this some late-night delivery? Ben wasn't party to all the technicalities of the business, but there was something about the way they were transporting the carcasses which seemed unusual. They were covered in black plastic and it took both men to move each parcel into the bay. A third man joined them from inside the building. He looked like he was in charge, he made no attempt to help. He was smoking a cigarette and supervising the operation.

Ben was satisfied that this was no break-in, so he returned to his car, with thoughts of an evening with Maisie occupying his mind. Her parents were out until ten o'clock and they had the house to themselves. In a rare moment of insight and with an embryonic sense of responsibility, Ben decided to call in at home first to mention the night-time activity to his father. There was something troubling him about it. It was that man. Where had he seen him before?

'Hi Dad. I didn't know you had meat deliveries at night,' he said to Tony, who was reading the newspaper.

'We don't. What made you say that?'

'Oh, I was dropping off my keys on the way to Maisie's. There were a couple of guys at the rear hatch - I didn't recognise them. They were taking a delivery of something or other, but it's not like any meat I've seen before.'

Tony put his newspaper down and was now paying more attention. Calmly, he gave Ben his explanation, but Ben could tell he was rattled.

'We sometimes take in game from local shoots. That was a small shipment of deer coming in. I allow a business contact of mine to use our equipment from time to time. The restaurants in southern Scotland like to buy it. You won't have seen that side of the business, it's more of a nuisance than anything, but it's popular with some of our more upmarket customers.'

'Oh.'

Ben was surprised that Tony had offered such a detailed answer. He was keen to get to Maisie's. He wouldn't need that long to accomplish his goals when he got there, but he was mindful of the time, nevertheless. He didn't push the subject, but he had an uneasy feeling in the pit of his stomach that lingered for some time. He didn't think Tony had been telling the truth. Sure, those carcasses might have been about the same size as a deer, he didn't know that much about it. But if he'd seen it in a movie, he wouldn't have been surprised to discover that they were moving human bodies in those plastic wrappings.

CHAPTER FOURTEEN

June 2018: Three Days Before The Party

Ben had it all worked out. The bags were packed and waiting by the front door. He'd managed to source a black support on Amazon in a pack of three and they looked pretty good. Granted, his middle-aged paunch wouldn't allow him to wear them quite as well as the six-pack model in the product description, but he was certain he could pass them off as an accidental pre-holiday purchase. Besides, he'd have plenty of ways to get undressed with Laura out of the room, what with their routines being disrupted by hotels and flights. He would only have to sit in the train to the airport, then sleep in the hotel, then sit on a plane, then sleep in another hotel. He was as certain as he could be that he'd get away with it. A small deception here or there would cover him: too tired from travelling for sex, changing in the bathroom rather than the bedroom in case the cleaners walked in. Laura would be none the wiser.

He'd even made a big deal about shaving his pubic area

and landed himself in Laura's good books for doing something for her. He felt like a plucked chicken, but it was a look that she preferred as a younger woman.

So, on his pre-vasectomy checklist, Ben had now ticked off everything he could think of. They had a taxi booked to the station; he'd distributed their packing over two bags so as not to make the lifting too unbearable; and they'd managed to borrow some lightweight travel kit from one of Laura's baby clinic friends so Harper's paraphernalia wouldn't weigh them down too much. As far as Laura was concerned, Ben would be at work all day, so he'd have plenty of time to lose himself in the local library or coffee shop to get used to having had the snip before he headed home.

He was pleased that Laura was still in bed when he left the house. He was feeling jittery, and he'd have had a difficult job hiding it from her if she'd managed to rouse herself out her slumber and join him for breakfast. Although all the men featured in the YouTube videos he'd watched had said the same thing – it's not as bad as you think but take it easy for a few days – Ben still didn't relish the thought of having a needle inserted into such a delicate area.

The staff at the clinic had seen it all before. So, when Ben pulled himself up on to the operating couch, completely naked below the waist, he tried to retain a sense of perspective. He'd hesitated over his socks – to keep them on or not? He decided not.

The doctor and nurse had heard all the nervous jokes before.

'Make sure you don't chop the wrong thing off!' he said as they pulled a sheet of blue paper over him to give him what little dignity they could.

The nurse smiled, laughed a little, then stuck the needle in. He could feel the local anaesthetic kicking in – he hoped that would be the worst of it. He lay back and tried to relax. It was a strange sensation, as if someone was doing the washing-up in his groin. He couldn't actually feel it, but he knew it was happening.

He thought of Alice and Ted and wondered how they were. He was desperate to see them. If only he'd had the money to take them out with him to the seventieth birthday gathering. Then he wondered how ridiculous he looked as he was snipped, clamped and manhandled by the doctor. Did they ever have a laugh at the patients after they'd gone? Ben suspected that it probably got quite boring after a while.

'And we're done!' the nurse said.

'Really? Is that it?'

'Yes, it's as simple as that.'

Ben began to breathe normally again. He hadn't realised how tense he'd been.

'I can't believe it's that easy. In fact, that was so easy, I'll come again!'

He smiled at the nurse, but she'd heard it before. She managed to force out a small smile before reminding him of what he could and couldn't do after the operation.

'If patients ever get into trouble, it's because they ignore the advice and do too much too soon. Take it nice and easy for a couple of days. Let the dressing come off in the shower and you'll be good to go. Remember not to have unprotected sex until you get the all-clear, it takes some time to flush out the last bits and pieces.'

Ben felt a massive sense of relief, he knew he could get this past Laura. After all, the following days would be taken up with travel and sleep. He was feeling fine. The videos had been right – there was absolutely nothing to worry about. By the time he arrived home, after an afternoon spent reading travel books in the library, he'd almost forgotten he'd had the operation.

Laura was all packed up, the house was clean, the baby fed and the two of them ready to go.

'I can't wait to meet your family,' she said. 'It's high time we put all the upset behind us and got on with our lives. Besides, they won't be able to resist our little beauty here.'

Harper made a happy gurgling noise and Ben ran his hand gently across her head, loving the feel of her freshly washed, downy hair.

'That's the taxi already. He's actually on time – that doesn't happen very often.'

Laura lifted up Harper, grabbed her travel bag and opened the door, leaving Ben to carry the suitcases. He walked to the door, hoping the taxi driver would jump out attentively to give them both a hand. He did no such thing, but sat as if glued to his seat, incapable of any movement which didn't include a steering wheel or gear stick.

Ben noticed there was now a third suitcase lined up next to the other two.

'I thought we'd got all the baby stuff sorted,' he cursed under his breath. They'd have to pay extra for that at the airport. Laura had assured him they'd be able to manage with just the two.

He stopped to check all was well after his operation. It was, still no pain. It was only when he swung that last suit-case into the boot of the car and caught it awkwardly at the side, nearly dropping it into the street, that Ben felt the first sharp twinge.

CHAPTER FIFTEEN

June 2018: Three Days Before The Party

The train was delayed. It was a regional train service too. Ben hated those. In the days before he and Laura had got together, he always travelled first class in those cattle trucks. It was the only way to achieve any sensation that even approximated to a comfortable journey.

This airport train service was overcrowded and ramshackle, a relic from a bygone age, yet in the north of England it's what somebody saw fit to describe as an express service. It was certainly much better than having to brave the Manchester traffic, and cheaper than paying the extortionate airport parking costs. So, cattle truck it was, standard class, via the UK's northern rail network.

All they had to do was to complete the journey of less than two hours, which would drop them off right in the heart of the airport. As long as they arrived at a reasonable time they could meet up with Gaby and Jaxon, enjoy a pleasant evening of catching up in the hotel restaurant, and then get a decent night's sleep before checking in for the early flight. Just like Ben's operation, it should have been so straightforward.

The late arrival of the airport train coincided with the late arrival of a CrossCountry train, meaning that it was packed. As the three-carriage vehicle came to a stop at the platform, Ben glanced inside the windows of the first-class section, recalling better days. There were seats to spare in there and the occupants looked relaxed and contented. Meanwhile, in standard class there was about to be a bun fight. There was no way all the people who were now clustering around the train doors were going to fit on that train.

'We're in carriage B, seats 21 and 22, it's a table seat,' Ben reminded Laura. 'You grab the seats, I'll do the bags. It's every man for himself. And woman. And baby.'

Laura didn't look amused. This was the first time she'd had to perform a manoeuvre like this with a new baby and she didn't fancy her chances.

The doors opened and those who were waiting to get in begrudgingly stood back to let off the passengers who were exiting the train. Then the battle began. Ben waited, watching Laura skilfully move herself into the slipstream and get on board.

She'll save my place. Everybody will get out of the way for a woman and her baby, he thought to himself.

The guard was now standing by the train door, monitoring the progress of those boarding. He saw Ben struggling with his three cases.

'Do you want a hand with those, mate?'

'That would be great, thanks.'

Ben picked up the two lightest bags and left the guard with the heaviest. He felt a slight twinge, but nothing too bad. It was probably just the way he'd twisted while he was putting the case in the taxi earlier. The luggage rack was full, but the man adeptly slung the other bags around and made room for Ben's cases.

'Brilliant, thank you!'

The guard would never know just how grateful he was. The third bag Laura had packed felt as if it was crammed with bricks. He scanned the carriage. People were having to stand in the aisle. At least Laura would have his seat saved.

'Excuse me, excuse me,' he said, one person at a time, slowly working his way from one end of the train to the other. At last he arrived at his seat. He almost walked past it because there was a man sitting there. He was completely bald, wearing polarised sunglasses, a black Johnnie Walker T-shirt, cargo shorts and white trainers. No socks, as Ben observed. Laura was squashed against the window with Harper in her baby carrier fast asleep. The man's legs were wide open, and he sat there, proprietorial, surveying his domain. This consisted of two discarded cans of Special Brew and a half-eaten sandwich.

Laura made a face at Ben and shrugged her shoulders. Ben decided to play it passive-aggressive. He took the train tickets out of his pocket and went through an elaborate performance of checking his seat booking against the ticket that was sticking out behind the bald man's head.

Still he stared into the distance.

'Excuse me, I think you're sitting in my seat.'

'Not me, sunshine. Looks like it's mine now.'

The man didn't even bother to turn his head as he spoke to Ben.

'Do you have a booking for this seat?'

The people who were standing in the aisle on either side of Ben visibly began to tense, sensing they were about to be bang in the middle of a stand-off. They shuffled as far away from the epicentre as they could. Ben was painfully aware that he was on his own.

'Not sure I need one, mate. When the trains are all late the bookings go out the window. Looks like I got here first.'

'But that's my girlfriend – my partner – you're sitting next to. We booked a seat together. I'd like to sit next to her please.'

'Leave it, Ben,' Laura cautioned. 'Don't make a fuss.'

'Exactly, darling,' the man sneered. 'It's not worth the fuss.'

The people on the opposite side of the table buried their heads in their phones. In the train-seat lottery, they'd just bought losing tickets. They could have been seated anywhere in the train, only they were sitting right next to the brick shithouse who thought he was entitled to sit in the weedy man's seat. And the weedy man was going to have a go at making him see reason. Everybody but Ben saw how that was likely to play out.

Ben felt a surge of indignation. He was sick of brawny guys throwing their weight around thinking they could do anything they wanted. Besides, he was surrounded by witnesses. Surely the bald guy wouldn't get aggressive with so many people around? And they all had their phones too. It was getting more difficult for bullies, racists and sexists to get away with things in public places. There was usually a witness there ready to supply evidence in the form of a grainy mobile phone video on social media.

'Look, here's my booking for that seat on this train. It doesn't matter if the trains are late or overcrowded. You don't have a booking for that seat and I do. Now please, move aside and save me the trouble of calling the guard to sort this out.'

The man sat up and spread his arms, revealing the

bulging muscles that were barely contained within his T-shirt. Sensing the disturbance, Harper woke up and began to cry.

'Now look what you've done.'

Ben was exasperated. Bald guy just felt in his pockets and pulled out a pair of lightweight headphones which he plugged into his mobile phone. Ben could hear the tinny beat of the music helping him to drown out the shrieks from the baby.

'Okay, I'm going to speak to the guard!'

Ben wagged his finger so the man would pick up a sense of his mood, even if he couldn't hear what he was saying.

'See you in a moment,' Ben mouthed to Laura, as he began to work his way back up the train to find the guard. He'd bonded with the guard. He'd take Ben's side, he was sure.

It took him a good five minutes to locate him hiding in the toilet area right at the top of the train. Ben explained his situation. The guard listened patiently, then, like a judge, delivered his ruling.

'I'd give it a few stops if I were you, mate. I'm not even thinking about checking tickets until some of these passengers have got off. It's like a cattle truck in there. It's generally not worth the bother. These pricks just don't get it, they think the world revolves around them. Your wife's got a seat with the baby, that's the most important thing.

Ben didn't want to annoy the guard, but he was getting more and more frustrated at the situation. In fact, he had such a head of steam on him that he pushed his way back down the train towards his seat, ready to pick a fight. Even the people standing in the aisles were getting annoyed with him now, as if to say, 'Leave it, mate, it's really not worth it.'

Ben drew up to his seat and puffed out his chest to make

himself bigger than he was. He was just about to launch into a 'Now look here ...' diatribe when he saw that the seat was empty. A rancid smell of soiled nappy permeated the atmosphere.

'Oh, you're back! About time too,' Laura said.

'What happened to our friend? Did he realise I had a fair point?'

'No, just take a deep breath. Harper took a crap then sicked up all over him. I've never seen anybody move so fast in my life. Now, take the baby, will you? She needs a change of clothes.'

CHAPTER SIXTEEN

1998: The Fifth Lie

There was to be no house party for Richard's birthday. He was not considered trustworthy enough. He'd recently brought shame upon the family for being caught smoking weed at school. He was persona non grata as far as Tony was concerned. The faster Richard moved on to university or whatever was coming next for him, the better. So Richard organised his own birthday celebration. A few friends in the pub – the ability to drink legally at last, it was all he needed.

The fact that all his siblings had long since moved on made things particularly hard at home. Ben – who he'd always had an affinity with – was in a serious relationship with a girl called Diana and seldom seemed to get home to give him some respite from the relentless hounding from his father. Gaby had always disapproved of him, and the recent incident with the weed hadn't helped him to improve his popularity ratings. Steve gave him the time of day, but he was so busy posing in his new Porsche that Richard tended to cramp his style. Besides, Steve had made things very clear when Richard was just fifteen years old: there was no place for him in the business. He was not required, Steve had things under control. Besides, his week-long work placement from school had proved that Richard and Harrington Meats were not a good fit, he wasn't suited to the work. The business had turned Ben into a vegetarian and Gaby had once protested outside the factory unit with her vegan friends, but Richard had been rejected out of hand. He would have to make his own way in the world, whether he liked it or not.

Steve had his own flat now and was living an affluent bachelor lifestyle. Richard looked up to his brother and admired his confidence, wishing that he too could feel that sure sense of his place in the world. But the truth was, Richard had never really known how he slotted in.

On the evening of his birthday he sat with Susan, opening his cards and examining his gifts.

'Do you think Dad will get back in time? It would be nice to catch him before I head off.'

'I think he's going to be busy all day, Rich. I'm sorry, I'm sure he wanted to be here.'

Richard wasn't so certain about that.

'Thanks for the cheque for the driving lessons, Mum. It's so expensive to get started – my paper round pays next to nothing, it's really hard to save.'

'Well, don't tell your dad about it. That's come from my writing money, he doesn't need to know. It's just my extra gift to you. I love you, Rich. You do know that, don't you? I know things feel tough for you sometimes. It's just that we worry. With all that business at school and you not knowing what you want to do next. We're concerned about you.'

'It's okay, Mum, honestly. The weed thing is no big deal,

it's not like I'm going to turn into an addict or anything. We just got caught, that's all. They had to do something to punish us. I get that. Don't worry. I've got a plan. I'll make you proud of me ... and Dad, he'll see, he'll be proud of me too one of these days.'

Susan reached out to squeeze his hand.

'I'm already proud of you.'

'I'd better be off. I said I'd meet my pals at the pub at eight o' clock. Tell Dad I said Hi. I'll be back after closing time, don't wait up. I'll be as quiet as I can.'

He gave Susan a hug, checked his hair in the mirror and headed out of the house to catch the bus. Within half an hour he was sitting in the pub with his friends. It felt good to be able to drink a beer without having to lie about his age. It was such a frustrating time of life, to be part-child and part-adult. He was ready to shed his child's skin and move on.

Richard had big plans. He shared them with his friends. There would be no university for him, he was going to set up his own business. He would work hard, build it up and make his family proud. They'd see that he was no waster. He didn't need a university degree to achieve his dreams.

Soon the conversation changed as the beers began to flow. They talked about music, TV, relationships, moving on from school. There was laughter and fun. Richard loved his friends, and this was just the way he wanted to celebrate his eighteenth birthday.

The final bell was rung from the bar. It was drinking-up time. He looked up at the clock on the wall.

'Oh no, I missed my bus!'

'They've got a payphone on the bar. Give your brother a ring, he'll give you a ride home in that cool car of his.'

Richard followed Ali's gaze, and fumbled in his pocket for some change.

'Good idea. I take it you're all okay for getting home?'

His friends nodded, they'd all got plans. Trust the Harringtons to live off the beaten track – none of them would be driving by their affluent estate.

'Steve, hi. It's Richard. Can you give me a lift home? I missed my bus – I'm a bit drunk but nothing too serious. I don't want Mum or Dad to see me like this.'

'Damn it, Richard. I've had a couple of glasses of wine myself. I wish you'd warned me beforehand. But, okay. I shouldn't really be driving but I feel fine and it'll give me a chance to give you your card and present. Happy birthday, by the way. Where are you?'

'The King's Head. I'll wait in the car park. Thanks, Steve.'

As he put the phone down, he heard the landlord's voice calling across the pub.

'Drink up, please. Time to go. I'm locking up now.'

They moved outside, chatted for a few minutes before saying their goodbyes, and headed off in different directions.

Richard waited in the semi-lit car park for his lift. It wasn't long before he heard the distinctive growl of Steve's Porsche making its way up the road.

'Hi bro! Happy birthday!'

Steve handed Richard a gift and a card as he lowered himself into the seat. His speech was a little slurred.

'Thanks Steve, I appreciate it. I'm a little worse for wear. I want to sneak back into the house without waking Mum and Dad. You know what they're like if I have a few drinks. Dad always gives me a hard time about it.'

'Fancy going for a spin before I take you home? The

motorway's quiet this time of night, so we can thrash this thing a bit – drive it the way it's meant to be driven!'

'You are alright, aren't you?'

Richard wasn't so drunk that he couldn't see Steve had had a drink or two himself.

'I'm fine, Rich. Unlike you, some of us are old enough to take our drink. It was just a bit of wine. I'm pretty sure I'm not over the limit. Besides, it's your birthday. Let's have some fun!'

Steve set off, carefully at first, keeping within the speed limit while they were still within the city boundary.

'Wow, thanks Steve. This is brilliant!' Richard said, admiring the mobile phone that Steve had given him for his birthday. 'This one's got the Snake game on it too, thanks so much.'

Steve was into a 60-mph stretch of road now, so he moved his foot down on the accelerator, the low growl of the engine daring him to go faster.

'It's no problem, Rich. I figured you'll need one of those things now you've left school. I've paid the contract on it for a year too. I'm pleased you like it.'

Steve slowed as they reached the roundabout which led to the slip lane of the motorway. As soon as he was able to straighten the steering wheel, he floored the accelerator. The car surged forward pushing Richard back into his seat.

'Jesus, Steve. This thing goes fast!'

'Watch this,' Steve grinned at him, pushing the accelerator down a little more. 'Keep an eye out for the cops. They're not usually out on a quiet stretch like this, but you never know.'

Richard was watching the needle on the speedo.

'Wow, that's over 100 mph!'

At 120 mph Richard called time on Steve's demonstration.

'Steve, I'm scared. That's enough. Drop it down a bit, will you?'

'It's fine, the car can handle it, it goes faster than this—'

At that moment a deer leaped out of the darkness in front of them. There had been a warning sign a couple of miles back, but they'd both ignored it.

Steve slammed his foot on the brake and the Porsche swerved, crossing from the first to the third lane, scraping the safety barrier, then veering back across onto the hard shoulder, coming to a rest on the grass bank.

Silence. The road was quiet, the motorway in darkness. The twin airbags had activated, but Richard looked to be in a bad way. Blood was pouring from a gash on his forehead. His seatbelt was undone – he hadn't fastened it properly when they'd left the pub.

Steve unclipped his own seatbelt and gave Richard a gentle shake.

'Fuck!' he shouted. 'Fuck! Fuck!'

He climbed out of the car and walked round to his brother's side, wrenching open the door. Clumsily he felt Richard's neck and wrist in a desperate attempt to find a pulse. He screamed at the lifeless body.

'Wake up, Rich!'

Steve forced himself to stop for a moment. He needed help. He straightened up and looked at the car, checking the damage. He stepped forward and searched by Richard's feet for the mobile phone. He retrieved the packaging and the card, then closed the passenger door and made one last sweep of the vehicle, removing anything that would place him at the scene of the crash.

Steve climbed up the grass bank and walked into some trees for cover. He pulled out his mobile phone.

'Kyle, don't ask any questions. Just listen. It's important. I need your help. There's been an accident. I need you to place a call from my flat. Use your spare key to let yourself in. Make sure nobody sees you. You need to pretend to be me. You need to report my Porsche missing. Tell them your brother took it and that you're worried about him because he seemed to be a little bit drunk at the time. Then I need you to pick me up. I'll walk along to Junction 36 – I should be there in about fifteen minutes, I'll wait for you, away from the road.'

CHAPTER SEVENTEEN

June 2018: Three Days Before The Party

'I need to warn you about Jaxon,' Ben said. 'He can be a little devil.'

'I notice you kept that one quiet,' Laura replied. 'In what way?'

'Well, Gaby is into new-age child rearing. She believes that kids should be free to express themselves and Jaxon certainly likes to make the most of expressing himself.'

'Crikey! How old is he?'

'Eight. To be fair, I haven't seen him for some time, so if we're lucky he'll have grown out of it.'

'Yeah, good luck with that. I've heard about these new-age types, they're a bunch of hippies. Anyway, thanks for the warning, forewarned is forearmed and all that.'

The train pulled into the airport hub. Ben stood up to retrieve the cases. He was relieved to feel no twinges – the two-hour sit down had been good for him. He'd find a trolley and wheel the luggage to the hotel. He could do this, he was certain. Laura would be none the wiser.

He had to suppress a smile as bald guy shuffled along the corridor pretending not to notice him. There was a waft of dried baby sick as he brushed by. It couldn't have happened to a nicer person.

Ben carefully lifted the bags onto the platform and waited for Laura to join him.

'Let's get checked in – hopefully Gaby will be in the hotel already. We can eat in the restaurant tonight. Wait here while I get a trolley.'

Things were looking up. Not only was there a trolley available, but its wheels seemed to run in a reasonably straight line too. Ben found that if he lifted by bending his knees, it avoided any tugs or twists in his sensitive area. He just had to let different muscles take the strain while the wound was healing. He could keep that up for a couple of days.

The hotel was linked to the airport, so they just had to work their way through the terminal to get there. It was more expensive than the hotels on the outskirts of the airport, but it would minimise the bag lifting for Ben. His mum and dad would pick up the bill. With the extra funds from the bank now safely in his account he only had to get to the island and then he wouldn't have to spend any money for a whole nine days. It would be bliss.

Within half an hour they were in their room, all bags intact and feeling remarkably fresh after having sat in a train for a couple of hours. Ben checked his phone.

'Gaby's here. She wants to meet at the restaurant in ten minutes. You know, now we're here I'm beginning to look forward to this. It'll be nice to see the family again – birthdays are a great excuse to get everybody together. They're a lot more fun than funerals.'

Laura was warming a bottle of milk for Harper by sitting it in the kettle on the tray with the tea and coffee. Ben frowned as he watched her.

'We're not going to have problems getting the milk through airport security, are we? I hadn't thought of that.'

'It'll be fine,' Laura replied. 'We're allowed to bring enough on board to last the journey. I've got enough bottles for 24 hours and the whole trip is only 18 hours plus a two-hour stopover. I'll mix it up tonight and keep it in the cooler pack.'

Ben wasn't so sure but let it go.

'Okay, good to go?' he asked. 'Let's do this. Harrington sibling number 1: difficulty level, moderate. Let's go and find Gaby.'

As the lift reached the reception area, a remote-controlled toy car whizzed past the opening door.

'Jaxon!' Ben said, raising his eyebrows at Laura.

Sure enough, it was Jaxon.

'Uncle Ben!'

A small boy hurled himself at Ben, burrowing into him.

'Woah, careful!'

Ben felt a small pang as he flinched to absorb the impact. It was still okay – nothing he couldn't cope with.

Jaxon had grown since they'd last met. He was a good-looking boy. Why on earth did Gaby insist on dressing him in a pink top? Poor kid, he'd learn to hate that one day.

He could see his sister smiling indulgently at her son from a seat on the other side of the reception area.

'Nice to see you again, kiddo,' Ben said, and walked over to her. They embraced – a little tentatively at first but then warmly. They were genuinely pleased to see each other, even with all the water that had passed under the bridge.

'You're looking good, Ben,' Gaby said, surveying her older sibling. 'Introduce me to Laura then, and let's see this lovely baby of yours.'

Gaby had chosen the route of peaceful engagement and Ben was grateful for that. It seemed she'd decided not to pick any fights. Not yet, at least.

'Pleased to meet you, Laura.'

Gaby opted for a handshake at first, then thought better of it and moved in for an awkward hug. As they pulled apart, a suited man from the reception desk interrupted them with an apologetic cough.

'Excuse me, madam. I wonder if you would refrain from letting your child use that toy in here.'

Jaxon's radio-controlled car had cleared the central area as people hovered on the perimeter of the lobby, trying to avoid the random movements of the plastic vehicle around their feet.

Gaby was having none of it.

'He's a kid, let him play!'

The man was a little taken aback by this.

'It's just that it's a matter of health and safety, madam. We wouldn't want to cause an accident with one of our more elderly guests.'

Ben intervened. It was always best when Gaby was being challenged about her child-rearing choices.

'Let's head for the restaurant, I'm starving. Jaxon, come on. It's burger time!'

The man in the suit gave Ben a grateful nod and offered to escort them over to the restaurant to make sure that they were seated swiftly. Jaxon picked up his toy and handed it to Gaby, who passed it to Ben.

'I want to cuddle this gorgeous baby of yours. Hello Harper.'

Laura handed the baby over, looked at Ben and gave him as big a smile as she dared. The ice was broken. One down, several more family members still to go.

Jaxon's table manners hadn't improved since Ben last shared a meal with Gaby. He ate with his hands, ignoring the cutlery. The spillages were many and the table began to resemble a war zone. Gaby was oblivious to it all.

'Mummy says you left Auntie Diana to make a baby with Laura. Is she my new auntie now?'

Laura's face turned red, and Ben shifted uneasily in his seat opposite Jaxon. His nephew had turned into the Grand Inquisitor.

'Well, yes, that's right, Jaxon. Auntie Diana and I don't live together anymore and now I live with Laura and Harper.'

'Does that mean Alice and Ted don't have a dad? What will Alice do now she doesn't have a dad?'

Ben considered for a moment that Jaxon might have direct and open access to his conscience. The kid couldn't have asked more pertinent questions. Had Gaby set him up for this? Surely not, she wasn't paying much attention, she seemed completely preoccupied with the baby.

'No, I still love Alice and Ted,' he replied. 'And Diana and I will always look after Alice, as she needs lots of extra help.'

He tried his best to sound calm and measured, after all Jaxon was just a kid, not Saint Peter at the gates to heaven, even though it felt that way. Or was he destined for hell?

Ben was bracing himself for whatever was coming next, when Jaxon came up with a complete show-stopper.

'Mum, I need the toilet! It's a big one.'

Gaby handed Harper back to Laura who'd been enjoying being able to eat a meal without having to sit a baby on her knee. She'd also been enjoying Ben's discomfort under the unrelenting questioning of Jaxon.

'I'll take you, darling,' Gaby said. 'I don't want you using the male toilets in a strange place.'

They left the table, Jaxon in somewhat of a hurry.

'Please tell me they learn to control their bowels by the time they're his age?' Laura said, once they were out of earshot.

'Most of them do by the time they're two, but as you can see, Jaxon is a special case. What do you think? She seems like she's playing nice, doesn't she?'

'Well, she loves this little one. Maybe she just wanted more kids, perhaps she wasn't ready to stop at Jaxon. Though frankly, from what I've seen of him already, I'd want to stop at Jaxon. I mean, he's a nice kid but he's just a bit ... feral!'

Ben laughed. 'That's exactly the right word, feral. And you're right, he is a nice kid. She just doesn't set any boundaries for him.'

Laura put her fork down and leaned towards her bag to take out a face wipe for Harper.

'Oh, I forgot to tell you, this came in the mail today. I thought you'd want to see it. It's been forwarded from your old address by Diana. That's her handwriting, isn't it?'

Laura drew an envelope out of her bag and gave it to Ben. Instead of opening it, he turned it over in his hands, examining it as if it was some historical artefact.

'Yes, that's her handwriting on the redirect. I don't recognise the handwriting on the original address though – and that's a London postcode. Strange, it's unusual to get a handwritten letter these days.'

'Open it then. Don't just look at it.'

Ben tore it open and read the letter. There was no date and no address. Just a scrawled note in handwriting that he didn't recognise at first, until he saw the signature.

Ben, we always got on as kids. Just wanted to give you a heads ups about Dad's party, it's going to get a bit tense but it's time we sorted things out. Hope you're okay, Rich x

CHAPTER EIGHTEEN

June 2018: Two Days Before The Party

Ben slept badly that night. He hadn't heard from Richard for such a long time. His brother's life had come to exist as a series of third-party reports, gossip and hearsay. He'd felt guilty when he read the short letter. Guilty that he hadn't shown more interest in him. He'd been so preoccupied with his own life and troubles – he didn't even realise that his brother was living in London.

It was the tone of the letter that troubled him most. What on earth would possess Richard to write something like that? And without an explanation too. He decided to keep it quiet from Gaby, he needed time to think it through. When it came to Richard, Ben always felt wretched at the sudden turn his life had taken. In fact, he'd been like an afterthought his whole life. As Rich had said, they used to get on, but after the crash it was a mess for everybody.

Ben had to put the letter out of his mind. They had

arrived at the terminal and it was time to make their way through security.

'I've never done a flight this long before,' Laura said. 'I'm getting a bit nervous now. It's a long time to be in the air.'

'You won't notice it,' Gaby replied. 'You get films to watch, you can have a doze. It'll be over before you know it.'

Ben doubted that. He hoped that he wasn't sitting too close to Jaxon; at least they'd booked their flights separately in the end. As they waited to get their bags scanned, the sounds from Jaxon's tablet were making Ben increasingly agitated. If only he'd turn the volume down! Other people in the queue were looking at him disapprovingly while Gaby appeared to remain oblivious.

It was quite a kerfuffle moving Harper from person to person, taking off shoes and belts, throwing keys, wallets and coins into the plastic trays. As Ben had anticipated, there was the inevitable delay with the baby milk. He was tempted to tell the guy to suck on a teat to try the milk for himself.

Eventually, they passed through, the point of no return. Ben kept checking his pockets – passports and boarding passes – everything was there.

'Oh shit! Shit, shit, shit!'

'What?' Laura asked.

'I can't believe what I've done!'

Laura looked at him.

'You know you put the small case inside the wardrobe, so you didn't keep tripping over it?'

'Yes ... Oh hell. You didn't, did you?'

'It's still there. Damn it!'

'Jeez, Ben, didn't you realise when you were checking them in?'

'I completely forgot about it. What's in there?'

'Clothes, underwear, things like that. I'm not sure.'

'It's too late to go and get it. Besides, they won't let me out now we've checked in. I'm sorry, Laura. What an idiot!'

'Don't worry. We can get some stuff at Kuala Lumpur airport if we need to. We're not cut off from civilisation until we get to the island and anyway Robinson Crusoe managed alright without a change of clothes. It'll be fine, Ben, honestly. It won't be the first time you've worn a pair of underpants for three days in a row.'

Jaxon's tablet game started playing a loud and sustained tune, celebrating the fact that he'd completed another game level. Ben was feeling tense and agitated, not the best frame of mind to begin a long journey. They started to make their way through the duty-free shop, a yellow brick road in Mammon's kingdom. Getting to the end without buying something superfluous to add to their baggage felt like some kind of endurance test. The smell of perfume made Ben sneeze.

He decided he needed to chill, to focus on the upside not the downside: they were checked in on time, Harper was sleeping soundly, they'd got the baby's bag - which was the most important bag of the lot, and they were on their way to a rather nice island break somewhere off the Malaysian coast. It would be an equatorial paradise, a chance to escape his troubles, if only for a short time.

Boarding was straightforward and it wasn't long before they were in their seats, their seat belts fastened, waiting for the safety briefing and pre-flight checks. Ben twisted round, scanning the other passengers.

'Can you see where Gaby and Jaxon are sitting? I lost track of them.'

'They boarded via the rear staircase. We can take a look when we're in the air and they take the seatbelt light off.

Look at this little one, she's fast asleep. If we're lucky she'll sleep like this for most of the flight.'

'I'm just going to call the hotel while I think about it, before we take off. Better warn them about that suitcase.'

Ben searched online for the hotel's number and dialled it straightaway. The flight attendants were working their way along the overhead lockers, making sure they were all closed properly. One of them spotted Ben using his phone.

'You need to turn that off now, sir.'

'It'll only take a minute or two.'

The call was answered almost immediately.

'Hi, Ben Harrington here, we were in room 213 last night. We left a small case in the wardrobe.'

His phone vibrated. A text, what great timing. He'd look at it after finishing the call.

'Yes, it's blue and has a name tag on it. We're back in the UK next week and we'll get it then. Can you keep it safe for us? We're booked into your hotel on the way back. That's great, thanks.'

Another flight attendant was standing by the seat.

'I'm sorry, sir, but all phones need to be switched into flight mode now. You need to end your call.'

'I'm done now!' Ben said. 'I've just got a text message to look at—'

'Sir, it needs to go off now!'

She spoke louder this time, startling Harper out of her slumber.

Three seats or so behind, Ben noticed the sound of a computer game being played. It was piercing and persistent over the hubbub of conversation.

Ben managed to sneak a quick look at the first part of the text message before turning off his phone. It was from Steve.

You'll never guess who's going to see you there at Kuala Lumpur ... go on, three guesses!

He'd have to wait nine hours to get his answer at Hamad International. Nine hours to think about Steve's stupid, cryptic message. Why couldn't he have just told him straight out?

As the plane began to taxi along the runway, the safety announcement began, accompanied by the tuneful sounds of Jaxon's computer game from the seating behind. And now, woken by the flight attendant and deciding that there was no more sleep to be had, Harper began to cry. It was the shrill, persistent cry of a tiny being determined not to sleep for the next nine hours.

CHAPTER NINETEEN

1975: Tony Harrington

Tony Harrington looked over the edge of the cliff face. Could he be certain of death? The last thing he wanted was to end up in a wheelchair, paralysed for life. Like the proverbial albatross, it would be a constant reminder of his complete failure in life. No, if he jumped he had to be sure that would be the end – there could be no half measures.

Tony had just learned his biggest lesson in business, but it looked like it was going to be the one that would destroy him. Cutting corners had seemed like the right thing to do at the time. With soaring rates of inflation the business had been under gruelling, relentless pressure. At just 26 years old, it seemed that he was going to be the member of the Harrington family responsible for the demise of the business which had kept roofs over heads and food on tables for over fifty years.

He took a couple of steps forward and sat on a large stone a couple of feet away from the edge. Behind him, his car was still idling. He'd dismissed the idea of a length of hosepipe and a reel of heavy-duty tape some time ago. It would take too long. When he began to cough and choke he might not be able to stop himself opening the door before the fumes took their deadly effect. Besides, it had to look like an accident. Life insurance was Susan's only hope of getting through this, especially with the two boys and the new baby.

Tony cursed his bad judgement. The offer had seemed so straightforward, it was a way out. Surely those ridiculous inflation rates couldn't go on forever? His costs had gone up: his suppliers were screwing him on price and his staff wanted higher wages so they too could navigate the financial challenges of daily life. Prices were going up every week, yet things like wages, mortgage payments, feeding a family and running the delivery fleet had to continue, the obligations were the same.

He was on his own too. His dad had his stroke at the worst possible time. Tony had been thrown into managing the business too young. His father should have been around to mentor him for at least another five years. And there he was, a partially paralysed shell of the man he once was. Tony was in over his head – no parents to advise him, no siblings for guidance, just his own inadequate abilities and a lack of judgement which was going to bring down the entire house of cards. But was it so bad that he needed to do this? When it came to it, could he really jump?

Tony lit a cigarette. He heard Susan's voice in his head: *You say we're hard up, but you can still afford to smoke those things.* She didn't get it. She didn't understand the stress he was under. The cigarettes were his release.

That was it for kids, he'd resolved. No more children. Three was enough. Gaby couldn't really have come at a worse time. Bang in the middle of 24 percent inflation. Never was an extra mouth to feed so badly timed.

It was growing dark. He'd come up to the cliff edge as part of the cover story. The one they'd piece together after his death. He'd set it up over the course of the past month. He'd pretended to re-discover his father's old camera while clearing out the house after the stroke - the proceeds from the sale would just about cover his care costs if they were lucky. Tony feigned a new interest in photography. He'd taken a few pictures, got them developed, shown them to Susan. He'd made a big deal of catching the sunset after he finished his day at the office.

'I'll be home later tonight, Susan. I need to practice a low ISO small aperture set-up.'

Her eyes had glazed over at the sound of technical talk – that was his plan.

'That's fine, Tony. I'll keep your dinner warm in the oven.'

It was the ideal cover. The cliffs were a popular suicide spot but he'd make it look like a fall. The headlines would describe how a local businessman had tragically plunged to his death while pursuing his new-found love of photography. Susan would get the life insurance and his legacy would no longer be as the imbecile who wrecked a family business.

'Hi, it's beautiful, isn't it?'

Tony turned around. He'd thought he was alone.

'Er, yes, hi, you caught me by surprise. Where are you parked?'

'I left my car further along the track. You're not here to jump, I hope?'

'Oh no ... er ... see, here's my camera, I was taking

photographs of the sunset. I'm an amateur photographer, just learning the tricks of the trade.'

'You might want to take the lens cap off,' the man smiled back at him.

Tony took a good look at the man who had just walked in on his plan to scam the life insurance company. It wouldn't be happening that evening. He'd have to spin Susan some yarn about ruining the film or missing the correct amount of light. The man was about the same age as him, perhaps a little older. He seemed rough, well-built, in a military way, sure of himself and his right to be there.

'Aren't you Tony Harrington, the meat guy? I've seen your photograph in the evening paper, haven't I?'

Tony was relieved that the light was beginning to fade, he felt his face going red.

'Yes, you'll have seen the big story, no doubt. Fined for selling sub-standard meat. It's been all over the local press, there's no hiding from it.'

'These are tough times, Mr Harrington. You can't be blamed for cutting a few corners to make ends meet. This high inflation is killing us all, it's a very difficult environment in which to do business.'

'Are you in business yourself?' Tony asked.

He was in professional networking mode now. He'd have to postpone his plans to die.

'I guess you could say that. I have a number of business interests in the city.'

'Would I know any of them?'

'Probably not ... No, I doubt it,' he replied. 'The funny thing is, I was thinking about you when I read about your recent problems in the newspaper. A man like me, in my line of business ... I could use a partner like you.'

'How so?' Tony was intrigued. 'What is your line of business?'

'I have fingers in a number of pies. But probably my biggest interest is in people management.'

'Oh, personnel?'

'A bit like that. Hiring and firing, you know the sort of thing. But I could make use of a premises like yours, it could be very handy.'

Tony examined the man's face. He seemed to be in earnest. This was the last topic of conversation he'd expected to be having at the top of a cliff. If he hadn't been such a coward, his head should have been dashed on the rocks below. Perhaps this man might have been the one to discover the body.

'What's your interest in my business premises?'

'You open from 7am until 7pm, is that correct?'

'You seem to know a lot about my business.'

'I like to know what's going on. As I said, I read about you in the paper. What happens at your industrial unit overnight?'

'Nothing. It's empty. We switch everything off, lock the doors and go home. Until the next day.'

'Exactly! So, for twelve hours every night you're paying for that unit and it's sitting there redundant.'

Tony was beginning to feel a little uneasy now. This man seemed to know a lot about him and his business. And what seemed to be a chance meeting in a remote location was feeling more and more as if it had been engineered.

'I want to make you a proposition, Tony. I know things are tough for you at the moment. I also know that you didn't come here to take a photo of the sunset this evening.'

'Hang on a minute!' Tony protested.

'It's fine, really it is. You're a family man and a businessman. Sometimes the pressure gets too much, I understand that. But I'm going to help you out. I will take care of your fine and I will pay you £500 in cash every month for night-time access to your premises. Between the hours of eight o' clock at night and six o' clock in the morning, it's mine. I will probably use it, at most, twice per month. You will ask no questions and you will tell no one. In return, you will receive that cash payment of £500 dropped through the office letterbox on the first working day of every month. It will be marked for your personal attention. If there is ever any evidence that we have been in your premises, I will pay you an additional £250 for each and every instance. That's my offer, Mr Harrington. It's a very good one.'

Tony was shocked. He had not expected the evening to end in this way. He should have been dead. Yet, like some angel, this man had come from nowhere and offered him an alternative. At last, a way out which didn't involve screwing up everything.

'May I ask what you'll be doing there at night?'

'You may not. There are two steps to proceed with this arrangement after our conversation today, Mr Harrington. Firstly, you need to give me a firm verbal agreement that you wish to go ahead. You will then make up a package containing access details, codes and any keys that I require to access your premises at night. After that there will be no record of our business together and you will never know that I've been in your unit overnight. There will be nothing to link us as business partners. Your fine will be paid in cash tomorrow morning along with my first month's rent. It's a very sweet offer, Mr Harrington, and I would encourage you to take it.'

Tony knew he didn't have a choice. Leave his wife a widow with three children or take the cash and walk away from his financial problems? He was going to live, things were going to be okay at last. He held out his hand and looked the man directly in the eyes.

'You promise me there's no comeback on this? This is the deal, no questions asked?'

'It's as simple as that. You make the unit available to me, the money continues to flow. You won't even know we've been there. Ever. Besides, it's the perfect partnership. I'm kind of in the meat processing business myself.'

'I do have one question,' Tony said, as he shook on the deal. 'What's your name? I am allowed to know your name?'

'Of course,' the man smiled. 'We're business partners now, after all. I'm Kyle Hunter. Pleased to meet you.'

CHAPTER TWENTY

June 2018: One Day Before The Party

'I feel sick,' Laura said from the back of the car.

Ben had had quite enough of travel problems. In fact, he'd had his fill for a lifetime.

'I told you to take travel-sickness pills. Especially as we have a boat transfer to the island. It might be choppy on the waves.'

'And I told you that I don't like the taste.'

Normally, Ben would have let it go, but he was nearing the end of his tether. Laura would like the taste of a mouthful of vomit even less. Why didn't she just take the pills? Jaxon had been driving him spare, the journey in the plane had been excruciating: nine hours of disapproving looks, tutting and intolerant glances. There was a short reprieve at Hamad International. Jaxon's tablet had run out of batteries by that stage and Ben had offered to go and buy some more in the airport.

'Sorry, Jaxon, they don't have the right type of battery

here. They must use different batteries in this part of the world,' he'd lied.

Jaxon looked doubtful but accepted the answer. Ben wouldn't be winning any Uncle of the Year awards, but he would, at least, get some peace and quiet on the second leg of the journey.

As it turned out, Jaxon and Gaby were nowhere near them on the connecting plane, so he could have saved himself a few days burning in hell for the deception had he just bought the batteries. Harper had worn herself out too. So, apart from the obligatory screaming as the air pressure changed when they came in to land, they got some respite from her crying.

Ben was tired, stressed and irritable. And he was sore. That was troubling him. During the long hours sitting in the plane, a dull ache had begun. He thought nothing of it at first and decided to give his crotch some extra space and let it breathe. It was at that point things had got tense with Laura.

'Do you mind not man-spreading on the plane!' she said indignantly.

Ben was in the middle seat. Laura was by the window with Harper and another woman was sitting in the aisle seat.

'I'm just having a bit of a stretch,' he replied.

The other woman gave him a glance as if to indicate that she was in complete agreement with Laura. To illustrate the fact, she shuffled in her seat and placed her elbow on the central armrest.

'Jesus!' Ben whispered to Laura. 'Can't a man even give his bits a good airing anymore? It's alright for you, you've got a skirt on.'

'It's all about consideration, Ben. If we all sat like that, there'd be no room for anybody. And why should men have all the space?'

Ben sensed a small nod from the woman sitting at his side. There was no point picking a fight as Laura was completely right.

Ben closed his legs and decided to put up with the discomfort. It was more important that he avoid any suspicion from Laura. She was exhausted and irritable and that should mean there would be no risk of much physical contact for a day or two. By that time Ben reckoned all would be back to normal.

The thing that was annoying him most of all – and he had a good list to select from by this time – was the fact that his mobile phone had been rendered completely useless by being in a foreign country. He should have considered that beforehand, of course, but he'd tried to ignore the thought of paying for mobile data when out of Europe. He hadn't a clue how much it would cost but assumed that he couldn't really afford it.

Ben cursed Steve's last message. Why hadn't he just written it in full instead of messing around and sending it as a series of short texts?

You'll never guess who's going to see you there at Kuala Lumpur ... go on, three guesses!

He'd been running through in his mind who it might be.

Richard was top choice. Next in line was Susan's sister, Aunt June. She was in a home and had Alzheimer's, surely they wouldn't bring her to the island, however special the occasion. Aunt June could become aggressive at times. She'd need a carer too, so it couldn't be her.

Ben had one more guess left. Who else might Tony and Susan invite out to the island? It would have to be immediate family only. That's how these things worked.

Laura was sick all over the back of the car.

'Why didn't you ask the driver to stop, Laura? You're not a kid, for God's sake!'

'Have some sympathy, Ben,' said Gaby.

'I didn't know it was coming, it was so sudden.'

The driver pulled up and they got out. Laura was a mess.

Ben left the women to sort themselves out. The driver's patience and attentiveness was putting him to shame. He walked a few paces away, he didn't want to say anything that would make things worse. The only thought he had to offer was: Take a travel sickness pill if you're going to get car sick!

He surveyed the city in the distance and realised that he'd been a bit of an idiot since landing at the airport. The Petronas Twin Towers were ahead of him in the distance, and for the first time he took in a long breath of air and realised what a spectacular trip this was. He'd been so preoccupied with financial matters, family affairs, vasectomies, screaming babies, obnoxious nephews, over-indulgent sisters and vomiting wives that he had completely neglected to see what was in front of him. Tony and Susan were picking up the tab for this holiday. The towers were an amazing piece of architecture, the sky was a beautiful and invigorating blue and for the next eight days he was going to stay on an island paradise, all paid for by somebody else.

He thought about Wendy in the office, the woman who talked about mindfulness. She'd gone on about mantras and being present in the moment, but he'd dismissed it as hippy stuff. But maybe Wendy's way was the right way for the next few days. He looked around him. He was in a different country with a different climate, a different language and a different culture. His troubles would wait. He'd take a leaf out of Wendy's book and appreciate what he had at that moment. The money worries and family nonsense would still be waiting for him when he got home, along with the grey skies of the UK.

Before long, Laura had managed to change her top and jogging pants with some other clothes out of the top of her suitcase. In his mindful moment, Ben showed inner appreciation for the fact that they'd both bought a few bits and pieces at the airport stopover to make up for the suitcase that he'd so stupidly left at the hotel. Laura threw the soiled clothing into a handy skip by the side of the road.

'I can get by without those for now. I've got plenty of T-shirts and a couple of pairs of shorts. I'm not carrying that stuff with us in the car.'

They arrived at Port Klang's cruise terminal.

Gaby was examining a print-out of an email. She looked around, trying to orientate herself.

'We just need to find where the boat is leaving from.'

Ben scanned the harbour. A ferry was disembarking at the end of the long jetty.

Then, to his side, he heard a voice – one that was familiar, very familiar. Was he imagining things? Surely not. This was Kuala Lumpur, what was she doing here?

It was Diana. Walking alongside her was Ted. And just behind them, using her stick and wary in this strange environment, was his daughter Alice.

CHAPTER TWENTY-ONE

June 2018: One Day Before The Party

'Diana! What the hell?'

Now he knew the surprise Steve was alluding to in his cryptic text. He'd have appreciated some forewarning about that.

'Great to see you too, Ben!'

She moved in for a half-hug, half-kiss. It was as awkward as it should have been.

Ted and Alice stood to one side, they looked uncomfortable to see their dad after such a long time.

'You never told me ....'

'We haven't spoken for a while ...'

'Why did you come ...'

'Why wouldn't we? I've known your mum and dad for years, not to mention that they're Ted and Alice's grandparents.'

She paused and then turned towards Laura who had baby Harper in her arms.

'I take it this is your family?'

Ben wasn't sure if Laura's pallor was due to the car journey or the sudden appearance of his family. His original family.

Gaby was hugging the children, Jaxon was greeting his cousins, Alice was fussing over Harper.

'Diana, this is Laura, Laura this is Diana. And this is Ted, my eldest, and Alice. Come here kids ...'

They were tense, not sure what to say or do, but when Ben opened his arms to them, they were straight in. They hugged him as if they hadn't seen him in four months. They hadn't. Ben wasn't sure how to handle the situation. He was delighted they were there, but he also knew how difficult this was going to make things.

'Tony and Susan asked us to come. They told me to keep it quiet, in case it put you off. They wanted the kids at the party, and why wouldn't they? You know I love your mum and dad, Ben. I wouldn't miss this celebration, whatever has happened between us.'

'It would have been nice to have known!' Laura muttered under her breath.

'It's time to get on with our lives, Ben. These kids have missed you. You have a new family now. And just look at this gorgeous baby, she's beautiful, Ben ... Laura.'

'How are you doing, Alice?' Ben asked, squeezing his daughter's arm. 'God, I've missed you lot. You look wonderful.'

'I didn't realise how bad my eyesight was until I saw you just now, Dad,' she smiled. 'You look so young!'

Ben gave her another long, hard hug. His eyes began to tear up as he looked at what he'd walked away from. He loved his kids. He had loved his life, in spite of its difficulties.

The other family members gelled immediately in a mess of excited chatter, news exchanges and hugs. Laura stood to the side, watching her baby being passed from person to person and looking to Ben as if for some acknowledgement that she was there – or that she even mattered.

A driver walked over with Diana's cases and deposited them next to Ben's. Diana thanked him and gave him a tip.

'You brought currency?' Ben asked.

'Yes,' Diana replied. 'I'm working again. For my sins, I've returned to teaching after all these years. I'm finding it much easier now I'm older, and it's made things a lot better financially ... since you left.'

'Oh, that is good news that you can support yourself, now we've got the baby to look after,' Laura interjected.

Ben looked at Diana and gave her a shrug of apology. She was far too gracious to take the bait. No doubt they'd have to talk about practical matters when they got to the island, but for now it was all about the kids. They were happy to be reunited and the difficult conversations could wait until later.

'Okay, we'd better find this boat. Any idea when Steve and his family are joining us?'

'Steve's been delayed,' Diana replied. 'Are you alright, Ben? You're walking funny.'

'Oh, it's all fine.'

Trust Diana to notice. Still, she knew him better than anybody.

'You look a bit uncomfortable. You haven't pulled anything, have you?'

She touched Ben's arm but pulled her hand away immediately as she noticed Laura's hostile stare.

'No, just a bit stiff from all the travel,' he replied, picking up one of the suitcases, as if to demonstrate there was nothing wrong.

'Ow!' he grimaced.

'I'll take it, Dad.'

Ted lifted up their cases with no effort whatsoever.

'I must be getting old,' Ben laughed, a touch too enthusiastically.

The group walked along the harbourside, guided by Gaby who was looking at her printed email containing the journey details.

Diana hung back with Ben, waiting for Laura to walk a suitable distance ahead. She and Gaby had hit it off well and Gaby couldn't stop talking about the baby.

Ben had seen that Alice was using her callipers.

'How's she doing?' he asked Diana.

'You know Alice,' she replied. 'She just gets on with it. She has to use her stick more and more now in the city – she finds it hard to pick out the detail in crowds. It'll be lovely for her to spend a week on the island. She won't have to worry about anybody crashing into her. Poor kid, she's missed you, you know.'

'I know. There's not a minute of the day when I don't think about you all ... about Alice. And Ted. I wish it hadn't played out this way.'

'Ben, what's up? You can't fool me. Why are you walking so weird?'

'You promise you can keep a secret?'

'Yes, go on. What's happened?'

'I had a vasectomy!'

Diana burst out laughing.

The huddle walking ahead of them stopped.

'What is it?' Laura asked.

'Nothing,' Ben replied, his face reddening. 'Just a bit of family news.'

'You haven't, have you?' Diana was teasing him now, it felt good, like old times. They knew each other well. Their sense of humour, their teasing thresholds, what made each other laugh. It was still a bit of an exploration with Laura. Ben wasn't entirely certain that he'd ever seen her laugh like Diana did.

'Yes, I have. And it's sore!'

'She doesn't know, does she?'

'No, she doesn't. And I'd appreciate it if you kept it quiet. From everybody, I mean. She'll be really angry with me if she finds out.'

'I can't believe it. You said you'd never have the snip after Alice was born. Not after I had my hysterectomy.'

'There was no need, was there? I escaped with my crown jewels intact. We weren't ever having more kids after Ted and Alice, that was our lot after that second caesarean.'

'I'm sorry for teasing, Ben, but that's so funny. So, you've had to put on an act since you had it? I can't believe Laura didn't notice – you're walking like an old man.'

'It's getting sorer to be honest with you. I'll tell you something else that will make you laugh. I'm wearing a jock strap too.'

Diana burst out laughing again.

'What is it with you two?' Laura asked, turning back to look at them. She looked annoyed now.

'Sorry, more family news,' Diana replied, doing her best to keep her face straight.

'God, Ben, we've missed you. You do make me laugh. I hope Laura makes you laugh as much.'

'If you remember, I can't laugh. I'm trussed up in a jock strap and it feels like someone just booted me in my groin.'

Diana managed to restrain the volume of her laugh this time around, she could sense that Laura was now beginning to hang back, trying to catch a sense of what they were discussing.

'What about the ... you know what ... the s-e-x? Won't she get suspicious?'

'I'm hoping that a combination of exhaustion, a demanding baby and a family environment will keep me safe for the couple of days it'll take for it to heal.'

'You're not going to be able to hide it, Ben. You're hobbling terribly now – you'll have to come up with an excuse to throw Laura off the scent. And I hope for your sake that the equatorial climate doesn't make her frisky or it might create a problem with your stitches down there.'

'Not much chance of that,' Ben muttered under his breath. Laura didn't seem to like him very much these days. He was beginning to wonder what she saw in him in the first place.

CHAPTER TWENTY-TWO

1979: The First Lie

Tony knew what to do the moment the police officer explained why the house call had been necessary. He would contact Kyle. He didn't know how, but he'd figure it out. Kyle appeared to be a man who could get things done.

'I'm very sorry to inform you, Mr and Mrs Harrington, that your boys have been identified in connection with the theft of certain items from one of your neighbours along the road. I do appreciate the sensitive nature of this matter, with you being such well-known members of the local community and the like, but I'm sure you'll understand that we do have to investigate this matter thoroughly.'

Susan was in a state of high distress. They'd only just finished dealing with the paperwork after the death of Tony's father. They'd moved into his comfortable home, given it a makeover to stamp their own style on it, and been welcomed by the neighbours. The Harringtons were well-respected and influential. They could always be relied on to provide sponsorship for local good causes. People had been prepared to overlook the minor transgression of selling below par meat products that had occurred four years earlier; they were happy to support a fine, traditional family business.

The truth for Tony was that Kyle Hunter's payments had helped to dig the business out of a hole. An additional unaccounted income of six thousand pounds a year, plus the payment of the fine, had been just the break he needed. Hunter had been as good as his word. The money appeared without fail every month, it even increased with inflation every year and as far as Tony and his workers were concerned, the factory was completely undisturbed when they entered the premises each morning. If there was any evidence at all of somebody having gained access overnight, it was that the surfaces and flooring were even cleaner than they had been left at the end of the previous day.

It was a bizarre situation. He had never seen Kyle again, not even accidentally in the city centre, and there had been no further communications, other than the plain envelope of cash addressed to Tony, delivered like clockwork on the first working day of every month. The money was never declared for tax, it simply allowed Tony to take less cash out of the business for his own salary, hence making the finances considerably more comfortable.

At times, Tony would wonder what Kyle was getting out of the deal. Perhaps he was moving illegal meat products through the machinery. Maybe he was using the premises to negotiate shady deals. He would think it through, then move on with his life. He didn't want to know. He liked his new-found wealth. With three children and a large house it suited him to have the disposable income to accompany his lifestyle. If push came to shove, he would deny all knowledge and claim that Kyle Hunter had secured access to the industrial meat-processing unit through deception and subterfuge.

Tony understood that Kyle Hunter operated outside the normal boundaries. He was the kind of man who would get things done. And he'd been nothing but civil and polite with Tony. In fact, he wished there were more businessmen who stuck to their word like Kyle had. Tony needed a meeting. But how to find him?

In the end it was Kyle who found Tony. He was having a pint of beer at the pub after work when Kyle approached him.

'Hi Tony, remember me?'

Tony was sitting alone, but he looked around, making certain that there was nobody he knew who might place him with this man.

'Mr Hunter – Kyle – I'm so pleased to see you again. I've been wanting to speak to you.'

'Is this connected with the police visit to your property?'

'How do you know about that?'

'I make it my business to know. What did they want?'

Tony realised what this was about.

'It has nothing to do with our ... arrangement.'

'So, why were they speaking to you?'

'Hang on a minute, are you watching our house?'

'I hope you'll agree that I have honoured and upheld our deal completely since we first spoke, Tony. I also observe that you seem to be flourishing since we made our arrangement. So, please don't get all sensitive when I take measures to protect my business interests. But to answer your question, we're not monitoring your property. The tip-off came from within the local constabulary. I think I told you, I'm heavily involved in personnel matters?'

'Yes, it's no problem, I just wondered. I'm very happy with our arrangement and I have no desire to review it. It's working well for both parties. The police were speaking to us about an issue with our boys, Steven and Ben. They've got themselves caught up in some youthful trouble. I wanted to speak to you about it, actually.'

'Could it create a problem for us? The further away you are from the police, the better. Is this likely to go away?'

'The truth is, it is a bit of a problem. God knows what the boys were up to. I blame it on that kid Jed Staples—'

'Is that the Staples family from the Greenacres estate?'

'Yes, that's the one. How do you know them?'

'Personnel, Tony. I make it my job to know everybody. Go on.'

'It's breaking and entering. And just when we've managed to get Steve into Newton Redcoat School. A blot on their copybooks is all we need – it could create terrible problems for the boys as they grow up. Imagine being labelled a common thief at such a young age.'

'Did they do it?'

'Possibly. I don't think they like the neighbour, it was just an ill-considered, stupid prank. But he's giving the police a hard time about it, he's a local magistrate. It could be tricky.'

Tony felt ashamed as he spoke these words aloud.

'I hoped it wouldn't come to this, Tony, but our business relationship is going to have to become a little more intimate from now on. I need this to go away. Nothing must come in the way of our access to your industrial unit. Agreed?'

'Totally!' Tony replied. 'I could really do with some advice about this.'

Kyle smiled, then laughed.

'Advice, that's what we'll call it. But you need to understand, Tony, that from now on we will be forever connected as business partners. I'm sure you've worked out how you'll deny any knowledge of me if our little midnight visits ever get discovered by the police. However, if I provide this ... advice ... to you, you can never walk away from our connection. Think very carefully about it before you give me the word.'

Tony sipped his beer. The pub was quiet, their conversation was private. He checked the faces of the few customers. He was sure nobody would know him in there. This problem had to go away. Steve had to get to that private school. Tony had never had such an opportunity as a young man, but with Steve showing such great promise academically, the family had a real chance at shooting for something higher. With private school behind him and a university degree, Harrington Meats would gain a level of respectability. No longer would they be just a family of butchers, they'd be a business worth noticing with Steve at the helm. But not with a record of theft behind him, that simply couldn't be allowed to happen.

'I want you to take care of it,' Tony said, looking Kyle directly in the eyes. 'But you promise me, nobody gets hurt?'

'Nobody needs to get hurt,' Kyle replied. 'I promise. In my line of personnel management you get used to dealing with people. You find out what makes them tick. Everybody can be helped to make the right decision with a little encouragement.'

Tony didn't need to know the details. He wanted his sons cleared of any wrongdoing. He assumed that it would just take a confidential word with his neighbour, the police, or perhaps Jed's parents. Maybe Kyle would use a little money to oil the wheels.

'I can assure you that the next visit you have from the

police will be to confirm that the misunderstanding is all cleared up. When is your next appointment with the school? I'll make sure that I've popped in to make a social call before that date. I'll put a word in for ... Steve, did you say his name was? I'll make sure the headteacher understands what an asset Steve will be when he attends the school. And I suggest that you make a generous donation to help him decide. Headteachers can be a sanctimonious bunch, it's best to use a little carrot and stick. I'll be the stick, you're the carrot.'

'You're certain that will do the job?' Tony frowned. 'And it won't make things worse?'

'On the contrary, you're likely to find that the amount of respect you get in this city will increase. You could become a very influential man, Tony. I think our partnership will work out very well for both of us.'

'Thanks, Kyle. I appreciate your help. I'll look forward to hearing that it's all taken care of.'

The two men shook hands and Kyle left the pub. Tony finished off his pint, wondering how his business partner might go about resolving the issue to everyone's satisfaction.

As he was reading bedtime stories to his boys that evening, he would have shuddered to know how Kyle Hunter was deploying his skills in personnel matters. At the same time as Tony was finishing the story of *Charlie and The Chocolate Factory*, a member of Kyle Hunter's staff was hanging Mr Hodges B.Ed. (Hons) by his ankles out of the third-floor window of his private school. After that, Kyle was moving on to visit Jed Staples' father in his working man's club, where he'd be informed of a potential sexual harassment claim by two women, both of whom were unknown to him.

CHAPTER TWENTY-THREE

The Island: One Day Before The Party

'I can't believe this is the island!' Gaby screamed.

'Oh my goodness, it's like some tropical paradise! Your parents must be loaded, Ben. It's incredible!' Laura screeched with excitement.

Their boatman, Mr Aquino, had just pointed out their destination to them. His English was poor, but he understood well what the money shot was.

Laura had complained about feeling seasick five minutes after leaving the harbour and Ben had done his best to communicate some tips for happy boat travel, but she was having none of it and insisted on letting everybody know how rough she felt. Harper slept through the entire journey, lovingly cuddled by Gaby. Alice seemed smitten by Mr Aquino's assistant, a young lad called Jeremiah who was about the same age as her. Ben felt the pangs of guilt returning as he saw how she had to retreat to the stability and security of the seating area because she was having problems with her balance. He longed for her to be able to throw off her callipers and experience the life of a regular teenage girl. He was grateful for Jeremiah's kindness. Her disability didn't seem to bother him, his English was good, and they immediately hit it off.

'Reading between the lines, Laura doesn't travel well I take it?' Diana said, as she moved alongside Ben who was admiring the sea from the back of the boat.

He snorted.

'You reckon? She was fine on the plane, although we only hit very minor turbulence. She really struggled in the car and now she's not getting on well with the boat either. I never realised it was a problem for her. But then I guess we've never really made a journey like this before.'

'I won't chat long. Have you seen how she watches us when we're together?'

'Can you blame her?'

Ben felt irritated, but it was more at his own feelings than at Diana's words.

'To be honest with you, Diana, I'm delighted the kids are here. But it's going to make things tense you being on the island. It's not that I'm not happy to see you – and I'm even happier that you're all talking to me again now – but have some sympathy for Laura. This is hard for her.'

'I get it, really I do, Ben. But I came for the kids. I know how much Alice misses you.'

'Look at her with that lad Jeremiah. She's growing up, she's a young woman now.'

'Just look at that boy's face. You used to look at me like that ...'

'Come on, Diana. We can't do this, not here and not now. Let's just agree to keep things chatty and polite for the sake of the kids and my mum and dad. They were naughty inviting you all without telling me. Did Steve know? Or Gaby?'

'To tell you the truth, I didn't know we were coming until the last minute. Tony and Susan invited me some time ago but the money was an issue. My new job makes things easier now. When they said they'd pay for every-thing – well, Alice and Ted wanted to come. They're still angry with you, but they miss you too. You must know that.'

'Of course I do. They're teenagers, their hormones will be raging enough already without me adding to the mix. I'm so pleased Ted is here to entertain Jaxon. I was in danger of killing him earlier. If Ted hadn't been here, he might have had an unfortunate accident at sea.'

Diana laughed and shouted up to Mr Aquino.

'How long until we reach the island, Mr Aquino?'

He held up the fingers of both hands, indicating ten minutes. She quickly touched Ben's shoulder.

'I don't want to give you marriage guidance or anything like that, but if I were you, I'd go and check in on Laura. She looks like she needs some attention.'

'You're probably right.'

Ben turned away from the sea and looked up towards the covered seating area. The boat made a sudden turn and he stumbled against the wooden seating. He winced.

'Ouch!'

'Still sore?'

Ben nodded.

'Again, this is not marital advice, but I'd tell her about it. It'll come out eventually and she'll be furious that you didn't discuss it with her. What if she decides she wants another baby?'

'I don't think that will happen. And by the way, for the

time being, you're still my wife. Laura is just ... Laura is my girlfriend. My partner.'

Ben walked away, leaving Diana to rejoin Gaby and Harper. Perhaps Gaby would have liked to have had more babies. He'd never given it much thought. She and Nigel had started a family late and the marriage was over before there was time for more children. He felt another pang of guilt. So many lives were affected by what men did. It seldom seemed to be the women who were at fault. They were the ones who had to pick up the pieces afterwards, putting the fragments of their broken lives back together into some semblance of normality for the sake of the kids.

'Hi Laura. How are you feeling now?'

Ben hadn't realised what a breeze there was out on the deck, it seemed so quiet without the crashing of the waves and the hum of the engine.

'I feel like crap, Ben. I didn't realise I'd be so bad. I've never been on a boat like this before. You don't think it's something we ate, do you?'

'I feel fine. I don't think it's the food.'

'Only, when I was watching you out there talking to Diana – again – you looked like you were standing awkwardly.'

Ben's face reddened.

'Oh no, just struggling to keep my balance. No sign of having the trots. I'm pretty sure I'm fine.'

He tried to ignore the dig at Diana, but Laura was obviously feeling wretched and appeared to want to make him to feel the same way too.

'You're not going to spend all holiday with your ex-wife, are you?'

Ben was going to correct her but thought better of it.

'It's just that you seem to prefer her company to mine. I

thought you might need reminding that your youngest daughter is out there with your sister and her mother is stuck in here trying not to throw up.'

'It's okay, you know. I can speak to her without it being a big deal. We were married for years. I can't just walk away from my family—'

'You have a new family now. Remember that. Did you know she was coming?'

'No, I hadn't got a clue—'

'Are you sure about that? Would you have even told me?'

'Laura, honestly, it was as big a surprise to me as it was to you.'

'But you're pleased they're here, aren't you? I can see it in your face.'

'Of course I'm pleased they're here. I'm delighted to see my kids again. Of course I am—'

'Nan and Grandad are out on the beach waving to us, Uncle Ben. We're there now!'

'Thanks Jaxon.'

For once Ben was relieved to see the child interrupting their conversation. He offered his arm to help Laura up from her seat.

'Look Laura, they wouldn't have invited us here if they didn't want to see us. This is a peace offering. They're trying to make things right in the family. I don't know about you, but I'm pleased everybody is here. It might make things more pleasant for everybody if we try to heal a few wounds.'

He looked at her. Her face was white.

'I feel terrible,' she said, taking his arm. 'I'm in no fit state to meet your mum and dad.'

'Nan! Grandad!'

The boat was pulled in towards the makeshift wooden

jetty with a small bump. There was great excitement among the children as Tony and Susan welcomed them, gave them hugs and commented on how much they'd grown. Ben got a little choked up when he saw how Jeremiah helped Alice off the boat. He was the perfect gentlemen. Alice's face glowed at his attentiveness and consideration. There was much fuss made of Harper, who had barely left Gaby's arms since they'd stepped on the boat. She almost had to be prised from her.

'We're on terra firma now,' Ben reassured Laura as he climbed on to the jetty and helped her off the boat.

'God, I'm feeling even worse,' she said.

'Ben!' Tony exclaimed.

Ben walked up to his father and they gave each other a firm hug.

'You look well, Dad. You've lost a lot of weight.'

'It's all this travel with your mum. Anyway, we're being rude. Hadn't you better introduce me?'

'Dad, this is Laura. Laura, meet Tony, my dad.'

Laura stepped forward to take Tony's outstretched hand, but she could contain herself no longer. As she went to say how pleased she was to meet him, her stomach finally gave up its resistance and she was sick all over Tony's Hawaiian shirt.

CHAPTER TWENTY-FOUR

The Island: One Day Before The Party

It wasn't the best of introductions to a new family but as Tony noted it was difficult to see the mess Laura had caused due to the garishness of his terrible shirt. Laura looked horrified, but Ben was thankful for his father's joke. It was the parental meeting from hell, but it had certainly broken the ice.

Ben was pleased to see how relaxed and well his parents looked, and he couldn't get over his dad's weight loss.

'It's all that traipsing around with me on my book tours,' Susan smiled. But Ben could see it was hollow, a rehearsed answer. It could wait until later; he'd ask once they'd all had time to freshen up and were installed in their accommodation.

The island was spectacular. It could easily have been the location for a castaway movie or some TV adaption of *Robinson Crusoe*. There was a beautiful sandy beach, palm trees, an expanse of jungle and the most incredible treehouse to the side of the beach built from dried leaves and bamboo and the size of a large shed.

'First call on the treehouse!' Ted declared, running ahead to take a closer look and followed by Jaxon who'd swiftly adopted the role of his shadow.

A man and a woman came to greet the family at the end of the long pathway leading to the main cluster of buildings. Everything was built from materials which must have been locally sourced – dried grasses, broad leaves, aged timber and bamboo. It had been designed for comfort and relaxation, there were even luxurious seats and loungers, though these were from the mainland, with their well-padded upholstery and flashy designs.

'This is Mauricio and Analyn Villanueva,' Tony said, introducing the couple. 'They're here during the daytime to take care of things. They'll take the rest of the bags up from the jetty.'

Ben looked back towards the boat. Still chatting, Alice and Jeremiah were slowly making their way towards the accommodation area.

'Does Jeremiah work on the island too?' he asked.

'He is our only son,' Mauricio explained. 'He is here to help you all. Please ask if you require anything.'

Ben nodded and the Villanuevas headed off to retrieve the bags.

'It's amazing in there!' Ted shouted from the doorway of the treehouse. 'Can I stay in there, Mum. It's brilliant!'

He darted back inside, too fast to hear Diana's reply.

'How do the rooms work round here?' she asked. 'Is it like a hotel?'

'There's a lot of flexibility,' Susan explained. 'We're in the big house – there are four more double rooms in there.

There's the treehouse too and four more self-contained cabins, so plenty of room to spread.'

'What about electricity and Wi-Fi?' Ben asked.

'The electricity runs off generators. Each house has one, but it's mainly used for the lights and low-powered stuff.'

Tony had already checked out all the technical matters.

'There's no Wi-Fi out here and no phone signal. You have your mother to thank for that.'

'Yes, I thought it would be good to have a family holiday where none of you have your heads buried in your phones and iPads. It's Tony's birthday, so I thought it'd be nice if we all spoke to each other for a change. And it'll take a desert island to achieve that goal.'

'What if someone gets ill or has an accident?' said Ben.

'The Villanuevas are here every day between eight in the morning and five in the afternoon. We have a satellite phone in the bar area over there. If we need help, we use that. All the numbers are printed on a piece of paper taped underneath it.'

'How long would it take to rescue everybody – if there was a fire or something like that?' Diana asked.

'There are no places to land a helicopter. The only way to reach the island is by boat. It's about – what – an hour from the mainland?'

Tony nodded.

'You'd best hope that operation of yours doesn't give you any more trouble,' Diana whispered to Ben.

'Okay everybody, feel free to explore and find your favourite rooms. I'd like to save one of the family cabins for Steve and his family. Other than that, everything is fair game. And when you're all sorted out, come and join us back here for drinks and nibbles.'

'Shall we stay in the main house?' Ben suggested to

Laura. 'It'll help you to get to know everybody better. What do you think? Mum said they've got a cot in one of the rooms there.'

'I want to get showered and out of these clothes, that's what I think!' Laura replied curtly. Then she softened her tone. 'You're right, we should stay in the main house. If Harper cries a lot, maybe we could consider relocating to one of the smaller cabins then. But for now, let's be sociable.'

The room was comfortable and nicely furnished with bamboo matting and carved wood ornaments. The bed was modern and luxurious, and towels and toiletries were provided. Ben checked his phone, out of habit.

'Dad's right, no signal,' Ben said as Laura placed Harper on the middle of the bed and began to tear off her clothes.

'Where's the shower?' she asked.

Ben looked around and then peered out of the doorway. He drew in his head, smiling.

'Out there. You might want to take a towel or two.'

It was an open-air shower, heated by the sun. It hadn't occurred to them that there might be anything other than mains electricity and gas, and hot running water.

Laura cursed and instructed Ben to watch Harper and make sure she didn't roll off the bed. Ben checked his phone again as she stepped out of the double doors and walked over to the shower. No signal, no broadband, no outside life. They were cut off in a first-world kind of way. It would be strange having no communications, but from the little Ben had seen of the island, it might be a blessing in disguise.

There was a tap at the door. Ben walked over to open it. It was Susan.

'Sorry to disturb you, Ben, but I wanted to have a quick word with you while I saw that Laura was taking a shower. I've brought you a bag for her clothes. We've put Tony's shirt out with the rubbish. We can't give it a decent wash out here.'

'Are you alright, Mum? You look worried.'

'Yes Ben, I'm fine. I take it Laura's okay with the shower arrangements. And look at that gorgeous baby! She's beautiful. But then so were Ted and Alice when they were born.'

Susan gathered up Laura's clothing which she'd wrapped into a ball on the floor, making sure that none of the contaminated surfaces came into contact with the matting. She handled the clothing with the hardened nonchalance of a mother accustomed to washing the underwear of three boys from childhood to their teenage years.

'So, how's things, Mum? The new book looks like it's doing well?'

'Not as well as I'd hoped,' Susan replied. 'But well enough, I suppose. It's paid for this lovely holiday, so I can't complain.'

'That's great. You look well, Mum, really well. And I can't believe how much weight Dad has lost. He looks like a new man.'

Susan dropped the bundle of clothes onto the floor and began to cry. Ben walked over to her and put his arms around her.

'What is it, Mum? I thought you seemed a bit off when we arrived.'

'Oh Ben, you and I always did love to chat. You were always the best company out of all our kids, the others were always in a rush. You always had time for your mum.'

She wiped her eyes.

'I'm sorry, Ben. I shouldn't have done that. You've only just arrived, you've got Diana – you've got Laura to take care of and beautiful Harper. Let's get rid of these clothes and I'll leave you all to get settled in.'

'What is it, Mum, you can tell me. Is it something to do with Dad's weight? Is he ill?'

'Is who ill?' Laura asked, stepping into the room with a towel wrapped around her and looking all the better for her shower.

'Oh, it's nothing, my dear,' Susan said, attempting to smile. 'I was just saying to Ben that I hope you're not ill after your long journey.'

CHAPTER TWENTY-FIVE

1980: The Second Lie

'I want you to follow her. I need to know what's going on. She mustn't see you, make sure of that.'

Kyle nodded. It was strange that they should be meeting there, the very place where five years earlier Tony Harrington had intended to end his life.

'Start with that man who's teaching her at the college – some posh bloke who talks about books and poetry all the time. I knew nothing good would come of that. These writing ideas of hers, she's got a young family to look after. Aren't three kids enough?'

Kyle knew better than to say anything. This was a difficult situation for any man. Besides, he and Tony had a remote relationship. They weren't what you'd call friends. Tony only got in touch when something – or somebody – needed sorting out.

'*Four* kids.'

Tony corrected himself. Kyle's face remained without emotion.

'We'd agreed, no more children. Three is enough, I told her. Now here we are with a fourth on the way. She says it's mine. I'm not sure I believe her. Things in the bedroom – well, you know what it's like with a young family and your own business ... don't you?'

Kyle said nothing. The less Tony Harrington knew about him, the better. In his line of work, that was how it should be. You never knew when everything could change. All it would take was a call to the police, a persistent investigation and too many awkward questions and he might have to hang Tony out to dry. A damning piece of evidence, a word in the right person's ear and Tony Harrington would become the fall guy for Kyle's own entrepreneurial sideline. It had made him a wealthy man already, and it was Harrington Meats that had got him there.

'Give me a week. I suggest we meet back up here. This is a delicate matter, it's best discussed away from public meeting places. Besides, if your hunch is right about this guy—'

'I don't want to know any of the details. Just deal with it. Make the problem go away. I want Susan back. Whatever is ... distracting her, whoever is distracting her, I want them out of the picture.'

'Consider it done,' Kyle said. 'Incidentally, I'm going to need access to the factory at weekend daytimes for a period over the winter. I'll increase what we pay you. Is that going to be a problem?'

'I've been thinking of introducing weekend working. It makes little sense to have all that plant sitting idle for two days every week. This Margaret Thatcher has some interesting ideas on productivity.'

'Have you costed it with wages and output? What would it be worth for you to hold off those plans until summer?'

'We'd start small at first. Just the profitable lines. But it could be worth a lot of money to the business. Over time, I reckon we could expand in a big way.'

Kyle gave him a cold stare.

'I need to access the premises at weekends over the winter. It's key to my own business growth. I'll remunerate you fully, but I need to you to delay those plans.'

Kyle was deadly serious. He was aware from his contacts that Tony Harrington had begun to think about business development plans like appointing a board of directors and pushing more aggressively into new markets. But it had been Kyle's money which had helped him to turn the business around. And now he wanted to grow it, possibly beyond what Kyle was offering him. Tony had to understand that already got himself a director, and not one who would be appearing on the books any time soon. He should take care not to kill the golden goose.

'Okay, I'll delay it. But I want to acquire the premises next door when they become vacant. I've got my eye on the entire row of units. If we knocked them through, we could grow Harrington Meats into a huge business.'

'Just keep me in the loop. Maybe let me look at the plans. I'd put the money in, but it suits my own business aspirations to be able to use your premises in downtimes.'

'Alright, I'll do that.'

This was the first time Kyle had interfered directly with the business. It might cause problems. There was a point at which the business growth would exceed what Kyle was was willing to pay him. Kyle could almost hear Tony mulling over what any severance terms might be. He had to understand they would be punitive.

Tony mulled over the issue in the intervening period before he met up with Kyle again. Susan was heavily pregnant, she was due any day, he wanted things tidied up. It was important to him to know that the child was his.

Babies seldom keep to adult schedules and, sure as anything, Richard Harrington decided to make his appearance at the most inconvenient time possible. It was a habit he'd maintain throughout his life. On the day Tony was due to meet Kyle, he ended up rushing with Susan to the hospital, hastily leaving the children in the care of a neighbour. The birth was straightforward and by late afternoon Tony was introducing Ben, Steve and Gaby to their new brother.

He thought back to the delight he'd felt when the other kids were born. He felt none of that with Richard. The poison of doubt had long ago contaminated his thoughts and he was convinced he wasn't the father. How could he be? He and Susan had barely had a sex life for some months now. The timings simply didn't work.

'It was that night after the policeman came round to tell us Steve and Ben were out of trouble. Don't you remember? Steve got his place at the school on the same day. It had been the first bit of good news we'd had for a while and the business was looking up. We cracked open that bottle of bubbly and ... well, you remember what happened. It was that night. Count the months. It works.'

Tony was no fool. Yes, the dates worked, but only just. And Richard was early. The other kids had all been late.

Susan had been very keen to make love that night, it seemed to have come out of the blue, after a lengthy period of famine between the sheets. It simply didn't feel right. And this writing nonsense, these aspirations to publish a book. He hadn't even met this professor or whatever he was. He couldn't understand why the meat business wasn't good enough for his wife.

Gaby couldn't leave the baby alone. Steve had gone off to find snacks. A nurse entered the room and told Tony that he had a visitor outside.

'I'm just nipping out for five minutes.'

Susan didn't seem to care, she was lost in new-baby-land.

It was Kyle Hunter. The man always seemed to know what was going on. Tony had no way of contacting him, yet whenever they needed a meeting, it always seemed to happen.

There was no greeting and no congratulations.

'Let's go into the gents, we'll be able to talk more freely there.'

The cubicles were empty, they took one each and talked through the flimsy wooden dividers.

'What did you find?' Tony asked.

'I don't know how Susan feels about him, but he definitely holds a candle for your wife.'

'I knew it!'

Tony thumped the side of the cubicle. It shook the entire row.

'I found evidence. He had photographs of her. They looked like they were ID pictures taken from her course files. This might be difficult to hear too ...'

'Tell me, I need to know.'

'They met up this week. For coffee. He touched her stomach to feel the baby. They looked very ... familiar.'

Tony thumped the side of the cubicle again.

'Are they having an affair? Is the child his?'

Kyle paused.

Tony wasn't thinking clearly. If his anger ran away with him, things would turn out bad, he didn't need Kyle to tell him that.

'Yes, I think they are having an affair. They've been exchanging notes in their pigeon holes at the university. I wrote down what one of them said ... if you want to hear it?'

Tony didn't want to hear it. But he listened anyway.

We're almost there. This birth is going to be wonderful. It's our own child, only more special. You're amazing, Bill. I can't wait.

Tony flinched. How could she? He loved Susan with all his heart. Things had been tough recently, but every couple has their difficulties. They'd work through it. These writing aspirations of hers – this relationship, whatever it was – it could wreck everything. They were a family. Harringtons was a family business and that's the way it would stay.

He could forgive Susan – in time – but this child, that was a different matter. She'd want to keep it, there was no way she'd ever get rid of it. But he would only tolerate it, there was no way he could love it.

'I want it to go away,' he said.

'I thought you'd say as much. I got an opportunity last night to make things right. This is all going to go away.'

Tony felt nauseous. He wanted this man out of his life, but he couldn't bear to consider how that might be achieved.

'Shh!' Kyle warned.

Tony did as he was told. He thought someone was coming into the toilets. He listened but could hear nothing. Kyle must have been mistaken.

'So, it's done? You're sure there'll be no fallout?' Tony

asked, taking the silence as an all-clear to carry on their conversation.

'It's all taken care of.'

'You're sure it's all watertight?'

Tony liked his messes cleared up but he didn't want to get his hands dirty. It was up to men like Kyle to sort out life's tricky problems. He didn't want to know the details, but he loved the results that Kyle was getting.

'It's good, Tony. Believe me, I've got it sorted. I'll need to use the depot tonight. Is the alarm code still the same?'

'It's all fine, no changes.'

There was the sound of footsteps and the washroom door banged shut.

Tony cursed.

Somebody must have come in, but they'd just kept quiet.

It was a good job they hadn't heard anything which might incriminate the two men.

CHAPTER TWENTY-SIX

The Island: One Day Before The Party

Ben had been chased out of his own room. Laura had got together with Susan and they were fussing over Harper.

'Why don't you go and find your dad, Ben? I'm sure he can't wait to catch up with you.'

Laura made a face at him as she spoke, making sure that Susan didn't see. He got the message. Laura was starting her charm offensive. She was probably right, Harper was a great way to soften even the sternest critic of their relationship. Whatever the family thought about his infidelity, Laura's collaboration in it, and the breakdown of his family, nobody could deny that Harper was a beautiful baby. And therein lay the path to acceptance.

Laura set to work on Susan, disturbing Harper's sleep to hand her over for a cuddle while she got dressed. Laura had a brashness which still shocked him at times. While Susan played with Harper, she let her towel drop to the floor and was happy to wander around naked as she gathered together her fresh clothes to get dressed.

Ben left the room and walked down the stairs into the lounge. Jaxon and Ted were laughing together as they played a game of Connect 4.

'You alright, Ted?' Ben placed his hand on his son's shoulder. 'It's great to see you. Thanks for babysitting Jaxon, that's really helpful to Gaby.'

Ted tensed, then moved his shoulders. It wasn't quite an eviction, but Ben understood the sentiment. It was too soon. Ted was angry with him. He'd need to take things slowly. Of course the kids would be cross.

'I'll leave you to your game,' he said, walking off. 'If there's anything you need, just let me know.'

Ted turned around. For a couple of seconds the game stopped.

Ben could guess what he wanted to say. He knew what his son wanted – his dad back with his mum, that would do to begin with. Then after that, knowing Ted, some food.

The game resumed, and Ben walked out of the house into the fresh air. It was hard to define where outside ended and inside began. The windows were all wide open, as were the doors, and the weather was perfect: warm and sunny with a soft breeze. The cabins were positioned in a semi-circle around a central area with its sun-loungers, bar and barbecue. Colourful umbrellas provided shade from the rays of the sun. In front of them was the beach and behind a dense mass of tall trees and shrubs. That must be the jungle, Ben decided.

He closed his eyes, breathed in the air and listened to the sounds around him. He could hear Tony and Diana laughing. They'd always got on well, ever since he'd first come home with her as a young man. He tuned out of their comfortable chatter and listened to the gentle ripple of the waves on the golden sand and the rustle of the wind as it caressed the green leaves of the palm trees.

For a moment, with Diana and Tony chatting away like that, he felt as if he might have gone back two years in time, to happier days when he and Diana were still together and Laura was just a colleague he got on well with at work. That feeling of family togetherness surged through him like a drug, nourishing him, making him feel more alive than he'd felt in months.

He waved at Diana and Tony as he passed them to join the boardwalk which led to the beach. He wanted to spend some time alone, taking in his surroundings. As he stepped onto the sand he saw Alice sitting on a fallen tree trunk. He stood still watching his daughter. She was a young woman now, no longer his little girl. He'd always felt closer to Alice, perhaps it was because of her disability, but he'd always been much more protective of her. Ted was his own man and had been so from a very early age, but however grown up Alice became, and despite her fierce independence, she would always come to her dad.

She was looking around, as if she was waiting for somebody. She spotted him watching her. Ben felt as if he'd been caught out and was suddenly embarrassed. But why shouldn't he watch his daughter? He'd missed her so much.

'Hi gorgeous!' he said, then thought better of it. 'Am I still allowed to call you gorgeous? Now you're a young woman and all that?'

Alice laughed. He loved to hear her laugh. It told him that she was still okay, regardless of recent events.

'Yes, you can call me gorgeous. Which girl wouldn't want to be called gorgeous, even if it is just her dad?'

'Mind if I join you?' he asked. He couldn't believe he

was on tenterhooks with his own kids, not wanting to try too hard in case they rejected him.

'You look like you're waiting for somebody.'

Alice looked behind her, then brushed off his comment.

'No, just admiring the sea. It's incredible, isn't it? I love it here. Mind you, it's hard to walk on the sand with my callipers.'

'How are you getting on with those things? They're a lot better than they used to be when we were kids, you know. Though I don't suppose that's any consolation.'

'My eyesight is getting worse, Dad,' she said, her eyes beginning to moisten. 'I don't tell Mum about it, but you and me – we always used to talk about stuff like this. I'm really scared. I can put up with all this crap on my legs, but I'm terrified of losing my eyesight.'

Ben's heart felt like it would explode. How could he ever have done something so stupid – something that took him away from his beautiful daughter?

'I'm so sorry, Alice,' he said, forcing back the tears.

'It's not your fault, Dad.'

'No, I mean for messing everything up with Mum and you and Ted. I'm sorry.'

'Well, Laura seems okay. And Harper is gorgeous.'

'I know, but I can't forgive myself for what I did to you all. You know you can talk to me any time? About all this and anything else that's going on. I'm still your dad, you know. I'll always be your dad.'

'It's been difficult. I won't lie to you. I was shocked when you left. We thought you and Mum were inseparable. Me and Ted never saw it coming.'

'Me neither. It just happened. That's the worst excuse in the book, I know. I found myself in a place I didn't want to be and I didn't know what to do. Me and Mum had been falling out—'

'About me? I know, Dad. I could hear you arguing when I was in my room. You don't have to feel bad about me. What is it they say? Shit happens? Well, shit happened to me. I just have to get on with it. It's not your fault – you don't have to keep blaming yourself. Blame Mother Nature. She can create a beautiful island like this and she can give someone like me CP. Life's a bitch and then you die.'

'Don't ever think that all of this happened because of you, Alice. It's all on me. I wasn't in a good place when we found out you were losing your eyesight. Me and Mum handle things differently. Your mum was always the strong one. I've always been weak. That's all it was with Laura, a moment of weakness.'

'Do you love her, Dad? I mean, do you love her like Mum?'

Ben waited before he answered. He closed his eyes and listened to the waves.

'I still love your mum, I never stopped loving her. That'll never change. We had you two kids, we had some great years together, that doesn't just go away.'

'You didn't answer my question, Dad. Are you in love with Laura? Only ... she doesn't seem to like you too much. Not the way Mum does. You and Mum just seem to – you seem to fit together.'

Ben looked behind him.

'What was that? I thought I heard something. Are there any wild animals in this jungle? We should probably check—'

'Answer my question. I won't tell anybody. Do you love Laura, the same way you love Mum?'

There was the crack of a twig behind them.

'I'm sure there's something in those bushes. Wait here, I'm going to see what it is.'

CHAPTER TWENTY-SEVEN

The Island: One Day Before The Party

A couple of minutes later, Ben was back.

'I don't know what it was, but there was definitely something there. Can you stay close to the house until I find out if there are any nasty creatures around here? I don't want my only daughter—'

Ben corrected himself.

'I don't want my *eldest* daughter getting eaten alive by some wild animal, do I?'

'It's only a small island, Dad. I don't think even the cast of *The Jungle Book* would have enough food to stay alive for more than a month. And anyway, nobody would have visitors on the island if they were going to get mauled by jungle creatures. I'm pretty sure it's safe.'

'Humour an old man, will you? How bad is your sight now, would you even be able to see a jungle creature if it came for you?'

Alice looked dubious but acknowledged that he'd

played his dad cards well. They'd all watched *I'm a Celebrity* on the TV, so knew what vile creatures could be found in a jungle.

Ben offered her his arm and they walked slowly along the sand.

'Hi, you two,' Diana called as they approached the seating area in the middle of the garden. Tony was sprawled out on a lounger, his Hawaiian shirt long ago discarded and a cocktail in his hand. Diana had taken off her T-shirt to reveal the top of a two-piece underneath. Ben clocked it but tried not to gawp. They were both only a couple of years away from fifty, but Diana still looked great.

'Do either of you know how dangerous this island is? I mean, in the jungle areas. Is there anything the kids need to watch out for?'

'There's a guidebook somewhere—' Tony began.

'Gaby took it,' Diana interrupted. She'd seen Ben glancing at her cleavage. She let slip a small smile. She knew that look of old. 'She's paranoid about Jaxon getting hurt. Why don't you see if she's got it? I suppose as responsible adults we ought to do a quick risk assessment.'

There was a dismissive grunt from Tony. Ben could see his dad's ribs, but he looked well enough – tough, tanned and healthy. He'd ask later, when he could speak in confidence, now was not the time, in front of Alice.

Ben walked off towards Gaby's house. In the distance he saw the Villanueva's boy appearing from nowhere. He wondered where the husband and wife were hiding – they'd be able to reassure him about the island.

'Gaby! I'm coming into your cabin!' Ben shouted.

He didn't want to walk in on his sister, even though everything that could be opened was open, including the front entrance.

'Hi Ben, I'm just staying the shade for a bit. The heat is fierce out there.'

She was lying on her front on the raffia rug, holding a folder up to read, on which was printed a bright logo: *Unique Island Getaways.*

'Did you know that they have a Robinson Crusoe experience on an island only a mile away from here? It's amazing. They actually strand people there and they have to fend for themselves.'

'No thanks,' Ben said. 'It's hard enough surviving in my office.'

'Still not getting on at work?'

Ben shook his head.

Gaby sat up a little, resting her weight on her elbow.

'That idiot boss still around? It only takes one dickhead to spoil a place.'

'Yes, he is. I'd expected him to have moved on by now, but he's showing no signs of looking for the next career move. And it's not like I dare risk a job change at the moment.'

'You could always work in the business—'

'I'm not working in the family business!'

Ben snapped at her. That was always everybody's solution.

'I'm sorry,' he said. 'But we've had this conversation before. Steve works there – Dad always wanted him to be head of Harrington's. Why do you think you and I were left to fester at that terrible secondary school? How many GCSEs did you get?'

'That was my own silly fault. You know, I never really got why you were so against working at the factory, Ben. You and Steve get along fine. You'd be able to take a reasonable salary. Steve would bite your hand off if you asked him. I sometimes think he'd like someone to share the burden.'

'No Gaby, I've said it before and I'll say it again. I'm not working for Harrington Meats. I'm a hippy vegetarian, anyway. How could I possibly reconcile that with my moral code?'

'You've managed to reconcile Laura with your moral code.'

Here it was, the old Gaby. The sanctimonious, pious, judgemental Gaby they all knew and loved. A couple of hours in the sunshine, a short time for the pleasantries to die down and here she was again, holding court over his life.

'Sometimes life takes turns which we don't see coming,' he began to defend himself. 'Look, Gaby, let's not do this now. Diana has seen fit to forgive me – or at least she's not scratching my eyes out. If she can let it pass for the sake of Dad's seventieth, I'm sure you can. Besides, who are you to decide how it sits with my personal code of ethics. If it makes you happy to hear it, it sits very badly. But that's my cross to bear.'

There was silence as they stared at each other. Gaby looked like she was thinking it over. Twist or stick? Stay quiet or have another go at Ben? She decided to stick. He quickly changed the subject.

'Is that the island guide you're reading? I wanted to check what it says about safety when we're walking around the place. I assume it covers the minor points, such as am I likely to die here?'

Gaby laughed and, just like that, the attitude was gone.

'Yes, I've been checking it out for Jaxon. The good news is that it is officially a jungle that surrounds the accommoda-tion area, but there's nothing too deadly in there. No gorillas, tigers, lions, hyenas or anything else that you'd spot in *The Lion King*. And absolutely no monkeys.'

'That's Africa, isn't it?'

'Who knows? It's hot so I assumed there'd be tigers. They have them in India, don't they?'

'I bet Steve would know. That's the difference between state and private education. Everything we know is based on Disney films, Steve actually learned some facts at school.'

'There are snakes. If you see one, the guide advises to leave them well alone and they'll leave you.'

'That's good to hear.'

'There are some spiders too ... oh and centipedes. Giant centipedes! The guide says to shake your shoes before you put them on. They bite, apparently, but they don't kill you—'

'Gaby – woah – stay still!'

'Oh, come on, Ben. You're not going to tell me there's a tiger standing on the veranda, are you?'

'Gaby, seriously. Don't move.'

She looked at him, waiting for a smile. He was the person who had once adapted her favourite doll to look like the Terminator, right down to a battery-operated glowing eye. She of all people knew what brothers were like.

'I want you to stay completely still. Don't move and don't panic. You've got a scorpion caught up in your hair.'

CHAPTER TWENTY-EIGHT

1988: The Third Lie

'This has to be sorted, Steve. I mean it. This mustn't bring you down. You're too young to be saddled with a kid.'

'Do you love her?' Susan asked.

Steve's face was bright red.

'Of course I don't! We were only messing about. We didn't do it properly. I don't want a kid yet, and certainly not with Jenny.'

'Why didn't you use protection? I can't believe you've been stupid enough to get caught like this, Steve. It's the oldest mistake in the book.'

Being questioned by his father wasn't Steve's idea of a great night in, but he knew he had it coming. When Jenny had told him she'd missed her period, he'd been horrified. It was a party, they'd had a lot to drink, it was just a bit of fun. He'd fumbled with a condom, put his finger right through it, then decided not to chance it. They'd messed around, kissed, taken some clothes off and done a bit of touching. But that couldn't have got her pregnant, could it?

Why had she been so stupid as to confide in her mum first? Steve cursed her. If she'd told him straightaway, he could have got inside her head before her mum did. Instead, she was on a no-abortion kick. Her parents had agreed to support her, they'd look after the baby to allow her to complete her education and they were now looking to Steve – and more specifically the Harrington family – to step up and help.

'They're only after our money!' Tony thumped his fist on the table. 'They've seen your success with the books and they've read about the expansion at the processing plant. They're using this as an opportunity. They don't give a damn about the baby, they're just seeking any cash that might be in the arrangement.'

'Would it be all bad if she had the child?' Susan asked. 'It's not like they'd have to get married or anything. We could easily help financially. You know what I think about terminations—'

With immaculate timing, Richard appeared at the door in his pyjamas.

'Go to bed!' Tony shouted at him. Richard flinched at the ferocity of it.

'Tony!' Susan scolded.

'I've got a stomach ache, Mum. Can I have a drink of water?'

Susan walked over to him, felt his forehead and moved over to the sink to fill a glass with water.

'Why can't you be a bit nicer, Tony. Come on, Richard. I'll settle you back down.'

Richard looked at Tony and Steve and could tell, even

at the age of eight, that something was hanging in the air like a fetid smell. Susan went out of the room with him, her arm round his shoulders. Tony watched as they headed off, up the stairs and out of earshot.

'You know, Steve, you're an adult now and you need to start taking some responsibility for this stuff. You've always been the one I want to take over the business. And with your mum's books going so well that's going to be sooner rather than later. You've got your entire life ahead of you, and you're going to be a wealthy man. You don't need to settle for the girl next door when you'll be able to have any woman you want. You need to up your game, son. Don't get caught in silly teenage traps like this.'

'What can I do, Dad? I don't want to have a baby, not at my age. But Jenny won't let it drop. She's all big on being an anti-abortionist, she reckons it's murder to get rid of a child, right from conception. Her mum and dad are right behind her, they want her to have the kid.'

'We'll have the meeting with her parents and I'll see what your mum and I can do to try and persuade them. Make sure Jenny doesn't say anything at school – we don't want everybody else piling in with their opinions. She has kept her mouth shut, hasn't she?'

Steve nodded.

'Yes, they're keeping it quiet until they've met with you and Mum. Only for now though, they want to talk to school next, see what arrangements can be put in place for Jenny to take her exams.'

'Okay, leave it to me. Let's get this first meeting out of the way. If we can't persuade them then, I'll see what else can be done to get them to change their minds.'

'Dad ...'

'What is it? Don't hold back now. If there's something I need to know, tell me.'

'When Richard was born ...'

'Come on, Steve. Spit it out.'

'I overheard you talking to a man. It was in the toilets at the hospital.'

Tony looked at Steve and encouraged him to keep speaking.

'I waited at the door to Mum's room to see who came out. I wanted to know who it was.'

'What did you hear?'

'Nothing really, but I wanted to know who you were talking to and why they hadn't come in to see Mum.'

'Why are you telling me this now?'

'From time to time I see him. Sometimes he's parked along our road. Occasionally I've seen him driving past the school when it's home time. Who is he, Dad?'

'Has he ever spoken to you?'

Tony looked concerned to Steve now, more worried than he'd been when they were discussing Jenny.

'No, never. I don't even see him that often. He has a great car. Is he a friend of yours?'

After a delay, Tony answered.

'He's a business associate of mine. When you move into the business, you'll probably get to meet him. We have an arrangement, a mutually beneficial one. He sometimes uses the processing unit at night when we're all shut up. He lives locally. It's only to be expected that you might see him from time to time.'

'Does Mum know him? He never comes to the house.'

'No, he's a part of the business that I like to keep separate from the day-to-day stuff. But, now you mention it, I've a feeling I might be seeing him again quite soon.

As if he had a sixth sense, Kyle made himself available to Tony at precisely the right moment. At first Tony was angry when he stepped out of the shadows one night as he was leaving the office late.

'Are you following me and my family?'

'It's good to see you too, Tony. How are you?'

'Tell me, do you follow us? My son says he's seen you. This is a business arrangement only. You have the keys, you let yourself in. That was our arrangement. I don't want you following my family.'

'I'm not following your family, Tony. I live in the area. I'm around and about doing business, just like you. I've seen you too – I might ask if you're following me?'

'Oh, come off it.'

'Well, the answer is no. And at your request, we are slightly more than business partners now, Tony. I'm thinking of the tragic death of Susan's tutor—'

'That was an accident.'

'But was it, Tony? Was it an accident? Suicide, they said at the time. What could have driven a man like that – with his promising academic career ahead of him and a wonderful student like Susan beginning to experience her first breakthrough as an author – what might have driven a man like that to suicide, Tony?'

Tony said nothing. He was pleased that Kyle had shown up. He'd been wondering how he could contact him.

'I need your help again,' he began.

'And I need to talk business first,' Kyle replied, looking around the office, scanning the year planner on the wall, picking up and putting down invoices that were piled up on one of the desks, ready for the next day.

'It's good to see you expanding here. That contract with the supermarket chain – you must be very pleased. This place is quite some size now. But I need to know it won't become a 24-hour operation. I need your guarantee that I will continue to get a minimum of six hours' access at night. We've been doing this for thirteen years. We've been business partners for over a decade. And it was my partnership with you that got you out of the mess you were in.'

'It's hardly a partnership, Kyle. You make it sound like we signed a contract.'

'We do have an unwritten contract, Tony, whether you like it or not. I think that troublesome neighbour of yours would agree that we had some sort of arrangement. And Steve's headmaster would confirm that too. Oh, and the Staples family, remember them? Their lad has been in court three times in the past year. He took a very different path from your kids. I'm certain he'd say that we had some kind of business arrangement.'

'Yes, Kyle. I promise I won't do anything to upset the status quo. But I'm going to need your help with something.'

When he'd expanded into the two new units, Tony hadn't been so foolish as to kill the golden goose. He'd left the car park to the original unit fenced off. It remained locked up and clean at night, supposedly to prevent cross-contamination. Effectively, Tony had created three processing businesses, one within each unit. He'd make the latter two units 24/7, the original unit could easily remain two shifts only, then idle at night. He'd grown to love Kyle's money. The relationship with Kyle suited him too, and it wasn't just because of the monthly cash payments.

'What is it?' Kyle asked, smiling.

'My son Steve has a problem at school. He's got a girl

pregnant. Her parents want her to have the baby. They're being very persistent.'

'Yes, I can help with that,' Kyle said. 'These kids, they do get themselves into some terrible scrapes. It'll be no problem, Tony. This arrangement of ours, I think it works out very well for both of us.'

CHAPTER TWENTY-NINE

The Island: One Day Before The Party

'Get it out. Quickly! Get it out!'

'Try and stay calm, Gaby. It'll get tangled in your hair if you make a fuss.'

'I don't care, just get it away from me!' she shrieked.

'I need something to brush it off.'

'Do it with your hand.'

'I'm not touching that thing! They're poisonous. I've seen one killing someone in a film—'

'Ben! You're not helping. Argh, I felt it move. Get it off, get it off!'

'For God's sake Gaby, stand still long enough for me to do something about it.'

Ben looked around for something to knock the creature off his sister's head. He was terrified that if he messed it up it would plunge its sting into her. It could be fatal.

There was a paper fan on the coffee table. He quickly grabbed it and folded its wings together.

'Come here, Gaby!'

She was feeling for the scorpion in her hair and as she levelled up to him, Ben saw its tail poised ready to strike.

'Stand still. *Still*, I said!'

She was chastened by his shout and did as he asked.

Ben moved to her side, found the creature and swiped it with the fan. He'd intended to flick it across the room and then run over to stamp on it. Instead, the scorpion flew into the air, coming back down onto Gaby's head and then bouncing across Ben's chest.

Both screamed.

'Where is it?' Ben shouted. 'Is it on me? Get it away from me!'

Gaby joined in.

'Oh my God, I felt it in my hair. Get it away from me. Get it off me!'

Their cries were interrupted by a thud on the wooden floor and the sound of Tony laughing.

'It's dead,' he said. 'Look, I stamped on it. I thought someone was dying in here. You should have heard the racket you two were making.'

Ben and Gaby began to calm down, still unsure they were safe. Gaby kept running her fingers through her hair, while Ben was patting himself down as if the creature might somehow have got into his clothing.

The rest of the family came rushing in – Susan, Diana, Laura, Ted, then Alice. She was followed by the Villanuevas.

'What has been going on in here?' Diana asked. 'I thought someone was being murdered.'

'Just a scorpion.' Tony lifted his foot. 'Look, it's only a tiny little thing.'

'These scorpions not kill,' said Mauricio. 'Their sting is bad, but not kill.'

'Check your room before sleep ... make big steps, they will hide,' Analyn Villanueva picked up from her husband.

'That's a relief!' Laura said. 'Is there anything else we need to know about?'

'Nothing that can really harm you,' Mauricio reassured them. 'We are so used to these creatures, we know what to do. Stay calm, most will run away if you let them.'

'So, you promise, nothing big and ugly on the island? Apart from Dad?' Ted grinned.

'No, you're safe. If you see snakes, be still and let them pass. Look out for spiders. There are none here that will kill you, but the bites will hurt. Centipedes are worst, they also bite. Get very angry.'

'That's good to hear,' said Diana, echoing everybody's thoughts.

'Where's Jaxon?' Gaby asked, now recovered from her trauma.

'I thought he was behind me—' Ted began.

'You left Jaxon on his own? I asked you to keep an eye on him, Ted.'

'I did. I thought he'd followed me over here. He'll be okay, we were just playing with a ball out on the veranda—'

'He's too young to leave alone, Ted. I need to go and find him.'

'I left Harper sleeping on our bed,' Laura muttered. 'She's perfectly safe up there, I put pillows either side of her.'

Gaby was becoming hysterical again.

'I need to find Jaxon, he mustn't be left on his own on the island.'

Humouring her, they walked out en masse towards the main house.

'Jaxon! Jaxon!' she called. There was no reply.

They arrived at the veranda where he'd been playing with Ted. The ball had been abandoned at the far end of the garden. Where the garden ended, the trees began. The accommodation had been built in a hacked out clearing, it was merely a guest of the jungle circling its borders.

'He will come to no harm, it is safe on the island. He is just a small boy, he won't—'

Mauricio's reassurances were immediately rejected by Gaby. He flinched as she shouted at him.

'Don't tell me what to do about my son. I'm his mother and I'll decide what's safe and what's not!'

Laura looked at Ben and raised her eyebrows. He turned away, catching Diana's eye. She gave a little smile.

'Jaxon! Jaxon!'

'Look, Gaby, calm down. He's probably curled up some-where for a sleep. Before we get over-excited, let's check the cabins and seating areas. He's more likely to be there.'

Mauricio looked crushed, as if he'd just been sacked from his job after a big dressing-down from his boss. Analyn gave his arm a squeeze.

'Okay, listen everybody,' Tony said. 'Ted and Alice, you search round the outside of this house. Laura and Ben, look upstairs. Susan, Diana and I will check the seating area outside. Mauricio and Analyn, check the smaller cabins please. Give it ten minutes and then we all meet by the bar ... okay?'

They all snapped into action. Everybody called out his name.

'Jaxon! Jaxon!'

Ten minutes later, having searched all the living areas,

they gathered back by the bar. It was hot. Ben passed round soft drinks as they decided what to do.

'We'll need to organise a more thorough search,' said Susan. 'It's very unlikely anything will have happened to him.'

'Excuse me, I'd better go,' Laura said. Harper had woken up and the cries could be heard from the open bedroom window.

'Feeding time!' she smiled, making a hasty exit. Ben suspected that she was pleased to be out of it. She'd already got a taste of his family and now was her chance to see Gaby in her true light.

'Did anybody check the beach?' Ted asked.

'Oh my God! Jaxon, he can't swim! What if he's gone to the beach alone? He might have drowned. Oh my God, Jaxon!'

'Gaby, calm down!' Tony said sharply. 'Your mum and I had four kids and you're still alive, aren't you? He'll be fine, he'll just have wandered off somewhere.'

Ben thought Tony's example was a weak one, bearing in mind they'd always gone to resort hotels whenever they went on holiday as kids. A jungle island was taking things to a whole new level, however luxurious the accommodation and however safe the critters were supposed to be.

'Alice and Susan, you go and check the beach. Ted, you go too, you're a good swimmer.'

Tony was back in charge now, the father organising his family.

'Ben and Diana, you take the right-hand side of the jungle. I'll search from the left-hand side with Mauricio. Gaby you check the accommodation again with Analyn and stay somewhere central in case he suddenly appears. He'll want his mum when he does.'

'Follow the paths in the jungle, they are very clear,' Mauricio advised.

They confirmed the plan and headed off in their agreed directions. It was late afternoon now and the light was beginning to fade. They'd have to hope he turned up fast or else they might be making an emergency call to the mainland.

CHAPTER THIRTY

The Island: One Day Before The Party

'I never thought we'd end up in the jungle together,' Diana said as she threw Jaxon's ball back into the garden and began to walk along the path into the undergrowth.

'Me Tarzan, you Jane!' Ben said.

Diana laughed. As they headed into the dense greenery, he noticed Laura watching them from their veranda. She was holding Harper, tracking them as they headed off in search of Jaxon. He gave her a wave as if to reassure her that everything was alright. To him, it still felt the most natural thing on earth to form a search party with Diana. He wondered if he should have suggested working with Ted or Mauricio instead, it might have been a little more diplomatic with Laura around.

'How are those stitches of yours holding up?' Diana asked.

'It's good of you to ask,' Ben chuckled. 'Very nicely thank you. They've been behaving themselves ever since we arrived on the island. Perhaps it's the sun. And then there was the distraction of the scorpion. It all helps.'

'Don't go trying anything too energetic. I'm sure Jaxon will turn up somewhere safe. He's just like his mum. He likes the attention.'

'Yes, the little devil! You should have seen him at the hotel. Some radio-controlled contraption frightening the life out of all the pensioners. And in the plane too. Gaby is completely oblivious to the mayhem he leaves in his wake.'

'Same old Gaby, eh? She doesn't seem to change with age. If you ask me, she needs a man in her life. That'd sort her out. Then, don't we all?'

Ben decided to ignore that. He looked at the path ahead of him, heading into the jungle. It must have been cleared with a machete; left alone it wouldn't be long before it was reclaimed by the vines, twigs and branches.

'I'm looking for snakes and beasties wherever I tread. That scorpion has spooked me. You always said you didn't marry me for my bravery.'

'And what of that, Ben? Our marriage, I mean. Are you really ready to get a divorce?'

He wasn't prepared for that one, it came left of field. He stopped.

'Listen,' he said. 'The birdsong is wonderful. And no engines. And just listen to the breeze in the trees. It's amazing.'

'Good evasion tactics!' Diana stopped too and turned to face him. 'I'm serious, Ben. We don't have to fall out over this, but what are we doing? Is this going to end in divorce ... or what?'

'You know I've been putting it off, don't you?'

'Never!' Diana teased. 'I know you, Ben Harrington. If

you'd really wanted that divorce, the paperwork would be in by now.'

Ben nodded, as much to himself as anything.

'You're right,' he said after some time. 'You've got to promise not to say anything. To anybody, I mean. This must be between me and you. Right?'

'Of course, Ben. I'm the woman that can spot your awkward limping a mile off. However bad our end was, we still know each other the best of anybody. We have two beautiful kids together. We survived your family all these years. That's got to count for something.'

'Can you give me a hand over that fallen tree?' Ben asked, seeing an obstacle ahead. 'I'm fine when I walk normally, but the stretching might pull my stitches.'

Diana stepped over the trunk first, then climbed back up to help Ben complete the manoeuvre in two stages. She gave him a hand up onto the trunk, then jumped down on the other side and offered him her hand again. Her touch felt so familiar. He and Diana had begun to get their first liver spots, and they'd laughed as they'd compared blemishes while watching TV together. Diana's hands were strong and safe, Laura's smooth, delicate and exciting. The symbolism wasn't lost on him.

They walked in silence for a couple of minutes.

'I can hear the sea,' Ben said. 'We must be close to the other side of the island. It's not very wide, is it?'

'Ben?'

'Yes?'

They stopped again and looked at each other.

'If Laura hadn't got pregnant would you even be thinking about a divorce?'

He looked directly at her. She meant it, she wanted to know the answer to this question. So did he.

'What could I do, Diana? You were angry with me for cheating on you – an emotion I fully understand, by the way. I was probably angrier with myself, if that's any consolation. What an idiot! And when Laura announced she was pregnant? You'd asked me to give you some space and she was asking me to move in with her. What else could I have done?'

'Do you want this divorce? You and Laura aren't like we were together. There's something cold about her. We always got on, even when things got difficult with Alice.'

'Jaxon!'

Ben thought they'd better get on with the job in hand. Besides, he was still working through those questions himself. He'd thought of little else since he'd moved in with Laura. And Diana was bang on the nail, he and Laura weren't comfortable together like they'd always been. At first he'd put it down to the new relationship, but it seemed to be getting worse, not better.

The jungle path suddenly opened onto the ocean. In front of it was a much narrower strip of sand, barely the size of a wide pavement.

'Hey look, there's some kind of lodge or cabin along there.'

Diana pointed into the distance.

'You're right. Let's take a look. Jaxon might be hiding in there. We'll have to be fast. The light is beginning to go and we need to get back.'

As they neared the hut, they could tell that it wasn't abandoned. It was part of the island's very limited infrastructure.

'Do you think people actually stay in there?' Diana asked. 'The Villanuevas didn't mention it.'

'Hello!' Ben shouted. 'Jaxon? Anybody in there?'

The door was unlocked. They stepped inside.

'Look at this, Ben. It's a proper cabin, it must be part of the island experience.'

'It's probably here for when there's the inevitable family bust-up and somebody needs to sneak off and lick their wounds. Maybe we could lock Jaxon up here and stop the little horror causing so much trouble.'

'Ben! Our kids had their moments too. He's only young, he'll grow out of it.'

'I hope so! He's a nice kid, there's not a malicious bone in his body. I just wish Gaby would—'

'Ben, look at this!'

'What?'

'Here, look!'

Ben moved closer to Diana to see what had got her so excited.

'It's an ashtray. Nobody in your family smokes any more so it can't be any of your lot.'

Ben touched one of the stubbed-out cigarettes.

'This one is still warm. These are fresh. How strange! There must be somebody else staying on the island.'

CHAPTER THIRTY-ONE

1992: The Fourth Lie

When Ben told Tony there was something going on at the factory, it piqued an interest in him that had been there since his first meeting with Kyle Hunter. The deal had been that Kyle's activities would make no impact whatsoever on his own business. Yet here was Ben, stumbling upon some night-time activity, effectively catching them in the act. That made Tony vulnerable. He'd had to lie to his son, he'd been caught off-guard. It also made him curious. He sat at the kitchen table, fidgeting and unsettled. He'd never known exactly when Kyle was using the premises, but he was there right then.

Every morning, after they'd first forged their arrangement back in 1975, Tony would open the factory and inspect the premises before the staff began to arrive. He would scrutinise everything – the floors, the machinery, the butchery equipment. There was never any sign of tampering, it was always left spotlessly clean. After several months,

Tony had tired of the checks. He simply concluded that Kyle Hunter barely used the premises and that their arrangement was a retainer for very occasional use.

What Ben had told him was weighing on his mind. They had been careless. By allowing Ben to see that they were doing, Kyle was bringing his activities to Tony's own doorstep. He couldn't accept that. As Susan called him through to the sitting room to watch TV, he made an excuse. He'd decided he was finally going to get an idea of precisely what sort of personnel business Kyle was running.

'I'm sorry, Susan. I've got to go back to the office. I left a document on my desk which needs posting – if I run it over to the main post office, it'll get sorted this evening. I can't believe I was so daft as to leave it there.'

'Okay, drive safely!'

Tony picked up his car keys and left the house. For a few moments he sat in the car with the engine running. Did he really want to find out what was going on? Was he being an idiot sneaking off to the factory unit when he knew Kyle was there? What else could he do? It was Kyle who had upset their arrangement. If Ben had seen what was going on, even though he hadn't understood what was happening, this could become problematical.

By the time Tony arrived on the industrial estate, he was sweating. It was dark and cold. He was nervous, uncertain if the information he was about to glean about Kyle's business might change things forever. He parked his car two roads away. He didn't want to draw attention to himself – he hoped he could sneak in and look without anybody realising he'd even been there. Surely the worst it could be would be butchering poached meat, or perhaps processing sub-standard meat products? He knew he could distance himself from that. There was no money trail and no direct contact. Tony could always claim that Kyle Hunter had gained access to the meat processing area without his knowledge.

He turned off the engine and reached for his coat. He got out of the car and gently pushed the door shut. The chilly night air instantly cooled him, his sweat-soaked shirt cold and clammy against his skin. All was quiet. The dim night light was on in the office and the blinds were down. It looked much as he'd left it when he'd locked up earlier. He waited and listened. Not a sound. No voices, no vehicles. Had Ben been mistaken?

He walked up to the front of the building, then along the side. It was in shadow, the light cut out by the high metal fencing and an overgrown hedge. A bit of foliage suited Tony. It was amazing how squeamish some people could be. They were perfectly happy to buy neat slices of bacon or beautifully trimmed joints of meat, but the minute they saw an animal carcass they ran a mile.

Tony was close to the edge of the building now. Cautiously, as Ben had done earlier that evening, he peered round to the car park at the back. This was where the meat arrived in refrigerated vans ready to be processed, packaged and labelled. The van was there, exactly as Ben had described. The loading bay shutter was down and the back door ajar. Somebody was smoking out there, he saw the red tip of a cigarette. Tony pulled back into the shadows. He watched as the man finished his cigarette and stubbed it out on the bottom of his shoe before placing it in a sweet tin which he had in his jacket pocket. This was why the place was so clean, these people were professionals, they didn't even throw their cigarette stubs on the ground.

The man had gone back inside the factory. Tony waited a few moments, making certain that the coast was clear, before he crept along to stand by the door, which was still open. He listened, straining to hear what was going on inside. All was quiet, except for the sound of one of the meat-grinding machines. Something was being turned into mince. What kind of animal could it be? Ben had seen a carcass being carried by two men. Could it be a pig or a sheep?

He decided to sneak a look through the door. Then, out of nowhere, he heard a footstep behind him. The last thing he was aware of was a violent blow across the back of his head.

He came round to the whirring of a machine.

'Jesus Christ! Bloody hell!'

Tony knew what this was. He thrashed his feet, desperate to escape the grasp of whoever was holding him, but they had him firmly secured, one man clutching his legs and another supporting the top of his body. They were feeding him into the mincing machine. Its sharp cutters were spinning just beyond his face.

'Stop! Stop it!'

'I thought you'd knocked him out, Joe. There's no way we can put him in there while he's struggling like that.'

'What the hell is going on here?'

Tony recognised the voice. It was Kyle. Thank God.

'You bloody idiots! You damn amateurs!' he screamed.

Tony felt himself being drawn away from the blades of the mincer and dropped on the ground. He looked around. Beside Kyle was a man dressed in blood-soaked overalls, holding a human arm in his hand, as if it was an everyday occurrence.

'For fuck's sake, Tony, you knew the terms of our arrangement. Now you've screwed it all up, I told you to stay well away. Our arrangement here has to be at arm's length.' He smiled at his own joke.

The two thugs who'd been restraining Tony looked at each other, sensing what was in play.

'Make your choice, Tony. What's happened here tonight can't ever get out. Do you want to go home to that family of yours again?'

'Don't hurt me, Kyle. I want to live.'

'So be it,' Kyle said calmly. 'You just stopped being a sleeping partner. I can't allow you to see what we've been up to here and let you walk away. So here are your choices. Either I let my two friends here carry on what they were doing or you become complicit in what's going on here. Let's call it insurance to make sure you don't open your mouth.'

He signalled to his thugs. They guided Tony to a metal table on which a partly cut up human torso was placed. The man in the overalls handed him a cleaver. Tony threw up.

'It looks like you're going back to the shop floor, Tony. Clear up that vomit then start processing this body for the machines. We've got a consignment of meat to get sorted before the night is out and it won't mince itself.'

CHAPTER THIRTY-TWO

The Island: One Day Before The Party

'Who could it be? You don't think people from the mainland use this place, do they?' Diana asked.

Ben was examining the cigarette stub, not sure what he was looking for. He shook his head.

'Dad said it's a private island. Just the Villanuevas come here – and Mr Aquino the boatman, of course. The company which owns this place does have a couple of other islands dotted around here, though. One of them is a Robinson Crusoe experience. Gaby was telling me about it.'

'You're kidding! Do you mean to say people actually get stranded on their own desert island?'

'Yes, that's right. Apparently, it's a big thing with survivalists. They get off on this stuff. They need to prove to themselves that they can survive without technology and supermarkets, all that kind of nonsense.'

'Wow! I'd rather have a luxury island with Wi-Fi and all amenities. A cinema would be rather nice too!'

Diana laughed and touched his arm as she did so.

'Sorry, force of habit. I'll try not to do that when Laura's around.'

'It's okay, I feel the same way.' Ben placed the cigarette stub back in the ashtray and turned to look at her. 'It feels so normal being here with you and the kids – if you can describe being on a tropical island as normal, that is. But you're right. Don't let Laura see anything. She had a face like thunder when she saw us heading off into the jungle together.'

'We ought to go or you'll really be in the doghouse, Ben. We need to leave now. It gets dark so much earlier than it does at home.'

'That must be something to do with being on the equator. It's years since I did geography, but I think the poles get 24 hours of light or 24 hours of darkness, depending on the time of year, and around the equator, it's 12 hours of each.'

'That sounds about right. Anyhow, regardless of the science, we need to think about moving.'

'I'm intrigued by who's been here though, aren't you?'

'Yes, of course I am. I'd like to know who we're sharing the island with. For all we know it could be Tom Hanks filming the sequel to *Castaway*.'

'Come on, Diana. Let's walk a little way along this stretch of beach, see if we can find a boat or something to give us a clue who's been here. It'll only take a few minutes. We can head back straight afterwards.'

'Okay, but I know you and your detours. Remember that time we took a shortcut to the pub when were on holiday at that static caravan park? You made me walk through a field that had been freshly sprayed with cow dung ... and I was wearing sandals.'

Ben burst out laughing.

'Ouch!' he said, squirming.

'What?'

'My vasectomy. It's been fine all day and now you made me laugh – that was a real sharp pain.'

'Are you okay?'

'I think so. I've got a horrible, dull feeling down there. I'm sure it'll go away. Let's check the beach.'

There wasn't much sand on that side of the island and it was clear why they'd chosen to build the hut on the open land near the jungle path. Sometimes the beach was a little wider, but most of the time it was no more than a narrow strip. After a couple of hundred yards, the sand disappeared and was replaced by jungle.

'Nothing here. Nobody here,' Ben said.

Diana looked up at the sky. The daylight was rapidly turning to dusk.

'Ben, we'd really better head back.'

Walking as fast as they could, they made their way back along the beach towards the hut. Ben was still puzzling over the identity of the mystery smoker.

'I think I know who it was,' he suddenly exclaimed. 'It'll be the Villanueva's kid – what's his name? The one who seemed to have his eye on Alice?'

'Jeremiah? Yes, he seems like a nice kid. Although if he's got his eye on Alice he'd better not be a smoker – she'll blow him straight out of the water.'

'I bet this is where he comes to smoke cigarettes and jerk off. This place is a teenager's dream. And it's well away from the visitors. Most of them will be sat on the beach or in the bar area getting drunk. I bet nobody ever comes this far out.'

'You're probably right. He was nowhere to be seen when we were hunting for Jaxon ... Ben, can you see where the path was?'

'I was just thinking the same thing. I'm sure it was over there, along from the beach hut.'

'I can't see it in this light.'

'Shhh!'

Ben stood still and listened.

'There's something over there in the trees. I can hear rustling.'

'I heard it too. Do you think we should shout for help? Have you got your phone on you?'

'They don't work out here. I left mine in my room.'

'There it was again. I'm scared, Ben.'

'Maybe we should take refuge in the hut.'

'It's so early, Ben. I wish it didn't get dark this soon. They'll go spare if we don't get back tonight – they'll think we've had an accident.'

'Some chance of that. When we were kids, Mum and Dad just let us do our thing. No one thought about health and safety in those days. When I look back, we did some pretty risky things. I often think what a horrible life Jaxon has with Gaby breathing down his neck all the time. So long as we were back for meal times, Mum and Dad weren't worried what we got up to. They probably won't even notice we're gone.'

'You're going to be in a lot of trouble with your girlfriend – partner – or whatever it is you call her.'

Ben let out a small cry of pain.

'Oh Jesus!'

'What now?'

'I must have twisted something. It's feeling really sore, Diana. I'm going to have to sit down in the hut. There's no way I can trek through the jungle now. It's too dark and we'll never make it over that fallen tree trunk.'

'Why do we always end up like this, Ben? You and me? It's not the first time we've got stuck out on a limb like this.'

'I know, but what else can we do?'

'And what if whoever has been in this hut comes back and finds us here?'

'I thought we'd agreed it's probably the kid. He'll be back on the mainland by now – the Villanuevas will have gone home for the night.'

'Okay, we'll stay. I suppose we can be up and out by the crack of dawn and we'll be back before they're even out of bed.'

They made their way to the hut, Ben walking gingerly, keen to avoid more pain in his groin.

'It's going to be a long night!' he said, as he sat down on the low bed, grunting with discomfort. 'We've no light and nothing to do. Mind you, maybe it's not a bad thing. I'm knackered after all that travelling. I'd welcome a good night's sleep – I want to be at my best for Dad's party tomorrow evening.'

'We're going to have to share the bed,' Diana said cautiously. 'I mean, I can sleep on the chair if you want, but that seems silly. After all, we slept together for years. We may as well be comfortable.'

'Yes, it's fine, just be careful around my crotch area please. And don't whatever you do say anything to Laura tomorrow morning. As far as she's concerned, I slept on the chair in the corner and played the gentleman with you. She mustn't know we shared a bed.'

'Don't worry, I'll keep my mouth shut. You're going to have enough making up to do when we get back as it is.'

It was dark in the hut now. Ben made himself comfortable in the bed and closed his eyes. Diana settled in beside him. She kept her distance, but instinctively put her arm around his waist. She withdrew it immediately.

'Sorry! Force of habit. I won't do it again.'

Ben said nothing. It felt good to have her back by his side again.

They lay in silence for a while, each thinking things through, waiting for it to get completely dark, listening to the sound of the sea lapping on the sand outside. Then Ben spoke.

'Diana?'

'Yes.'

'You know you asked me earlier if I still wanted the divorce? And I didn't give you a proper answer?'

'Yes.'

'I needed time to work out what I thought about it. But I've got my answer now. I think I knew it the moment I saw you walking up to me at the harbour. I don't want to get divorced, Diana. I don't want us to split up for good.'

CHAPTER THIRTY-THREE

The Island: The Day Of The Party

It was the waves they heard first. Then the birds. And finally Laura's voice.

'You treacherous pieces of shit!'

Diana and Ben jumped up from the bed as a large sea shell ricocheted across the wall above their heads, bouncing off onto the floor.

'Woah, hang on a minute, Laura.'

'It's not what it looks like.'

'It's exactly what it looks like!' Laura screamed at them.

In the doorway Tony made a face at his son. Ben and Diana were barely awake, but a nuclear missile had just landed on the hut. He tried to intervene.

'Laura darling—'

'And don't keep calling me darling!' she snapped.

That's the formalities out of the way then, Ben decided.

They'd thought that waking up in time for dawn would be no problem, but they were more exhausted than they'd expected after the flights. That meant Laura and Tony had been able to go out searching for them before they were even awake. And now here they were, sharing a bed together in their underwear, Diana's bra draped over the chair.

'Laura, you've got to believe me. Nothing happened, honestly. We got caught in the dark and had to stay here overnight for safety.'

Ben saw the smirk on Tony's face. He and Susan had always loved Diana. They knew what they were doing when they invited his family over to celebrate Tony's birthday. But he owed it to Laura to be fair.

'I was worried sick about you last night! You could have fallen from a rock, got eaten by a tiger or anything.'

'There aren't any tigers ...' Tony began.

Ben moved to get up, intending to put his arm around her. He grunted with pain.

Laura's tone changed.

'You've hurt yourself. What have you done?'

Ben's face turned red, he tried to fight it off.

'He had a slip,' Diana said quickly. 'Did you pass that tree trunk on the way over here? He had a small fall and he's pulled something. He'll survive.'

'I told you. It's all a storm in a teacup,' said Tony, seeing it was now safe to enter the hut. 'Laura and Gaby were beside themselves last night when you didn't come back. They almost had the Villanuevas calling out the rescue services from the mainland. We told them you'd be fine. There's nothing that can harm you on this island. So long as you keep your eyes open and you don't drown, it's safe as houses here.'

'Did you find Jaxon?' Diana asked.

'The little devil was hiding all along,' Tony said. 'I tell

you, Diana, I don't remember your kids being like that when they were younger. He could see we were all going spare looking for him and yet he thought it perfectly acceptable to hide inside one of those huge plant pots while we were all running around calling his name. I still don't think he gets it.'

'Well, so long as he's safe,' Diana said.

She picked up her bra and wriggled it on under her T-shirt. Laura watched her, still looking doubtful that they were telling the truth.

'I'm really sorry, Laura,' Ben said. 'We got the times wrong. I never thought it would get dark as early as that. We tried to find the path, but it was too late. And we heard something in the woods—'

'That'll be a tiger!' Tony ventured, feeling more confident now.

They all smiled at that, Laura breaking into a grin last of all.

'Okay, okay you piss-takers,' Ben laughed.

'How about we get back for breakfast?' Tony suggested. 'It's seven o'clock now. Oh, and by the way, guess who arrived on the boat with Mr Aquino last night?'

'Not Richard?' Ben replied.

'Richard won't be coming!' Tony snapped.

His tone caught them all by surprise. Laura looked at him, Dan thought she looked shocked.

'No, it's Steve and Kiki. He's brought the kids too. They're asleep now, a tiring flight, I think. But they're all dying to see you.'

'Have you met them yet?' Ben asked Laura, steering the conversation onto safe territory.

He was pulling on his trousers. He hoped no one noticed him having to tackle them from three directions before he found a way to get them on without buckling over with the pain.

'Yes, Mina is amazing. You never told me she was so clever. And Henry, I never realised there was an older son in the family. The way you spoke about him, I assumed he was younger.'

'You know how it is, I remember them all as toddlers. It only feels like five minutes ago I was changing his nappy along with my kids'. It's sometimes hard not to see them all as babies. Speaking of which, who's looking after Harper?'

'Alice. She's gorgeous that daughter of yours, she loves Harper. She's a complete natural with babies. I wish I could bottle half her talent and keep it for myself.'

'We're very proud of Alice,' Diana said, beaming. 'She was lovely from the minute she was born. A ray of sunshine that one, even though she has so much to put up with.'

Ben felt his eyes begin to well up with tears.

'We'd better get back,' he said.

As they left the hut he touched Laura's arm, keen to reassure her.

'I promise,' he said. 'It's all fine. We just shared the bed. You can see that we were both out like a light. We must have slept for almost twelve hours.'

Laura was still tense, but she seemed to have accepted their explanation. Diana left them together and hung back with Tony.

They made their way back through the jungle. How different it looked in the bright morning light, the sun shining strongly through the leafy canopy. It was alive with birdsong.

They reached the fallen tree.

'This is where Ben slipped,' Diana said.

'My darn knees play me up these days, I'm not entirely

sure I could get over that. Look, you can squeeze by at the side,' Tony said.

Ben was relieved to discover that there was an alternative route. As soon as they got back to the house he'd search for some paracetamol to ease the pain. If anyone asked, he'd say he had a headache brought on by too much sun.

At last they reached the clearing which brought them back to the garden of the main house. Jaxon's ball was exactly where they'd left it. Ben heard Steve's distinctive and confident laugh coming from the bar area. He was feeling sore now but tried to conceal his discomfort as he walked towards his brother. Steve stood up to welcome him and give him a hug.

'Ben!' he said loudly. 'You're alive! Now, you're walking like a man who's just got himself a vasectomy!'

CHAPTER THIRTY-FOUR

1998: The Fifth Lie

Steve's rise in Harrington Meats was meteoric. Something had happened with Tony the year he finished university and he was propelled through the business at a great velocity. For some reason his dad couldn't wait to move on and rinse his hands of all obligation.

With Susan's writing taking off, she increasingly needed to be out on the road, attending book signings and author events throughout the UK. Tony seemed happy to accompany her, distancing himself from the day-to-day running of the business.

It was true that with Richard about to turn eighteen they'd done their time as parents. The intensive bit was over and they could reclaim their adult lives. Susan's career as an author allowed them to move around the country on expenses-paid trips, discovering new cities and towns and distancing themselves from the meat-processing business. To be the husband of a popular author suited

Tony. It made him feel more like the man he'd always wanted to be. The reflected glory and the cultured company invigorated him in a way factory work had never come close to.

Tony had spent the summer teaching Steve everything he needed to know about the business. But there was one handover item he saved until last. He hadn't a clue how he was going to raise it with his son but raise it he must. He had been badly shaken after his encounter with Kyle Hunter in the factory. Not only had he been terrified for his own life, but the nature of their arrangement was now crystal clear. Kyle was a killer and he was using the meat-processing plant to dispose of bodies. Tony was rigid with shock when he realised that Kyle might have been passing the meat through the freezers. Had Harrington Meats been distributing human flesh through the food chain?

He'd run through all his options: telling the police, setting Kyle up so he got caught red-handed, or even trying to buy him out. They were all non-starters. Perhaps he could sell the business as a going concern? But it still supported him, Susan and the kids. It was their inheritance. He felt the weight of history on his shoulders. The family business, in truth, was a curse. It was like a baton passed on in an Olympic relay. He didn't want to be the person who dropped it and ended the chain reaction.

Susan's writing was becoming a way out. She was beginning to make a decent second income – it had the potential to free them from Kyle Hunter. But Kyle's money was still useful. It sustained their lifestyle. In fact, Steve's entire private education had been sponsored by Kyle Hunter.

The paperwork for the restructuring of the business had just been signed and Tony and Steve were having a celebratory lunchtime drink in one of the city's quieter pubs. It was before midday, the offices hadn't yet spilled out, so Tony felt free to speak.

'There's something I have to tell you about, Steve, something which must never appear on the books.'

He gave his son an outline of the demands Kyle made on the business and he made him swear that he'd never attempt to interfere with the goings-on in the small hours of the night.

'It's a long-standing arrangement with an old friend,' he explained. 'All you need to do is collect the money every month and split it 50:50 as we discussed. That's it. That's all you have to do. You have to swear that you'll do that.'

Steve had taken it well – remarkably so, and he swore to his father that he'd stick with the arrangement. Once Tony had finally passed the albatross around his neck to his son, he felt a huge sense of relief.

Steve was a different beast from his father. He was competitive, proud and ambitious. Where Tony had had limited educational prospects, Steve had been groomed for success ever since he'd entered private school. After a difficult start at the fee-paying school, Steve had learned to mix with the rich kids and had even picked up their attitude. And he had none of his father's hang-ups. He could see he was being gifted a money machine. He was only 22 years old and he was earning more money than many of his student friends would make in their lifetime. There would be no poverty-stricken years building up a business from scratch or working his way up the corporate chain for Steve. He was starting at the top. He had big plans to expand, maybe even franchise the operation, start to export and move online – that seemed to be the future to him, the worldwide web was a new universe waiting to be explored and exploited.

But there was more to Steve's easy acceptance of the situation. He knew Kyle Hunter already – he had done for four years – and he knew what Tony was going to tell him about the business before Tony broached the subject in the pub. Steve was not like his father. When the problem of the unwanted pregnancy magically disappeared at the age of eighteen, he wanted to know why. And he knew it had happened before. He remembered the problem of the burglary which had mysteriously gone away when he was only nine. Steve knew he and Ben were guilty, but Jed had taken the blame. There seemed to be some angel in their lives taking care of troublesome events.

He'd got his answer after pushing Jenny hard after their break-up. There was a lot of heat from their parents at the time of the pregnancy, and she wouldn't talk to him after the termination. Eventually, he discovered the truth about what had happened, or at least part of it.

'That was you, that was your family!'

She spat her words at Steve, furious at how they'd been threatened by Kyle. It had troubled him. He wondered if that was how the situation with the burglary had been resolved, by intimidation. So Steve did some digging and it didn't take him long to figure out the connection with Tony and Harrington Meats. At first, he was outraged, his moral indignation kicking into overdrive. How could his father use the threat of violence to cover up family messes? And he remembered too that hushed conversation in the hospital toilets, as a child. He'd known things weren't right even then.

All the messes that had been covered up were Steve's. It

was he who'd been responsible for encouraging Jed and Ben into breaking into their neighbour's house. If that hadn't been taken care of, he'd have spent his years at a secondary modern, like Ben and Gaby, or even worse, some juvenile detention centre. And it was he who'd taken the risk of not using a condom with Jenny. If that hadn't been sorted out, he'd be a young father now, trapped and without his university degree.

The more Steve thought about it, the more he realised he could do with a fixer in his life. He was a young man, not yet married and with far too much money. Fast cars, drink and cocaine followed as sure as night follows day. Steve had other problems that needed to be sorted out, and he couldn't wait to make the acquaintance of his father's secret friend, the one who'd been lurking in the shadows for so many years.

Steve ensured that he got to know Kyle Hunter well before he took over the family business from Tony. It was remarkable how easily cocaine bills could disappear with a friend like Kyle. It was also incredible how gambling debts could be forgiven with a connection like that.

So, when Steve came round at the wheel of his car, dazed and bloodied, high on wine and cocaine, he knew that Kyle Hunter would have to be involved. Richard was dead, he had to be, his body was completely still in the passenger seat next to him. There was no way a respected businessman could take the rap for something like that, it would be the end of his career and the end of Harrington Meats. He'd bring shame on the family and destroy everything his father and his forebears had built. He was sorry for Richard, of course he was, but Kyle had taught him there was always a way out. Richard would just be collateral damage.

CHAPTER THIRTY-FIVE

The Island: The Day Of The Party

Ben moved his eyebrows to warn Steve off the delicate topic.

'What's the matter, Ben? You don't need to be embarrassed. We've all had one – I'd be surprised if you hadn't at your age.'

'What's he talking about, Ben?' Laura asked. She was tense again.

'It's nothing, Laura, honestly. Just a bit of discomfort after that incident with the tree trunk. I thought I was Tarzan and it turned out I wasn't.'

'It looks like somebody hasn't been telling the whole truth ...'

Ben needed to shut this down. Steve could be a cocksure little prick at times. He was being one now.

'Steve, I hurt myself in the jungle, right? Leave it alone please, you're wrong.' He tried the eyebrow thing again. Steve finally took the hint.

'Anyhow,' he said, 'let me call the family over, they're dying to see you. They'll be fussing about that lovely baby of yours. No wonder you got a vasectomy!'

Steve punched Ben's shoulder playfully. Ben wasn't feeling playful.

'Kiki! Henry! Mina!'

The names of Steve's family always made Ben smirk. It sounded just like it was: wealthy, successful and confident. Everything that Ben wasn't.

Steve's family left the main house and made their way over to the bar area. Ben gave Kiki a warm hug. Kiki had been good for Steve. There was a period in his brother's life, before he was thirty, when Ben feared his older sibling might turn into a complete and utter idiot, but Kiki had come into his life and changed everything. He couldn't have met her at a better time. It was after Richard's accident, just when they were all reeling from the fallout from those events. Kiki had steadied him, given him a family, and made him focus on what was important. However much Ben resented his brother's success, he couldn't help but admire what he'd done with the business.

They were all groomed to within an inch of their lives. Kiki looked immaculate, her haircut oozed class, the jewellery was perfect, not overdone but clearly boasting wealth. The kids wore the latest trainers and clothing brands, but even Steve's money couldn't rid Mina of her sour, disdainful teenage face.

'Am I still allowed to give you a hug?' Ben asked.

'I'd rather you didn't,' she replied bluntly. 'But hi anyway, Uncle Ben.'

'Great to see you, Ben,' Henry said, holding out his hand and giving Ben a firm handshake. He was the natural successor in the business.

'Mina has brought her violin and will be performing for us at Tony's celebration tonight,' Steve announced.

'God help us!' Tony mumbled so quietly only Ben could hear.

'Dad! I told you, I don't want to do it.'

'There are many things that I don't want to do, Mina, but I do them anyway. We've spent a fortune giving you private violin lessons and it would be nice, from time to time, to see the benefits of that. Besides, Grandad would love to hear you play, wouldn't you, Dad?'

'Of course, I'd love to,' Tony replied.

'How about you, Henry?' Ben asked. 'Still swimming?'

'Yes, still swimming for the county. I've got trials for the British team next month.'

Of course you have, Ben thought, trying not to be petty.

'Well done!' he replied. 'We could have used your skills earlier, when we thought we might have lost Jaxon.'

'How are your kids doing?' Steve asked. 'Is everything fine with them? I've barely seen Alice and Ted - or Jaxon come to think of it.'

This was always the bit Ben dreaded. Whereas everything in Steve's life was always about achievement and attainment, Ben's battles were very different. With Alice, the wins in life were related to the practical support she was being given and health problems for which the outcomes were, perhaps, marginally better than had been predicted by the medical profession. The successes were often about getting to town without a bunch of idiot teenagers teasing her about her callipers or an ill-informed shop assistant asking her if she would leave the shop because she looked drunk. That didn't make for a sexy update with Steve, but that's how life was in Ben's little part of the Harrington world. As for Ted, he was bright enough, but couldn't match the achievements of Steve's two, and besides, the continual battles around Alice's provision and welfare tended to over-shadow his successes in life. They relied on Ted to just get on with it. He was a good kid. He took care of his sister just as he was taking care of Jaxon, even though he was over ten years his junior.

'Oh, they're fine, you know how it is, we're all toddling along.'

Ben had been giving Steve that answer for more years than he could remember.

The introductions over, everybody dispersed into the comfortable seats, drinks were poured and the conversation began to flow. The sun was shining, the sky was a rich blue and for the first time in a long time Ben felt at peace.

'What's the plan for tonight, Dad?' he asked after a while. 'I know it's all starting at seven o' clock, but you've been cagey about arrangements.'

'Nothing to tell, really,' Tony said, sipping a bright pink cocktail. 'The caterers will be over on the boat soon to set up the dining area for us, get it decorated and bring over the booze. They'll be off on the last boat before dark and leave us to it. Then they'll be back first thing tomorrow morning to clean up. Simple as that, and no washing up for anybody either. We've kept it nice and simple. A family meal, around one table, just good conversation, plenty of laughs and a lot of memories.'

'Plus, a special announcement from your father,' Susan interjected.

'Oh yes?' Steve said.

Everybody stopped talking to listen.

'I thought we weren't going to say anything about that until the time came.'

'I want to make sure it happens, Tony. I know what

you're like. So, I'm committing you to it. We're all here together and I insist you tell everybody at your party this evening.'

'You can't keep us hanging on like that,' Ben protested. 'At least give us a clue.'

'No, I'm saying nothing,' Tony replied. 'Only that it's something that you all need to hear, and I can't think of a better time to tell you than when we're all together like this, enjoying each other's company.'

'And no mobile phones, either,' Susan said. 'You kids and your phones. I can't believe we had to bring you all this way just to make sure we can spend an evening with you away from those cursed devices you all carry around with you.'

Susan was a bit of a fascist when it came to tech. She was always moaning about the kids being on their tablets and phones. It was alright for her and Tony, life was a medieval when they had young kids. The shops didn't open on Sunday, they had to use phone boxes, the internet wasn't invented, and the TV was rubbish. If Ben had had access to computer games and mobile phones at that age, he'd have been all over them. It was easy for Susan to be all snotty, she hadn't had to bring up kids who were surrounded by a Pandora's box of technology.

'I think that's the boat coming in!' Steve changed the subject.

'I think you're right,' Ben replied. 'Fancy a walk over to the jetty to watch the caterers arrive?'

Ben wanted to get Steve on his own. This seemed like a good opportunity.

'Sure, bruv!' Steve replied, getting up. 'So long as you can still get about alright after your operation!'

'I thought you said—' Laura began.

'I'm teasing!' Steve smiled at her. 'Ben's just an old man now, always has been really. You still a vegetarian? You've got a shareholding in a flipping meat-processing business, imagine becoming a vegetarian.'

'Some of us are vegans, Dad,' Mina began. 'I can't believe my family makes its money from slaughtered animals. I'm ashamed. We'll burn in hell for this.'

She stood up and headed for the main house.

'Ray of sunshine, isn't she?'

Steve shrugged it off.

'Come on, Ben. Let's go for a catch-up.'

When they were out of earshot, Ben picked up their conversation. He didn't want to tease Steve, but it seemed too good an opportunity to miss.

'So, Mina's a vegan? How does that one play out at home?'

'Mina is anything that causes a pain in my arse. She's at that stage. If I told her the last thing I wanted was for her to play that bloody violin this evening, she'd be up there rehearsing now until it was honed to perfection. I can't get anything right with her. Isn't Alice the same?'

'No, Alice is a good kid. Ted too. They're angry with me, of course, for breaking up with Diana. But who can blame them?'

'Still, you've done alright, Ben. Laura is gorgeous. You do know you're punching well above your weight, don't you? What's the age difference? If me and Kiki ever went our separate ways, I'd be very happy if I'd done half as well as you have.'

'Be careful what you wish for,' Ben warned. 'And hold on to what you've got with Kiki. There are beautiful women all over the place, but not that many you could make a life with.'

'Is all not green in the garden?' Steve asked. 'Oh, and by the way, why are you lying about your vasectomy? You can't kid a kidder! I know that walk very well. The one where you make small careful steps in case you pull anything you shouldn't. Don't tell me you got the snip on the quiet and you didn't bother telling Laura? How well do you reckon that's going to work out, Ben?'

CHAPTER THIRTY-SIX

The Island: The Day Of The Party

The boat was nearing the jetty and the sound of its engine made it difficult to speak at a normal level and be heard. Ben was glad for that, he didn't want to answer Steve's question. He was bang on with his assessment. Ben did wonder how well it was going to pan out. With the discomfort he was feeling after his walk back through the jungle, it was becoming increasingly difficult to hide the pain. Laura was already prickly, the overnight sleeping arrangements with Diana hadn't gone down well and now Steve had opened his big mouth about the operation. If only they could get through the birthday without it all exploding in his face.

'There's another boat out there in the distance,' Steve remarked as the engine was turned off and the boat firmly secured.

'Probably just a fishing boat. I can only just see it,' said Ben squinting in the glare of the sun.

The boat was packed with ready-prepared food, drinks,

glasses, plates and all the paraphernalia required for a party. The catering team had little English, so the conversation was limited and superficial.

'I'm sure that boat's heading over here,' Steve insisted. Ben shrugged it off, disinterested.

'Maybe they forgot the birthday cake. Shall we take a walk along the beach before we head back? I want to ask you something.'

'Oh yes? What's up, bruv?'

Ben wanted to challenge Steve about the bruv thing, but it was too early. They hadn't yet settled back into their family grooves.

'Did you get a letter from Richard?' he asked. The firm sand that had been soaked by the sea was easier for him to walk on than the soft dry sand further up the beach.

'No, I haven't heard from him in ages. You know how it is with Richard and me. He hates me for the accident. Even after all these years he's still saying I set him up. He needs to let it drop. We had witnesses to confirm that I wasn't at the wheel. He's in denial still. He was pissed and he stole the car. Period. He should move on.'

'He's never let that one drop, has he? It's like a conspiracy theory – he won't let it go. There's so much anger about that. You'd think he'd just be delighted that he escaped with his life and only spent a short time in prison. What an idiot though, doing it on his eighteenth birthday. If he'd pinched your car the day before, he'd have been tried as a juvenile. Poor guy. I always liked Richard, but he's got this chip on his shoulder. He thinks everybody's against him. You don't think it's mental illness, do you?'

'What, Richard? I know we're supposed to be all touchy-feely about this mental health stuff nowadays, but there's nothing wrong with him. He just needs to man up and admit his mistake. Anyway, why did you ask about Richard? You know I always go off on one whenever he's mentioned.'

'He sent me a letter. It was weird. He advised me not to come to this party.'

'Really? Why?'

'I don't know. He just said that we'd always got on and that I should consider coming here. Maybe he knew it was all going to be a tense. No change there then.'

'It's true that he always liked you – it was only you and Mum who went to visit him in prison. I'm surprised Mum invited him, to be honest with you. Have you talked to them about it?'

'Not yet, no. But what's this thing Dad wants to talk to us about? Have you seen how thin he is now? I wondered if he'd been ill. You don't think he's going to tell us he's dying, do you?'

'Jesus no, I hope not. It'll probably be something related to the business. If he's 70 now, he's bound to be thinking about that stuff. Now his own kids are all grown up, he'll want to distribute some shares probably, maybe even exit the business. They haven't taken money out of Harrington Meats for years now. They live on what Mum makes from her books.'

'I didn't know that,' Ben replied, thinking it over. 'I assumed that the meat business kept them going and Mum's book money paid for the holidays and cruises.'

'No, Mum does really well from her books. She's no 50 *Shades*, but she has money coming in all over the place. I saw one of her books in the airport shop at Kuala Lumpur. She's amazing.'

'It just shows you how little you can know about your

own family. I knew it was going well, I just never realised it was that lucrative. Good for her!'

'I hope he doesn't get into share allocations at the party. I have strong feelings about all that. After all, I've run the business all these years and built it up. I've no intention of screwing over you and Gaby, but you're a veggie, for Christ's sake, you haven't worked there in years. Any share allocations should reflect that.'

For the first time, Steve's words made Ben think about what money might be residing in the family business. He'd grown up with it, accepted it running in the background, and knew that in some way they were all invested in it. But it didn't create an income for him, it was all tied up in shares.

'Could I ever extract my share?' he asked. 'You know, in theory? I'm not saying I'm going to. But could I, if I wanted to?'

'Yes, in theory you could sell out. It's not quite as straightforward as that because it's a family operation, but yes, you could. I wouldn't recommend it, the way the business is growing. You'll miss out on future growth.' Steve paused and scanned the horizon. 'You know, that isn't a fishing boat. It's definitely heading over here.'

'You're right, it is. Do you think we should head back to the others and stop being anti-social?'

'Probably. It is supposed to be a family occasion, after all.'

'Oh look, Laura's waiting for me at the top of the beach. She doesn't look very happy.'

'You look like you're in trouble, bruv. I think I'll leave you to it.'

Ben did his best to walk normally, but he was struggling

now. He felt sore and uncomfortable. Laura was giving him a look that said she knew exactly what his game was.

Like the treacherous man that he was, Steve strode ahead, greeted Laura with a beaming smile of innocence, then walked back to the chattering group gathered around the bar, leaving Ben to fend for himself. As he walked up to Laura, ready to face whatever the music was, he noticed the quieter engine of the second boat drawing up the free side of the jetty behind him.

'Steve was telling the truth, wasn't he? I watched you walk down the beach with him and now it's even worse. You have had a vasectomy, haven't you? Tell me the truth, Ben.'

The game was up. He couldn't hide it anymore. In spite of the aggravation Laura was about to give him, it would be a relief to get it out into the open. At least he would be able to grimace freely wherever he went.

'I'm sorry, Laura. I wanted to tell you, but I ... I just couldn't. I don't want any more kids. I'm sorry about that. I'm too old for it now—'

'You might have mentioned that before we had Harper. It's a bit late now, isn't it? You're a grown man, Ben – why didn't you tell me? Do you think I wanted to have a child with you? It was only supposed to be a bit of fun. It's not what I planned for my life either. And I know you and Diana slept together. I can see she's still in love with you. I can see how you are with Alice and Ted. You're not like that with Harper. You're a piece of work, Ben Harrington. I'm furious with you!'

Ben opened his mouth to speak, but she stormed off, avoiding the group in the middle of the garden area and skirting around the edges to the sanctuary of the big house. In the distance, Steve gave Ben a big thumbs up.

Bastard! Ben thought to himself.

He wasn't ready to face the humiliation of the group yet, so he turned around and faced out towards the sea. Somebody was getting off the boat, which had now been tied to the jetty. It was Mr Aquino. He had a single passenger whose back was turned to the shore so that Ben couldn't get a good look at the face. He didn't need to. There was only one person he knew who had blond hair like that. It was Richard. Their youngest brother had arrived.

CHAPTER THIRTY-SEVEN

1975: Kyle Hunter

It was no coincidence when Kyle Hunter met Tony Harrington at the top of the cliffs. Only four hours previously he'd been in bed with Tony's wife in the house they shared with their three children.

'I'm worried about Tony. I think he may be on to us,' Susan said.

She studied Kyle's face. He was a young man with dark hair and chiselled, masculine features. He was strong and fearless in a way Tony was not. For Susan he was only a fling. She was run off her feet chasing after the baby and the two young children. A chance encounter with Kyle – in the doctor's surgery of all places – had resulted in this affair.

It felt good to Susan, it was like the child-free, uninhibited passion of her youth. The way Tony had been behaving recently, you'd have thought he was the one who'd given birth to three kids. He was constantly tired, always fretting about the business and the lack of money coming in. Susan loved her husband and she had no intention of leaving him. Kyle was just an escape, a release, a bit of fun. It'd be over soon, she'd end it and he'd be out of their lives forever.

'That's unlikely,' Kyle replied. 'He's stuck at that factory unit from first thing in the morning to early evening. I'm not sure when he'd find time to catch on to us. Besides, relax. I've got the baby and Ben out of your way for the afternoon and Steve's at school until 3.30. This is perfect, isn't it?'

It was perfect, but Tony was not her husband and Susan was struggling to get her head around what she'd done. What a crazy moment of weakness. She still couldn't believe she'd gone through with it. It was partly release from the post-partum depression after Gaby's birth, but also a way to claim back her identity after being poked, prodded, and drained almost dry by three demanding kids. Kyle was like an oasis in the desert, an escape from the drudgery of the day. He was wealthy too – he'd brought in a nanny to take care of the kids while he and Susan lay upstairs in the marital bedroom. She'd get the baby and Ben out of the house for the afternoon and bring them back in time for the school pick-up. When the kids were gone, Kyle would turn up at the house. It was a snatched two hours of release from being a housewife and mother. True, it interrupted her first attempts at writing, but she'd struggled to reclaim her routine after Gaby – she'd pick that up after she'd finished with Kyle. She kept telling herself 'just one more time' but she was finding it hard to end it.

She regularly asked herself if she loved him. She didn't, she loved Tony, but she didn't like her husband very much at that moment. He was aloof with the kids, totally preoccupied with work and obsessed with how little money the business was bringing in. He felt the looming burden of shame. He was terrified of it all collapsing under his management. Susan was less concerned. As far as she could see, a family business was an albatross which was handed on from generation to generation. It might have been somebody's dream several decades ago, but Susan knew it wasn't Tony's. He was an only child and he'd felt the weight of obligation since he was a boy. It was always assumed that he'd take his father's place. He never really had a choice.

Susan had always encouraged him to walk away.

'Just sell it. Or become the owner in name only and let some other poor soul run the place.'

'I can't do that,' Tony would reply. 'I'd be a traitor to the family name. I will not be the Harrington who runs this business into the ground. It's got to keep going to hand on to the next generation.'

And there it was in a nutshell. Tony was forever bound by the pressure of family legacy. There was no way he would walk away: he'd have to thrive or the business would break him.

She had a plan of her own. When it came to the family business, she'd always been on the margins. Tony didn't require her input, it was a part of his life that was Harrington only. She had no intention of sitting on the side-lines. She'd had great feedback from her writing group on her short stories and once Gaby was a little older, once this thing was finished with Kyle, she'd get back to her typewriter.

The machine was an old one Tony had been throwing out at the office. She was determined she would dig them out of that Harrington family legacy by writing a book written on a Harrington typewriter. It seemed a fitting way of breaking the chain of responsibility he'd been saddled with.

It was hard for Susan to both love Tony and at the same

time, resent what he'd become. She despised herself for cheating on him, and she hated herself even more for what she was doing to her children. But, somehow, she needed this for her own survival. She was finding her strength again. Tony would never know, and in five years' time it wouldn't matter. It would be an insignificant fling with a married man that was well and truly parked in the past. It was all under control.

'Tony must never find out about this,' she said. 'You know that, don't you?'

'I do. I have a wife of my own – I also have a lot to lose, Susan. I understand what this is. I'll get one of my guys to keep an eye out for Tony, but I'm pretty sure he's not on to us. I know how to cover my tracks.'

'What is it you do again? I'm still not sure you ever told me.'

'You know how it is. I'm a local businessman. I have fingers in lots of pies. I have an interest in one of the local taxi firms, I'll ask a couple of the guys to keep tabs on Tony. Trust me. I'm good at this sort of thing.'

Susan wasn't sure she wanted to know what he meant by that. It was the first time she'd felt unsettled around Kyle. On the surface he was a perfect gentleman, well-groomed, polite, immaculately dressed, clearly wealthy. But there was a rough side to him too, an intoxicating confidence and masculinity which was making it difficult for her to give up their occasional encounters in the bedroom. She wondered if that side of him was also evident in his business dealings. Intoxicating as this fling was, when Susan was on her own she wondered what he might be capable of if pushed. It sent a chill through her just thinking about it.

When Kyle left the house that afternoon, he had no intention of assigning the task of watching over Tony to anyone else. He had his eye on a bigger prize. This was so important to his future enterprise that he would handle it himself. When Tony Harrington left his office that evening, Kyle Hunter was following at a safe distance, never so close that it would raise suspicion. For part of the way, Tony took his regular route, as if he was going to head back home to his wife. Kyle was about to leave him to it, but instead he took an unexpected turn. That caught Kyle by surprise. He cursed as another driver sounded his horn at him, annoyed by his sudden swerve in the road.

When Tony's car drew up at the cliff-top car park, Kyle knew immediately what he was planning. This was a beautiful place to look out to sea. It was also a well-known suicide spot. He parked further up the road and walked back down towards the car park, shielded from view by a bushy hedge. Tony was taking photographic equipment out of the back of the car. Had he read the situation wrong? Susan hadn't said anything about photography. She was more concerned about Tony's state of mind.

Kyle hung back as Tony walked up to the cliff edge. He assembled his camera and set up a tripod. Kyle moved closer, grateful for the cover of gorse bushes which kept him hidden. He watched as Tony stood right at the edge, holding his camera and closing his eyes.

Damn it, he's going to jump.

The permutations flashed through his mind. If Tony jumped, Harrington Meats had no natural successor. Susan would sell the business, denying Kyle the prize he was seeking – access to the factory unit. Their fling was good, he liked her, but he was simply using her as a means to an end. In addition to a couple of months of afternoon sex with a bored housewife, he'd get a copy of the keys to the meat-processing unit.

Kyle Hunter knew a lot about life and death. He knew Tony didn't have the guts to jump. Tony was not a suicide case, he was a desperate man with limited choices trying to figure out a way to make things right. For a moment, Kyle considered pushing him off. Nobody would be any the wiser.

But it was a long-term partnership that Kyle was after, and Harrington Meats was the perfect fit for his expanding business empire. Tony Harrington was a man who looked like he needed a deal. So, like all good businessmen, Kyle spotted his opportunity and made his move. As he approached Tony from behind, he decided to reach out to him instead. They struck their deal, made their pact and Kyle's objectives were secured. For him, it was just another arrangement, a fix for a problem that needed solving. That was one of his best skills and he knew it. When something needed sorting out Kyle was the type of man who took decisive and drastic action.

CHAPTER THIRTY-EIGHT

The Island: The Day Of The Party

Ben didn't know whether to run after Laura or greet Richard. In the end, he opted for Richard. Laura would need some cooling-off time – somehow he'd have to make things right before the birthday celebrations began.

As he turned to walk towards his brother, he thought he heard Alice's laughter coming from the treehouse.

'Ben!' Richard called from the jetty.

Ben held up his hand and waved. He couldn't even remember how long it had been since he'd seen his brother. He felt guilty at how he'd let him down.

'Great to see you, Richard,' he said, embracing him. 'Hi, Mr Aquino, good to see you again too.'

Mr Aquino had helped Richard onto the jetty and was now retrieving his case from the boat.

'This is amazing!' Richard said. 'What an incredible place for a family get-together.'

Mr Aquino placed Richard's case to his side on the wooden jetty and began to untie the rope securing the boat.

'Don't leave yet, Mr Aquino,' Ben said. 'Why don't you come and join the family for a drink? You've ferried enough of us over here. Please stay a while.'

'Your wife seemed very angry with me yesterday. Are you sure it is okay?' he replied, looking at Ben.

'I'm sorry about that. She was feeling ill. Please, join us for a drink, they'll all be pleased to see you. Let us make it up to you.'

'Okay then, if you're sure. It's Mr Tony's birthday, I think? I will say happy birthday to him.'

'It's tomorrow actually – he was born a couple of minutes after midnight. When we all lived at home, we'd always celebrate the evening before and wait until just after midnight to wish him happy birthday at exactly the time he was born. It was a bit like New Year celebrations.'

They turned to walk up the beach towards the houses.

'I'm still a bit slow with the stick, I'm afraid,' Richard said.

'Yes, I forgot. You're the Bionic Man, aren't you? How many metal rods did they put in that leg in the end?'

'Don't even ask – it was completely rebuilt. I think it's going rusty. It's been giving me quite a lot of trouble recently.'

Mr Aquino looked at them, waiting for a cue.

'Go on ahead, Mr Aquino. We'll follow you up the beach.'

Ben was relieved when Mr Aquino picked up Richard's bag. He couldn't allow Richard to carry it himself, yet he too was in pain. They were like a couple of old men.

'Ben, do you mind if I sit down for a minute. I'm feeling a

bit queasy after that boat trip. I didn't want to mention it to Mr Aquino in case he thought it was his fault. I think it might be easy to offend him – their culture is very different to ours.'

'Sure, no problem. You sit on the post, I'll stand.'

'Now, Laura is your new lady?'

'Yes, you know I split with Diana, don't you?'

'Mum told me. She was very upset about that. We all thought you two would go on forever.'

'You and me both, Richard. It's not how I planned it, believe me.'

Ben looked at his brother sitting with his leg stretched out in front of him.

'Tell me how you are. It's been years since the accident now.'

'Let's put it this way. I haven't received any calls from *Strictly Come Dancing* yet.'

Ben laughed.

'Seriously, I do get hassle from this leg still. I've been having physio for years. Mum pays. Did you know that?'

'No, I didn't.'

Susan had always been a lifeline for Richard. Ben was pleased about that.

'Are you working?' he said.

'Yes, I've still got my eBay business – it's served me well. The internet came into my life at exactly the right time.'

'I'm happy to hear that,' Ben said, and he was.

There was a silence. Ben breathed in the fresh sea air and closed his eyes to listen to the sound of the waves gently lapping the sand on the beach.

'You know, I'm sorry I don't keep in touch.'

'It's my fault too,' Richard replied.

'Things were so difficult after your accident. I thought

we were all going to kill each other for a while. It was horrible time. I'm so sorry you had to go through that.'

'It's okay, Ben.'

'It's not okay. You were treated really badly over that. I don't know how you survived that spell in prison. It must have been terrible. I should have been around more. The older I get, the more I regret some of the things I've done.'

'Ben, seriously, it's fine. You came to visit when you could, you carried on speaking to me, you didn't treat me like some pariah.'

'Why did you send me that letter?'

Ben had remembered the cryptic message he'd received before arriving on the island.

'I'm sorry, I probably shouldn't have. You know there's going to be a shit storm when I go up to see the family, don't you?'

'I knew it wasn't going to be easy, but why is it going to be so bad?'

'Dad doesn't know I'm coming. Mum invited me but told me to keep it quiet. She reckons Dad's mellowed in his old age, thinks it's worth trying for a reconciliation. I'm supposed to be a birthday surprise – I hope it isn't one which will go off in my face.'

'Jesus! How do you think he'll take it?'

'I really don't know. But he won't live forever. Before he dies I want to make it up with him, he's my dad. It's all I ever wanted.'

'I get that, but at his seventieth birthday, Richard.'

'That's why I thought you might like to give it a wide berth. You're the only member of the family who still speaks to everybody, aren't you?'

Ben snorted.

'I was until I got Laura pregnant.'

'Oh yes, I forgot that. You and I can be the family let-downs together. Somebody has to pave the way for perfect Steve and his perfect family.'

'I thought you two had made it up?'

'On the surface we have, but only for the sake of the family. I'll never forgive Steve for what he said. I told you I wasn't driving that night. My friends testified that I was only tipsy when I left the pub. I had to move on, it was eating away at me. I had to let it go, Ben. It was poisoning my life.'

'I can understand that. I still don't know what to think, even after all these years. Steve's my brother, you're my brother. I had to steer a course down the middle and support you both. I didn't know what else to do.'

'There's nothing else you could have done. Even I don't know exactly what happened. I remember laughing with my mates in the pub and then nothing until I came round in the car after the crash. It must only have been a matter of seconds, but it felt like there was somebody in there with me, moving me. After that, it's blank. I woke up in hospital eight days later.'

'I prayed you'd come out of that coma, Richard. I'm not religious, but I certainly prayed that night when I'd heard what happened. I know I'm really bad at showing it, but I do care. I think about you all the time. I just don't know what to believe. For me the only way through is to say that I love you both – even though you can never be as perfect as Steve ...'

Richard laughed out loud.

'Is everything still as perfect in his life? Totally pristine and tidy?'

'Yes, still married to Kiki. Henry and Mina are perfect too. We're getting treated to a musical performance from

Mina this evening ... that's if she gets over her teenage attitude.'

'Hah, even perfect Steve can't escape a bad-tempered teenager, that's great to hear. I think I might ask Mr Aquino to run me back to the mainland. I'm not certain I can face an evening of polite applause while we have to sit through a performance from Mina.'

'You and me both.'

Ahead of them they could see Tony. He'd got off his sun lounger and was storming down the beach. He left the wooden pathway and, feet bare, was walking across the burning hot white sand of the beach towards them.

'Oh shit. Dad knows I've arrived.'

Tony sounded furious.

'What's that little shit doing here?' he shouted.

'Tony! Tony! Stop!' Susan called after him, but he ignored her.

Richard's instinct was to stand up and face him. Tony was approaching with such velocity that it seemed to be the only thing that he could do.

'Hi Dad!' he said, cautious, not sure what was coming next.

'Just go back home, Richard. Leave us alone to celebrate in peace.'

'I love you dad, but you really can be a tosser at times—'

Tony punched Richard squarely on the chin and Ben had to lurch forward to grab his brother's arm and prevent him from falling into the water.

Tony clutched his chest, his knees buckled, and he fell heavily onto the wooden planks of the jetty.

CHAPTER THIRTY-NINE

The Island: The Day Of The Party

'Tony! Oh my God, Tony! Ben, feel in his pockets, find his pills.'

Susan had seen what was happening and had run down the beach to join them. Ben felt a sharp sting in his groin as he bent down to help his father, frantically feeling around in both pockets.

'I've got them. How many should I give him?'

'Just one. Be quick, Ben.'

Henry had arrived at the jetty carrying a bottle of water.

'Sit him up. Help him with the tablet!' Susan cried.

Ben did as he was told. There was silence among the gathered group which had now increased in size. Tony opened his eyes.

'You silly old fool!' Susan scolded him. 'You know you can't afford to get yourself worked up like that. It's your seventieth birthday and it would be really nice if you managed to get to the end of it without dying on us.'

There was uneasy laughter. Richard stood back, keeping well out of the way.

'Where is he, where is the little—'

'Enough, Tony. Shut up. I mean it. It's your seventieth birthday and I invited all the family and that includes Richard.' She looked at her youngest son. 'I wish you'd given me warning of your arrival time. I asked you to do that.'

Richard shrugged.

'Sorry Mum, I couldn't use my phone when I got off at Kuala Lumpur. It was completely dead.'

'It's so lovely to see you, Richard. We'll catch up later after I've taken care of your father.'

Henry and Mr Aquino helped Tony to his feet, taking his weight as they slowly climbed back up the beach. Susan gave Richard a long, hard hug before catching up with Tony.

Then it was Diana's turn to embrace him.

'I see you still know how to make an entrance. It's good to see you – you look well.'

'You too, Diana. I swear you look younger every time I see you.'

'Sweet talker!'

Steve moved forward and held out his hand.

'Richard.'

'Steve.'

It was taut, standoffish, but they managed to keep it civil.

Kiki was much warmer. She'd inherited the Richard situation after it had become part of the family history..

Ben looked ahead and saw Alice making her way carefully down from the treehouse. He watched for Jaxon following close behind, perhaps even Ted. She appeared to be alone. He thought it unusual but was quickly distracted by the conversation.

'So, I guess we now know what's up with Dad then,' Steve said.

'Yes, heart problems, I assume. I never saw that one coming. Did he tell anybody?' said Diana.

'They seem to discuss most of this stuff with Gaby, but she hasn't said anything. Did she mention it to you, Ben?'

'No, nothing.'

'I knew he was unwell,' Richard said.

'How did you know?' Steve said defensively. Then he softened his tone. 'When did they tell you, Richard?'

'Mum told me. She keeps me up to date with most things. It's one of the reasons I agreed to come today. I don't know the details, but I know she's really concerned for his health. I want to set things right with Dad if I can. I know most of you don't want me here, but—'

Kiki, Ben and Diana were quick to tell him how wrong he was in that assumption. Steve kept his silence.

Alice had made her way to the group, keen to find out what was going on. Her face was flushed. Ben assumed the walk on the beach had been difficult with her callipers. She'd taken them off and was holding them in her hands.

'Are you okay?' he asked.

'Uncle Richard!' she deflected.

She gave him a hug.

'You're a young woman now, Alice. I can't believe how much you've changed. I hope your mum and dad tell you how beautiful you are. It's great to see you. Look, I have a stick too!'

'Ha ha! You can join my stick club.'

Alice and Richard had always been close, ever since she was a toddler. They'd bonded the minute they'd met.

Richard couldn't have seen her more than three or four times in her life, yet they were thick as thieves. Ben liked it, it was nice. It felt like a small gift that he'd been able to give his brother, when he was out of ideas on how he could help him.

'How about we head back up to the house and find Richard a room?'

Diana took the lead, anxious to get back into the shade of the bar area.

Ted was entertaining Jaxon outside Gaby's house. In spite of the age difference between the two, they were happy in each other's company, running around, kicking a ball and burning off their energy in the sunshine. She came out on to the veranda when she heard him shouting across to greet Richard.

'Hey Gaby,' Richard said as his sister joined them on the loungers.

'Richard,' she said tersely. It was marginally warmer than Steve's greeting.

They embraced, but it was awkward. Gaby was a funny one. She could be very liberal with the judgement but not quite so generous with the self-knowledge. Ben thought back. Gaby had been twenty-four when Richard had his accident and was no longer living at home. She'd rushed over to the hospital to see her little brother, they'd always seemed close. After all, they'd been the last two children left in the house after Steve and Ben moved away.

He could see Jeremiah walking up the beach, heading over to the main house where the birthday preparations were underway. Where had he come from? Had he been moving things from the bigger boat?

'So, where is your new lady?' Richard asked, aware that

he was a bit of a fly in the ointment and keen to overcome the inertia as soon as possible.

Steve laughed, and Kiki gave him a playful punch.

'Ben's in the doghouse!' Steve said.

They were interrupted by his daughter who was walking across to join them.

'Look who's coming to grace us with her presence,' he said with a smile. 'It's Mina, finally emerged from her bedroom.'

'Hi Uncle Richard!' she grunted.

'Hey Mina, you're another one who's growing up wonderfully. It's great to see you.'

'Ben and Mum, everybody - I need to tell you something.'

'Not now, Mina. We were just asking Uncle Ben a few questions.'

'What happened to put you in the doghouse, Ben?' Richard asked. 'I hope it won't spoil the party. Mind you, I might already have done that all on my own.'

'Dad! Mum! This can't wait. I have to tell you now.'

'One moment, darling.'

Steve was enjoying Ben's discomfort far too much to listen to his daughter.

'It's a long story, Richard.'

'Dad!'

Mina was indignant. Steve and Kiki were used to her teenage impatience and they'd agreed not to indulge her. She'd have to wait until the adults had finished talking.

'In fact, I should probably head back to our room to make things up with her—'

'Okay, if you won't listen to me, I'll tell you right now. I've been thinking about it for ages, but we might as well get it out in the open while the whole family is here.'

'What is it, Mina?' Steve sighed, clearly tiring of her attitude and persistence.

'I need to tell you something – you all need to know. I'm gay. I like women. I've known it for two years. You're not going to get the white wedding you're always banging on about. Not unless I walk up the aisle with a woman, that is.'

CHAPTER FORTY

1979: The First Lie

Kyle Hunter was sailing close to the wind. Not only was he holding the ankles of a 76-year-old man as he dangled him from a dormer window three levels up, it was also becoming increasingly difficult to separate business and pleasure.

Tony Harrington had requested his assistance with a minor domestic problem. His two boys had got caught up in a silly little matter. They'd been messing around in Mr Ingram's garden, scrumping apples or something similarly trivial, and then Steve had spotted an open window. What had started as a bit of mischief ended as a police matter. Tony Harrington needed that sorting out – and fast. As far as Kyle was concerned, it was just a normal day at the office.

Need somebody scared witless, sir? Of course, that'll be £1000. Physical violence is extra. And if they need to be disposed of permanently and without a trace? Well, that costs considerably more, sir.

When it came to the Harringtons, things were slightly

more precarious. Kyle had struck up his affair with Susan as a way of gaining access to the business. Originally, he'd intended to do it by stealth, by stealing the keys and entering the premises, without anybody's knowledge, at night. But he'd listened to Susan talking about their money concerns and how Tony had become more and more remote as the business struggled to survive. It seemed she would happily see the whole set-up washed down the plughole. It was when Susan asked him to keep an eye on Tony and Kyle got to see the level of desperation in his life that he realised there was a better way to approach this.

Tony was a man in trouble and desperate for a deal. He was also weak. Kyle well understood the difference between a strong man and a weak one. He'd only ever had to kill one woman and she'd shocked him with her bravery. Right up until the moment when he snapped her neck, she was calling him every name under the sun. She'd struggled, tried to scratch his face and lashed out viciously. Even in death she had a scowl on her face. If he hadn't been paid to kill her he'd have considered inviting her out on a date.

Tony would be a wet-the-pants kind of guy. He'd sob and beg. Kyle hated that type. Sometimes they even soiled themselves in fear. He'd cleaned that little mess up once in his career, then decided it was time to hire staff. The boss doesn't clean up the crap.

Kyle enjoyed the kill. There was something godlike about it, the ability to give or take life – not that he ever offered any mercy. Where a contract was involved, Kyle always delivered. He'd turned his capacity for killing into a business, but if things had been different he might have become a random killer. He'd have done it for free.

He considered himself an entrepreneur, although the idiots on *Dragon's Den* might not agree. He could imagine

Duncan Bannatyne sticking his nose up at what he did, declaring 'I'm oot!' as Kyle explained to him the amount of profit that could be derived from the killing and disposing of some fool who needed to be got rid of. The cash flow, initial outlay and profitability of a business like that was great. He had no direct premises costs, no utilities to pay, and any HR issues with the staff ... well, they knew how the appraisal process worked in Kyle's business. You want to cause a fuss? Let me introduce you to the mincing machines at Harrington Meats. You threaten to tell the police? Fine, you go into the mincing machine ... alive. That's what a great boss he was.

It had made Kyle a wealthy man. The arrangement with Tony Harrington was perfect – in business circles they called it leverage. Tony had been in such a bad place, he was considering ending his own life. Rather than come up with a way to dig himself out of a hole, he'd rather go for an insurance job. Kyle had no respect for that. Tony was easy prey. He would take the money, ask no questions and allow him to use his factory at night. And that's what happened. For several years he would be the perfect sleeping partner. That is, until Susan complicated things.

Kyle had thought himself capable of breaking it off with Susan. That's exactly what he intended to do once the deal was struck with Tony. But he liked the arrangement – she was starved for attention from Tony.

Ingram was struggling and Kyle nearly dropped him. This was not a killing job, it was strictly intimidation. Kyle pulled him back up. He'd soiled himself. Goddammit, he'd messed himself! He hated it when they did that. This was a solo job, strictly private. Ingram would have to clear it up himself.

'Look what you've done, old man!' he scowled through

his mask. 'Do you know how they train puppies not to do that? They rub their noses in it. Do you want that to happen to you, Mr Ingram?'

Kyle was worried the old man might have a heart attack. He checked that the gaffer tape was secure across his mouth, held his breath and dangled Ingram once again from his ankles. He never got used to that smell. It wasn't something they ever showed in films. What did people think happened in situations like that?

He thought about Susan. She would never know about Tony's arrangement with him. The two men had agreed that on the cliff top. But, in any case, Tony would feel such guilt and shame at the slimy way he'd managed to keep the family business going that he'd never tell a soul. And of course Tony must never find out about his relationship with Susan. If he did he'd threaten to end their business arrangement and even report him to the police. Then he'd have to kill him. Perhaps he'd finish them both in a car crash, something clean like that.

This business with the boys had made things difficult. Susan had told him about it in bed and he'd listened attentively, offering useless advice and empty reassurances. He and Tony had already spoken about resolving the problem – hence his late-night visit to Mr Ingram. However, it placed him in the very road where Tony lived and where he was having an affair with Tony's wife. He'd masked up – not his usual style, as he was the last face that most of his victims ever saw. This was dangerous for Kyle. If he wasn't careful, a neighbour might spot him leaving Ingram's house and then notice him ducking into the Harringtons' driveway the next afternoon. It was time to end it with Susan.

Kyle pulled Ingram back in from the window and made him stand in his own mess.

'So, Mr Ingram. Let's go through this one more time. When the police ask you if your house was broken into, what will you say?'

Ingram wept as he replied.

'It didn't happen like I said. I'm an old man. I was mistaken.'

'When the police ask you who was involved, what will you say?'

'It was Jed, the third boy. He was the one who took my silver.'

'I'm going to take two spoons and a carving knife before I leave your house. That's what you're going to say was stolen. The other items that you reported missing were fool-ishly thrown away by you during one of your confused episodes. Two spoons and a carving knife, that's what's miss-ing. Got it?'

Mr Ingram nodded. He'd now wet himself, a big patch of urine spreading across his pyjama bottoms.

Kyle looked in the old man's eyes. He'd do what he'd been told. Living alone in a big house like that, he knew how vulnerable he was.

'Okay, I'm going to leave now. You need to clear up this mess you've made and get a good night's sleep. First thing tomorrow morning you call the police and explain how you were mistaken.'

Ingram nodded. He just wanted Kyle out of his house.

Kyle exited Mr Ingram's bedroom and headed down the stairs. He removed the items of silver with his gloved hand and placed them into a Safeway supermarket bag. That's where Jed's mum and dad shopped, he'd worked that one out when researching the job. He was pleased to be well away from the smell.

It was going to be a busy night. He had a house break-in

to squeeze in and then a follow-up visit to the headteacher of the local private school. Kyle wondered if he'd soil himself too. In his experience teachers were cocky little buggers who always tried to play the authority card. If he tried that, Kyle would threaten to cut out his tongue. That would show him who was boss. Dammit, Kyle loved his line of work.

CHAPTER FORTY-ONE

The Island: The Day Of The Party

'Why do you have to make me look like a prick every single time, Mina?'

Ben thought Steve was going to explode. His brother was usually cool and collected, a man under control, but what Mina had just told them had made him race from zero to 100 mph in less than 60 seconds. His face was red, convulsed with rage.

'Maybe because you are a prick, Dad.'

'Mina! That's enough,' Kiki intervened.

Steve shot an angry glance at his wife.

'Did you know about this?'

Ben had never seen his sibling like that before. To watch him and Kiki in action you'd think they had the perfect relationship. Well-dressed, immaculately groomed and respectfully supportive of each other, that was Steve and Kiki. It was as if they'd stepped out of the pages of a textbook about relationships, a perfect example of what every marriage should be.

'I've suspected for some time, but it's up to Mina. She's old enough to know her own mind. And does it really matter? I can't say it troubles me—'

'Of course it matters! It matters that she decided to tell everybody at Dad's party. It matters that she didn't think to let us know first. It also matters because we've talked about her wedding since she was a little girl.'

'I'll still be getting married, but to a girl not a boy, Dad. Same wedding, different groom.'

'And what will my associates think of that? We're a traditional family business, we can't have a gay wedding in the family.'

'To be honest with you, Steve, I don't think anyone will give a shit. Unless you missed it, this is the 21st century. Nobody cares.'

Steve turned around to face Richard. In that moment Ben saw fierce resentment – even hatred – in Steve's eyes. It was shocking. He decided to try to calm things down.

'Seriously Steve, it makes no difference. Surely you'd rather Mina could be honest with the family rather than having to hide it away? I know it's probably a surprise, but it's for the best. Nobody in the family cares and only a few bigots outside the family will even think twice about it. Richard's right, it's the 21st century now. Nobody's bothered in the slightest.'

'Thanks Uncle Ben. And Uncle Richard. This is no biggie. I've been wanting to tell you all for ages. So, now you know. It's out there. I haven't grown another head or turned into an axe murderer. I'm the same person I was ten minutes ago.'

'Yes, a precocious little—'

'Steve!' Kiki interrupted sternly.

It was enough to shake him out of his rage. He took a deep breath and attempted to calm down. His face was still crimson but from embarrassment now.

'I'm going to go and check on the caterers,' he announced. 'They should be almost finished by now. Mum asked me to see that everything is okay while she takes care of Dad.'

He crept off towards the main house, looking contrite after his outburst.

'That's unusual for Steve,' Ben remarked, once he was out of earshot. 'He seems very wound up. Is everything okay?'

'He's just a stuck-up prick!' Mina said.

Kiki ignored her and offered a more reasoned answer.

'He's under a lot of stress in the business. He's really pushing the export markets hard and I think he might have bitten off more than he can chew. You know Steve. He tries to make it all look smooth and under control, but between you and me, I think he may be struggling.'

'Exactly – he's a prick!' Mina repeated.

'Your dad has worked very hard to grow the business, Mina, and you'd do well to remember it. It's what will pay your university fees. Whatever you think of him, he's deeply committed to that business. He's determined to leave it in much better shape than he found it.'

Mina sat down where Steve had been sitting previously.

'Have you told your cousins yet?' Ben asked.

'Alice has known for ages. We message each other all the time. She was the first to know, actually. She knows how to keep a secret does Alice.'

'I always assumed Alice didn't even know what a lesbian was.'

Ben looked at Diana who had so far been quiet. She knew better than to get involved in Harrington family dramas.

'You'd be surprised, Ben,' she said. 'Our little girl is growing up fast. Don't be deceived by the walking stick and leg splints. That girl turns heads in the street.'

'Seriously, Mina, no one cares one little bit,' Richard said. 'In our day we had to keep quiet about our sexuality. Hiding secrets screws you up. Look what it's done to me.'

'Does that mean that after all these years you're finally coming out as gay?' Ben asked, even though he knew exactly what was behind Richard's words.

Mina wasn't sure if they were joking. She looked from face to face. Ben and Richard burst out laughing.

'We're kidding, Mina!' said Ben. 'But don't you worry about it, you did the right thing. Secrets eat you up from the inside. You can't hide them forever – they always come out into the open eventually.'

Kiki turned to look round at the dining area.

'It looks like the caterers have finished.'

'We don't have to serve ourselves tonight, do we?' Richard asked.

'No, the Villanuevas are staying overnight to do the honours. They're staying in the third cabin over there. Have you decided where you're sleeping yet, Richard?'

'No, I haven't had time. What's still free? I don't care where I sleep.'

'I must be leaving also.'

They'd all forgotten about Mr Aquino, who was sitting on a chair set back from the main group. He'd barely touched his drink. Ben wondered what he thought of their crazy family. The poor guy had come to take them to and from the mainland in his boat and had ended up bang in the middle of a family lesbian drama. As he spoke they all realised their lack of manners and were suddenly over-attentive in their concern for him.

'Mr Aquino, thanks so much for having a drink with us ...Yes, we'll pass on your best wishes to Mum and Dad ... You'll be over in the boat at midday tomorrow with some supplies? That's great, thank you.'

'He must think we're a bunch of western idiots!' Richard said, as they watched him walk off towards the beach and his boat. He looked like he couldn't wait to abandon them on the island.

'We should think about getting ready,' said Diana. 'Besides, Ben, don't you have some making up to do with Laura?'

'I've been putting it off.'

'Do tell,' Richard said.

'You can't talk,' Ben replied. 'You need to smooth things over with Dad before the party. It's going to be a bit tense otherwise.'

'I think we all need to chill out,' said Diana. 'We don't want to spoil this party for your father. The light seems to be beginning to go a bit. That's probably why Mr Aquino was getting so fidgety.'

'It's blowing up too,' Kiki observed. 'You don't get trop-ical storms out here, do you?'

There were shrugs all round.

'That's all we need, some crazy equatorial weather to completely screw up the party,' Richard laughed. 'Though, if you ask me, the storm feels like it's begun already.'

In the distance they could hear the engine of the larger boat revving up to leave the jetty.

'There go the catering team,' said Diana. 'I'm going to check in on Gaby to see if Ted is with Jaxon. He's a good kid

Ted, he seems quite happy entertaining Jaxon. It's done us all a big favour. He'll need to start getting ready.'

'I'll head over with you,' Richard said. 'I need to have a chat with Dad before everything gets going – see if I can smooth things over.'

'Me too,' Kiki said. 'Come on, Mina. Let's find your dad and see if we can calm him down before the celebrations begin. He'll get over your news. You just caught him off his guard.'

Ben was left alone. He had some smoothing over to do himself. As he went to get up from the lounger there was a sharp pain in his groin. He let out a groan. He'd got up way too fast. As he looked out to sea towards Mr Aquino readying his boat, he saw grey clouds in the distance.

Perhaps Kiki was right. It looked like they were in for a storm that night.

CHAPTER FORTY-TWO

The Island: The Day Of The Party

Ben thought it best to knock before entering. She was the mother of his child, but she was also furious with him.

'Laura, can I come in?'

It seemed a ridiculous thing to say.

There was no answer and he walked through the door anyway. Laura was curled up asleep on the bed with Harper at her side. Harper was awake and happy. When he saw her like that, unaware and content, he felt guilty. Somehow this beautiful kid had become caught up in his feelings of contempt towards himself. He loved her, however they'd got to where they were. He loved Harper as much as he did Alice and Ted.

'Come on, tiny,' he said gently as he leaned across the bed and picked her up without disturbing Laura – she'd been crying, he could see that her make-up had run.

Ben felt wretched. How had things wound up like this? He meant Laura no ill will, but they shouldn't have been together. They'd had a stupid fling, got caught out and now they were stuck with each other. For the first time Ben realised that Laura probably felt as trapped as he did.

He walked over to the veranda and looked out over the gardens to the beach. The sun was still shining on the island, but the grey clouds were closer now. They were unlikely to escape without at least a heavy shower.

Mr Aquino's boat was still at the jetty. It struck Ben as odd, but perhaps there was a good reason; as a local boatman he lived and breathed the tides, the weather and the sunset times. The storm was over the mainland – even Ben could see that. Maybe he'd decided not to risk it, he wouldn't have wanted to head off into that. He could have chosen to stay overnight instead.

Ben stopped thinking about Mr Aquino and took five minutes to admire the island. It was the most beautiful thing he'd ever seen. The sea, the trees, the gardens, the cabins – it was paradise. The perfect place for a seventieth birthday party.

'Ben? Is that you?'

'Hey Laura. I've got Harper. Are you okay?'

'Yes,' she said, suddenly aware that her appearance would give the game away. She wiped her eyes.

'I'm sorry,' Ben said, walking back into the room. 'I should have told you.'

'Yes, you should.'

He'd made the first move, and now he was on the defensive. She grabbed the ball and ran with it.

'Why didn't you tell me? Am I really that awful?'

Ben sat on the edge of the bed. Harper grasped a handful of his hair in her hand.

He gently unfurled her fingers.

'Ow! You're strong, little one.'

She giggled, and he felt a surge of love that was strong and impenetrable.

'We should have talked about it, I know. But Harper wasn't planned and it was a lot having another child at my age. I thought I was done with all that. I love her dearly, but I have two children already.'

'And what about me?'

'What do you mean?'

'Do you ... do you love me?'

Ben knew that his eyes had given the game away before he'd had time to let something more diplomatic come out of his mouth.

'It's not that I don't love you—'

He was too slow for her.

'It is because you don't love me!' she shouted. Harper flinched in his arms.

'It's okay, baby,' Ben said, stroking her little tuft of hair.

'And don't call me baby!' Laura snapped at him. Ben decided not to quibble with her over that one.

'Come on, Laura. It was a fling. You're a young woman. You're not really interested in an old bloke like me. I've got a middle-aged paunch; my hair is turning grey and you make me shave my pubic hair in an attempt to make me look vaguely sexually attractive to you. We're a different generation. You don't even know who Duran Duran are.'

'I do know who Duran Duran are! But only because you won't stop playing that greatest hits CD.'

She was right about that. It was a good CD. Why wouldn't he play it over and over?

'Can you honestly look me in the eyes and tell me that you love me?' Ben asked.

Laura studied his face.

'How did we get here, Ben? I love Harper, I loved our fling. It was exciting.'

She began to cry.

'But no, I don't love you. I thought it was just a short-term thing, and I actually considered having an ...'

She struggled to say the word.

'I was going to have an abortion. I really considered it for about a day. It was that day I said I was ill and skipped work, do you remember?'

Ben nodded. He did. He'd even covered for her. It was before they were out in the open about the relationship.

'But I couldn't. How could I have killed that beautiful baby? She's gorgeous. We made her – together. I just don't know what to do, Ben.'

Her eye make-up was a mess now. It would be unsalvageable. Ben glanced out towards the beach again. The heavy clouds were getting nearer, and he could see some movement by Mr Aquino's boat. He guessed he was probably securing it for the storm.

'That's how I feel,' he said quietly. 'We kind of landed ourselves in this relationship and neither of us really wants to be here. And we both love Harper. I'm the same, I just feel ... stuck.'

'What can we do?' Laura sighed, wiping her face.

'I don't know.'

'You still love Diana, don't you? You're so easy with her and the kids. I see it in your body language and your conversation with her. You two should never have split up. I feel such a bitch for sleeping with you—'

'You're not to blame for that. I was unhappy, we got on well, I did a stupid, middle-aged man thing. I was feeling lousy about Alice, I hated myself. If anybody's to blame, it's me. I thought I could have you and Diana and that nothing would change. Well, it did.'

Ben looked out of the window again. There were three figures by the boat now. One of them looked like Henry. There was a lot of movement.

'Diana's lovely, and Alice and Ted are wonderful kids. You should be with them.'

'And Harper?'

'I don't know, Ben. I just don't know. Shall I tell you the reason I got so angry when I found out you'd had a vasectomy? It's because when we started sleeping together I assumed you'd already had one. I thought a man your age, with grown-up kids, would definitely have had the snip. I love Harper to the end of time, but I wish to God you'd sneaked off and had that operation before we went to bed together. Are you even listening to me, Ben?'

There was outrage in her voice again. Ben turned his gaze away from the beach, back to Laura.

'I think there's something going on out there, over by Mr Aquino's boat. He was supposed to be on his way over to the mainland by now. It looks like there's a storm coming.'

Suddenly there was the sound of running footsteps and shouting at the far end of the house.

'Oh hell, I hope that's not Dad. He'd better not be ill on his seventieth birthday.'

Laura took Harper from Ben and went out onto the veranda, looking out towards the jetty.

There was a loud banging on the door. It was Ted.

'What's up, Ted? Is Grandad okay?'

'Yes Dad, Grandad's fine. It's Mr Aquino, the boat guy. He was supposed to have left by now but we think he might have had an accident and been swept out to sea. He's nowhere to be seen ... and there's blood on the jetty.'

CHAPTER FORTY-THREE

1980: The Second Lie

Kyle watched Bill Aitken as he crossed the college canteen carrying his lunch. He'd opted for burger and chips – and a pile of lettuce, a food choice that suggested he was slightly delusional about whatever health kick he was on.

Kyle adjusted his baseball cap. It wasn't an item of clothing he'd normally be seen dead in, but he had to be sure he'd blend in. His denim jacket and glasses with their black frames made him feel ridiculous. He needed to exude an air of 'college lecturer who wants to be down with the kids'. The canteen was filled with men just like that. There was an identikit example not three tables away, only this guy had a grey ponytail instead of the baseball cap. Kyle wanted to take a pair of scissors, cut it off and tell the man to grow up.

Tony wasn't the only one who wanted to know if Bill Aitken and Susan Harrington were having an affair. Kyle was invested in the answer to that question too. It wasn't that he was in love with Susan, though for a time the free and grateful sexual encounters had become somewhat addictive to him. She'd broken up with him anyway. Just over eight months previously. It suited him fine. No tears, no shouting, no threats. Of course, he missed the sex, but he'd got what he'd come for – access to Harrington Meats – and he'd had a little fun along the way.

Bill had been published in the past, Kyle had found that out in his research. He was still writing too, most of it crime stories and police procedurals. He was one of that rare breed of lecturers who'd achieved demonstrable real-world success at what they teach others day-in, day-out. Kyle had even bought his most successful book – he was thorough in his preparation. It was all about a husband who'd killed his wife after discovering her affair. The irony was not lost on Kyle.

He needed to find everything out about him. If Bill Aitken was going to disappear, Kyle had to ascertain who would miss him and which of his family members might cause a fuss. He also needed to look at opportunities – was Bill into drink, drugs or prostitutes? It was always easier to create a scandal or to find a way of frightening someone than it was to kill them.

However, if it came to murder, Kyle knew it would go smoothly. Harrington Meats had been a gift horse to his business. In the bad old days before his arrangement with Tony he'd had to go for the traditional option of cutting off heads and finger tips and separating them from the torsos. Headless bodies would be dumped in lakes, heads would be burned then buried, fingers would be placed in a hand mincer then fed to pigs. Teeth and heads were always the problem, they were so difficult to get rid of. Harrington Meats provided the perfect solution. Not only was it set up to manage the carving up and destruction of animal corpses on an industrial scale, it also gave him access to bone-crushing tools which would have raised far too many red flags if he'd bought them on his own. And the icing on the cake was that the human waste could be easily packaged to look like animal products. If he and his guys had ever been stopped it would have just looked like they'd done a run to the local cash-and-carry butcher's.

At one stage he'd considered slipping the meat into the Harrington Meats supply chain, but that idea had swiftly been dismissed. It was too dangerous. It would only take one connoisseur to realise that their shepherd's pie wasn't actually made of minced beef and the game would be up. Instead, Kyle fed the waste to pigs. His favourite trick was to locate pigs which were being reared organically. It tickled him to think of all those rich idiots exclaiming how delicious their hand-reared bacon was when there was every chance that that very animal had been fed on somebody they might have known. That's what made for a humorous situation in Kyle's book.

Bill Aitken was well-groomed, professionally turned out and a man whose career was on the rise. No wonder Susan liked him. Her hopes and dreams of writing success were all caught up in her relationship with this man. She was taking a creative writing course, Kyle knew that much from their pillow talk. It hadn't much interested him at first, until his encounter with Tony in the toilet cubicles at the hospital. There were a couple of things that worried him about that meeting.

Firstly, there was every chance that Susan's child was his. He'd never even thought about it previously, he'd just assumed that things were going better for her and Tony and that they'd cemented their newly rekindled love with a brand-new baby. But when Tony talked about the sexual famine and how Susan had quite clearly engineered a bedroom encounter with her husband – possibly to cover up an extracurricular sexual relationship – it had made Kyle's antennae go off. The timings would work perfectly.

The other thing that was troubling Kyle about that encounter in the hospital toilets was Steve, the oldest child. He and Tony had been in separate cubicles, with the doors locked, when he'd come in. Tony had carried on speaking, but Kyle had looked over the door of the cubicle to check out what was going on. At first he didn't place Steve with the Harringtons. It was only when Tony had returned to the Susan's room and Kyle left his cubicle five minutes later that the connection was made. He had hovered outside the room for a few moments, watching the family as they clustered around Susan's bed. That's when he saw Steve. He recognised his navy-blue shoes. That could be awkward. If Steve ever figured out that they'd spoken, if he ever put two-and-two together, it might create a difficulty.

As he sat at that canteen table looking like a young lecturer, Kyle thought about Bill and Susan. He really hoped they were having an affair. He'd faked the nonsense he'd passed on to Tony – all that *We're almost there. This birth is going to be amazing. It's our own child, only more special. You're amazing, I can't wait, Bill* and the rubbish about having Susan's photo from her student file. If Kyle hadn't been intending to make Bill Aitken disappear, he might have been tempted to take the creative writing course himself. With a mind for fiction like he had, Kyle reckoned he could go places.

Susan had now entered the canteen carrying her baby in a sling. She joined Bill who was sitting at a table with a couple of other students, two girls and a young guy, an arty type. Kyle hated blokes who looked like that. He wanted to feed them to the hand-reared pigs, only there wasn't enough meat on most of them to make a decent meal. Kyle knew a lot about people. Susan wouldn't be expecting to see him there, and if she did catch a glimpse, she wouldn't recognise him out of context and in his current attire. And to think they'd once been so intimate.

The members of the group were clearly comfortable with each other. As far as Kyle could tell from a distance, the baby was nothing like him. He didn't have kids of his own, so he hadn't a clue what kind of distinguishing features they might have. But Richard just looked like a baby to him. On the other hand, he didn't look much like Tony or Bill either.

Bill Aitken had to disappear off the scene – either by way of relocation or permanent re-homing by Kyle. Tony needed a result on this. But Kyle still wanted to know who the baby's father was. He didn't care, it wasn't as if he'd be offering child support or Sundays in the park. He just wanted to know.

So far, he'd got nothing on Bill and Susan. They got on well, they laughed a lot, he was clearly offering her every help he could with her writing. But that didn't place them in a bed together. In fact, Bill Aitken didn't seem to have a woman in his life.

Then Kyle saw it. It was only momentary, but he got all the explanation that he needed. And he got a solution that wouldn't have to result in a dead body. This was why he was patient. If you could be patient and wait, people would always betray themselves, they just couldn't help it.

Bill Aitken wouldn't be the slightest bit interested in Susan. He was gay – the male student who was sitting with them had just cupped his balls under the table, out of sight of everybody. Except for Kyle, of course. They'd exchanged a quick, collusive glance across the table. He'd got his solution. Bill Aitken would be leaving the university at short notice, either as a result of his own surprise resignation or under the cloud of scandal. University lecturer has forbidden gay affair with student, breaking all university student–lecturer rules in the process. And Bill wasn't openly gay, so family members probably weren't even aware of his sexuality.

Kyle didn't particularly care if Bill was gay or not. He was an equal-opportunities killer. But it gave him the leverage he needed to run the man out of town and give Tony the result he was looking for. Bill would be blamed for the affair – and the baby, and he'd disappear out of their lives.

Only it left Kyle with one problem. That meant Richard was most likely his child.

CHAPTER FORTY-FOUR

The Island: The Day Of The Party

'Do Tony and Susan know yet, Ted?'

'No, Uncle Steve told me to come and get you. He said not to worry Nan and Grandad.'

'Good, good. I don't want to mess up the party for them. Mr Aquino could have had an accident. It might not even be his blood. Perhaps it's blood from when Grandad hit Uncle Richard. Let's check it out properly first. Who's down at the jetty?'

'Uncle Steve, Henry, and the Villanueva's son Jeremiah. It's getting stormy out there, blowing up a bit of gale.'

'You go, Ben.' Laura said. 'We can speak later.'

'You sure?'

'Yes, go. If Mr Aquino's hurt, you need to find him. We'll leave this until after the birthday meal, let's not screw things up for your dad and mum. But we do need to talk.'

He looked at her face. She was serious. They were going to have to thrash it all out. The problem was, Ben felt guilty about all the options. There was nothing in the list of available choices that would not result in an injured party. Either Harper would be left without a dad or Ted and Alice would have to continue without him. And Laura had been brutally honest, a quality which he had perhaps not been endowed with. She'd said it out loud: the only reason they were together was Harper. But wasn't that the primary reason they should be trying to make it work? His head almost span out of control anytime he thought about it. Whatever action he took, it was going to cause pain for somebody.

'Dad?'

Ted's voice shook him out of his thoughts.

'Yes, sorry, we need to go.'

Ben walked over to give Laura a kiss. She was tense, offering only her cheek. Ben stroked Harper's head and gave her a kiss on her soft, dimpled chin.

'Are you up to a beach search? What with your operation and all?' Laura said, a hard edge to her voice.

Ben's face reddened.

'I'm in quite a lot of pain now, but if I take it easy, I'm sure I'll survive.'

Laura opened her mouth to reply, but looked at Ted and thought better of it.

'Right, let's go Ted!'

They walked along the hallway and across the lounge area which had been prepared for the forthcoming celebrations. There were gas-filled balloons, colourful streamers and a beautifully set table. In the adjacent kitchen the Villanuevas were taking care of the pre-cooked menu. For a few seconds Ben felt a pang of excitement. So far the entire journey had been about problems. He'd worried about the cost, his operation, his relationship with Laura; he'd been eaten up with embarrassment at his current predicaments. And in fretting so much, he'd neglected to focus on what was about to take place. Tony and Susan had organised this wonderful family get-together on a delightful paradise island. All his three children were there and everyone in his family was getting on together –with the temporary exception of Richard and Tony, and Ben was sure they'd work out a way of keeping the peace by the time they all sat down to eat. The entire Harrington family was in one place at the same time. This never happened, it was a one-off. He needed to stop focusing on the negatives – this might be the last time they ever got together as a complete family. Once they'd found Mr Aquino, he'd place his worries to one side and just enjoy the evening.

Ben walked over to the kitchen to ask if Mr Villanueva would join them on their search.

'We're going to have a storm tonight,' Mrs Villanueva looked up as she stirred a vat of something that smelled delicious. 'They blow up very fast in this part of the world. But it will come, and it will go. Tomorrow, it will be a beautiful day again and we will forget all about it.'

Mauricio Villanueva wiped his hands on a towel, removed his apron and walked up to Ben.

'Nimuel Aquino knows these waters very well. I would trust only him to take me in a boat across these waters in a storm. I think it is likely he decided to stay on the island, rather than risk the journey this evening.'

'Do you know anything about the hut on the other side of the island?' Ben asked.

'Dad, we need to get looking for Mr Aquino,' Ted interrupted.

'You go ahead, tell the others we'll be there in a moment. I just need to ask Mr Villanueva this one thing.'

Ted went ahead, anxious to begin the search.

'There is a hut there, but it is not used as part of the holiday accommodation,' Mauricio explained. 'Jeremiah uses it sometimes to avoid doing any work.'

'Is there anybody there now? Has Jeremiah been using it while we've been here?'

'Not that I know of. Is there a reason you have asked this thing?'

'No ... no ... I just ... It doesn't matter, I just wondered if anybody was using it, that's all.'

Mauricio nodded and began to make his way out of the main house. Ben followed, managing a smile for Analyn Villanueva in the kitchen.

As they walked out into the garden, Ben could see that the search was already underway. Steve was there, Ted had just joined them, and Henry looked like he was getting undressed, ready to leap into the sea.

He tried to trot over towards the beach, but it was impossible to go faster than a walk. He was too uncomfortable.

'Any joy?' he asked Steve when he finally reached the jetty.

'I'm trying to discourage Henry from jumping into the water and looking for a body, but I'm not doing a very good job of it. Tell him, will you?'

'I don't like the look of those waves,' Ben said, giving a worried look, as if that might convince Henry.

Henry was stripped down to his boxers, ready to dive in. He had a lean and athletic body. Ben could barely remember a time when he'd looked anything like that.

'Look, Dad, he's not on the beach and we can't find him in any of the rooms. If he fell into the water, he could drown, especially if he's not a strong swimmer.

'Nimuel can swim, but I think he would struggle in these waves,' Mauricio said.

'I can swim in this water, I promise. I won't go far out, Dad.'

Steve was still doubtful, but he nodded.

'Okay, but promise me you'll take care. Promise me, Henry!'

'I promise, Dad.'

He'd barely uttered the words before he was in the water.

'His mother will never forgive me if he has an accident out there. Look at him go, though. It's just like a big swimming pool to him.'

'I guess there's no point having a swimming champion in the family if we can't use his skills from time to time. Why don't you go to the end of the jetty and keep an eye on Henry and I'll work with Ted and Mr Villanueva to scour the beach one more time.'

Steve nodded.

'How did it go with Laura?' he asked, moving his gaze between Ben and the sea.

'Difficult! But all in all, positive, I think. Let's put it this way, we'll be able to sit through the meal without killing each other.'

'That's progress I guess!' Steve smiled. He turned and walked to the end of the jetty.

Mauricio and Ted were standing by the water's edge looking out to sea, trying to spot Mr Aquino.

'Come on,' Ben said. 'Let's cover the entire length of the beach. We'll check the water, the beach and the jungle – everywhere. It's possible he's just resting.'

He examined the blood on the jetty. There wasn't a lot

of it. He wondered if it was even fresh, it was already dry and browning.

Mauricio, Jeremiah and Ted walked along the longest stretch of beach to the right of the jetty and Ben took the smaller section to the left. He passed the treehouse. Perhaps Mr Aquino was inside, taking cover from the bad weather. He turned to shout to the others, but they wouldn't be able to hear him against the noise of the wind. Sand caught his eyes and he blinked it away.

'Anybody up here?' he called as he gingerly made his way up the wooden ladder. Every step intensified the pain in his groin.

He pushed the door open and peered in. There was nobody there. On the floor was a blanket with a magazine resting on it. It was probably just the kids hiding away from the adults.

Suddenly he heard shouting. He looked out of the window. Mauricio and Ted were running along the beach back to the jetty – Jeremiah was too far away to hear the excitement. He climbed down the ladder as fast as he could. On the third rail he stumbled badly. He gasped for breath as a sharp pain stopped him dead.

'Damn and fuck it!'

He stood still for a moment, waiting for the pain to subside before carefully making his way back to the jetty. He reached it just as Henry was hauling himself out of the water, breathless and exhausted. To his side, pale and sodden, was Mr Aquino.

CHAPTER FORTY-FIVE

The Island: The Day Of The Party

'Oh my God, is he dead?' Ben asked.

Mauricio was administering CPR while Henry struggled to catch his breath.

'Henry found him floating near that red buoy,' Steve said, pointing out to sea.

'Jeez Henry, how did you manage to swim that far?'

'With difficulty. For a moment I thought I was a goner. It's really come in fast, it's not like storms at home. You get much more warning—'

'Take it easy, Henry.' Steve rested his hand on his son's bare shoulder. 'Get your breath back.'

Ben watched as Mauricio tried to revive Mr Aquino. After a few minutes of compressions and blowing into his mouth, he looked up in despair.

'He is gone.'

Henry leaped back into action.

'Let me try. We do lots of this in swimming training. Tilt his head to the side.'

Henry was much more confident than Mauricio. He pumped Mr Aquino's chest hard and sent full breaths deep into his lungs, forming a seal around his mouth and exhaling with a sure and rhythmic touch. He stopped for a second to check Mr Aquino's chest was now rising and falling. He returned to the compressions, thrusting with all his remaining strength. There was the crack of a rib and Mr Aquino spluttered, the water that had been held in his lungs running out onto the decking of the jetty.

'Well done, Henry!' Steve patted him on the back.

'Thank God for that,' Ben said. 'Good job, Henry ... and Mauricio.'

'I cracked one of his ribs. I shouldn't have done that but perhaps the pain brought him back. We'll need to get him checked over straightaway.'

'Nobody is going out to sea tonight!' Mauricio said, assertively.

It took them all by surprise, he'd been so shy until that point.

'Nobody will cross the water while the sea is like that, we will have to make my friend here comfortable until the storm passes over.'

'Can we call somebody on shore? Maybe get some help or advice on how to look after him?'

'Yes, there is a satellite phone in the house that I use with my family. Ted, please find Jeremiah and let him know that we have Mr Aquino safe. Then return with him to get the phone.'

'Will do!' Ted said and began to run off along the beach towards Jeremiah.

Mr Aquino was struggling to regulate his breathing.

'What happened, Nimuel?' Steve asked.

Leave him, Dad. He'll need some recovery time. We need to keep him warm. His body has had a huge shock.'

'It's very impressive, Henry, what you did there. Very impressive.'

Ben meant every word of it. Just because Steve wound him up every time he boasted about his kids, it didn't mean he couldn't recognise a real achievement. Henry had just saved a man's life.

'Thanks, Uncle Ben. Best not tell Mum all the details though. She'll go spare.'

'There's a blanket over in the treehouse,' Ben remembered. 'We can wrap him up in that and keep him warm for the time being. Would you mind getting it, Mauricio?'

'I'll go,' Steve picked up. 'I suspect it might be a bit painful for Ben at the moment. I can see you're still suffering, bruv!'

Before long they had Mr Aquino out of his wet clothes and heading along the beach. Ever resourceful, Henry had suggested turning a blanket into a makeshift stretcher.

'I'll sit this one out for obvious reasons,' Ben said, embarrassed. 'After all, somebody needs to carry his clothes.'

'He's got a nasty bump on his head too. Have we got a first aid kit?' Steve asked.

'Yes, I have everything in our cabin,' Mauricio said. 'If we take him there, he can have the spare room. We can take care of his wound and make him comfortable. I will call the hospital on the shore and get their advice. I do not think they will come for him tonight though, it is too wild out there.'

The darkness was closing in now. Ben had barely noticed it with all the excitement. The lights were on in the garden and the hum of the generators could be heard over the wind.

'Do you think we should keep this from Mum and Dad, Steve?' he asked. 'Once we've bandaged up that wound and contacted the hospital for advice, there isn't any more we can do. I think it might spoil the sense of occasion, don't you?'

'Yes, I think you're right,' Steve replied after thinking it through. 'They'll only worry. But let's see what the hospital has to say when Mauricio calls them.'

'Some seventieth birthday this has turned out to be. Did you see the way Dad set about Richard? There's some real bad feeling there. What is it about those two? They never saw eye-to-eye.'

'Our family has way too many secrets,' Steve said, speaking almost to himself. 'I never figured out what made Dad despise Richard, but I can make a few guesses.'

'Really? What do you know that I don't?'

'Oh, it's nothing,' Steve said, looking ahead to see Ted approaching from the lodge. 'I've probably spoken out of turn. Let's put it this way, you don't get to seventy years of age and nearly fifty years of marriage without a couple of skeletons in your closet.'

'What sort of skeletons?'

Ben had seen the look on Ted's face, but he wanted Steve to stay in flow. His brother was always so guarded, he never gave away his true emotions. He had acted very out of character when Mina made her badly timed announcement.

'Things in the business, stuff like that. I know you think I drew the long straw when I walked into the business after Dad. And perhaps I did from a financial point of view. But you don't create a family business like that over all those years without making enemies. It's not all smiles, that's what I'm saying. Dad is not necessarily the Colonel Sanders that we'd all like him to be. And Mum's not completely without involvement too—'

'Dad, Uncle Steve, look!'

Ted was holding up what looked like an old-fashioned mobile phone. It had seen better days. In fact, it seemed to have been hit with a hammer.

'Is that the satellite phone?'

Ted nodded.

Henry and Mauricio levelled up with them. Mauricio indicated that they should rest Mr Aquino on the ground.

Ted handed over the phone to him. Mauricio took a closer look, attempted to coax the thing into life, then looked up at the small group. They stared at him expectantly.

'Can you fix it?' Ben asked.

He shook his head.

'It's broken. I don't know who would do such a thing.'

The first thought that came into Ben's mind was Jaxon, but he kept his mouth shut.

'But you have a mobile phone, right?' Steve asked. 'I mean one that works?'

'There is no mobile signal out on this island. We have to use the satellite phone. The satellite phone is broken. We are now cut off until the storm ends and the boat comes out to clear up after the party. We are stranded here tonight.'

CHAPTER FORTY-SIX

1988: The Third Lie

Jenny Hayes was a problem for the Harrington family. Steve was officially an adult, but 18 years of age was too young for anybody to be saddled with a baby. Particularly the son who'd been groomed to take over the family business. Her parents wanted her to keep the baby on moral grounds. Kyle knew that was the most troublesome type of objection.

The way he saw it, there were a couple of plays in this scenario. He could scare the life out of the girl and persuade her to have the abortion without involving her parents. That would be neat, but they'd find out eventually and maybe cause a fuss. The other way to play it was to scare the parents. If they had a sudden change of mind – encouraged by a well-timed conversation with Kyle – that would keep things nice and tidy.

From previous experience Kyle had learned that the best approach in this type of situation was to wait a while, gather information and see where the leverage point was. There was always something – whether it be Jenny or her parents. Everybody had secrets. If you're patient enough, they'll always rise to the surface.

Tony was putting pressure on him. Kyle was the one who was used to turning the thumbscrews and he didn't like it when a man like Tony tried to throw his weight around. But he needed that meat-processing facility – he had three bodies to get rid of that month in what would be a very lucrative deal for him. In fact, if all went according to plan, he was in line for a villa in Spain at the end of it. That wasn't a typical payday, but this was a complex job since one of the three was a senior police officer. It was risky disposing of a cop. That meant big money for Kyle.

Unusually for Kyle, he was jittery. He wanted this matter with Jenny resolved. He tapped on his steering wheel as he waited for her to leave her dance class. She'd recently passed her driving test and had use of the family car. She was a bit rough on the clutch – at one junction he'd almost run into her as she spluttered the car, then stalled it. He hung back a little after that.

She was out now and chatting to her friends at the door. There were no signs yet of the pregnancy, she was so young she probably wouldn't show for some time. As he watched them talking and laughing, he thought back to his own teenage years. Kyle had wanted to be an artist. He'd always had a flair for painting. He could remember a time when he might have been in a group just like that. He'd chosen a different path – the art was a distant memory now. It's why he was so hostile to people who'd had the guts to follow their dreams. Watching Jenny, he felt a rare sense of loss and a brief pang of regret for a life that might have been. Introspection was a very occasional indulgence for Kyle and it was normally only brought about by a long and boring wait in a car.

Jenny was off, kangarooing the car again. He wondered what her father would have to say about that. It would be an expensive clutch bill for him, no doubt. He waited until she'd pulled up at the junction, then started his own car and followed her at a safe distance. She made her way through the back streets until they arrived at the main road. She wasn't going home, that was good. There was more chance of finding out something interesting if she strayed from her normal routine.

Eventually she pulled up at a large house in a leafy suburban street. It wasn't so far away from Kyle's own residence. This was good. Jenny had paused outside the driveway, checked something about the house, then moved a little further along the road. Kyle pulled in on the opposite side, allowing her to park up and lock the car. He turned off his lights and sat in the darkness. He watched her as she checked her appearance in the wing mirror. She was going to see somebody and whoever it was she wanted to look nice.

She walked back up the street, looking around, checking to see if there was anybody to see her. Kyle recognised the signs. Whoever Jenny was visiting, she wanted to keep it secret. He was out of his car now, lurking behind a van parked a little closer to the house. Jenny walked into the short drive and up to the porch. The moment her foot touched the first step, the door was opened by a middle-aged man, generic in appearance: greying hair, open-neck shirt, work slacks. Nothing of particular to note. He had clearly been expecting her. Jenny entered the house and the door closed behind her.

Kyle surveyed the street and waited for an elderly lady

walking her dog to pass. As they moved along the road, Kyle entered the drive and ducked in under the lounge window. He could hear a television and their voices, but it was difficult to make anything out. He was grateful for the uncut hedge at the front of the small garden, it gave him more than adequate cover. Whoever this person was, he was unknown to Kyle. This looked like it could be something. Perhaps he was a tutor? But it was the way she pulled the car up at the drive first, as if she was looking for a signal of some sort. That's what made Kyle suspect this was something more.

He would need to enter the house. He couldn't use the front door, there was too much chance of being caught. He'd need to try the back. Kyle drew a pair of black leather gloves out of his coat pocket. There was a ski mask in there too, with eye holes cut out. He might need that later. With the gloves on, he listened once more to be sure they were still at the front of the house, then slipped around the side where there was a metal gate leading to the back garden. He twisted the handle gently and it opened. The back door was protected by an old wooden porch. Kyle cursed as he turned the door handle to find it locked. Then he saw a large stone to the side of the door mat - instinct made him lift it. There was a spare key. Kyle slotted it into the lock and opened the door. The interior door was already unlocked, he was in.

As he walked through the dark kitchen, he could hear giggling. They were heading upstairs. This was better than he could have hoped. He waited a while, knowing he had some time now, time that would be best spent getting to know who this man was. Jenny was seventeen, it was up to her who she fooled around with. Of course, it would scandalise her parents, but there was nothing illegal in it. It gave him no leverage as such, but he was beginning to see a likely scenario in his head.

He could hear them upstairs now, laughing and whispering, then it went quiet. Kyle turned on the kitchen light and surveyed the kitchen. There were school exercise books spread across the table. The man, whoever he was, seemed to be a teacher. He was halfway through what appeared to be a pile of badly written assignments. Kyle read his name on the front cover of the books. Mr Norris. Biology. He smiled at that one, sensing what was going on up the stairs. An extra-curricular biology lesson by the sound of it.

There were photos on the walls. A wife, children too. That was good. He needed to ascertain if the wife was still on the scene. There wouldn't be so much mileage in it if he was divorced or separated. He rummaged around in the man's old-fashioned leather briefcase which was propped up and open in the seat next to where he'd been working. There was a pocket at the side; it was in the pockets and concealed storage areas that Kyle Hunter flourished. Sure as houses, there it was. A folded envelope, inside of which were two school photos of Jenny. In school uniform. That meant they might well have been taken prior to her being in the sixth form. At best he'd had an inappropriate relationship with a student, at worst he was a paedophile. Either way, Kyle had everything he needed to close down this problem.

As Kyle made his way out of the kitchen, he saw the last piece of the puzzle. The family calendar was pinned up next to the door. Much of the handwriting was different to that which had scrawled comments in red pen on the school exercise books. That meant a wife or partner. One who was still around. Kyle checked that day's date. Thursdays were karate night for Josh and Terry, 8 to 9pm. That had given Jenny and her teacher friend just over an hour for their sordid little encounter. Jenny had probably slowed at the drive to check for an all-clear signal.

This was the staple fare of Kyle's work. People could be so predictable. Affairs, secrets, deceptions and lies. They were always there somewhere, lurking in the shadows, just waiting for a man like him to fit the pieces together and threaten to bring their seedy little lives crashing down around them.

Kyle walked through the kitchen door and along the hallway. Hanging on the wall were pictures of the man and his wife and school photos of Josh and Terry. Kyle didn't particularly care which was which. All family members were accounted for. And Jenny and the teacher were already at it in the upstairs bedroom.

Kyle didn't even need his mask. With the landing light off, he burst into the marital bedroom.

'Jesus, what the heck!'

'Bloody hell, David. Is your wife back?'

'Shut up, both of you. Do not touch that light.'

'What do you want?'

Kyle could hear the fear in the man's voice.

And just before he spoke, Kyle saw exactly what had happened. Sometimes he even amazed himself at how good he was at making the connections.

'I've found two photographs of Jenny in your briefcase.'

'How do you know my name?'

'What do you think you were doing—'

'Shut up, both of you. Here are the photos.'

Kyle threw them on the bed. They both flinched as his dark silhouette lunged towards them.

'This is an inappropriate relationship, however you spin it. And there's a wife and two kids back shortly who would be shocked to walk in on this little scene—'

'How dare you break into my house.'

'If you interrupt me one more time, I'll call your wife myself. Now, listen, both of you. This could end your marriage and your teaching career. Jenny, I know what you did. You blamed Steve for the pregnancy. It was a cover. Does your teacher friend here know you're pregnant?'

'Yes, but we couldn't say the baby is his.'

'Shut up! Jenny, you make sure that Steve is well and truly out of the picture by this time tomorrow. I don't care how you do it or settle it with your parents. But make it happen. If it doesn't, these pictures get delivered to this man's headteacher and I blow the lid on the entire set-up. I've got my own photos too.'

Kyle didn't have photos, but it wouldn't matter.

'He said that he'd leave his wife. We were using the thing with Steve as a cover, just until we could be together ...'

'How stupid are you, kid? That's the oldest lie in the book. Make sure it's done by this time tomorrow. Get rid of the baby, Jenny. Believe me, you'll thank me for it.'

Kyle picked up the two school photos and left the room. He could hear their scared voices arguing and blaming each other.

He smiled to himself as he let himself out of the front door. They were all the same. The truth was only skin deep. Scratch the surface and there's always something nasty below. Now he could get back to the chief constable – after a swift visit to Jenny's parents, that was, just to make sure the baby situation was well and truly contained.

CHAPTER FORTY-SEVEN

The Island: The Day Of The Party

'You can't be serious?'

'We're on a desert island, Steve. What did you expect? That there'd be a doctor's surgery perched on the end of the beach?'

'No, but surely they can get a helicopter out here?'

'You've been watching too many Arnold Schwarzenegger films, Dad,' Henry chipped in. 'They ground all light aircraft in weather like this. It's an occupational hazard when you live this far out at sea.'

'We should get Mr Aquino settled down and start thinking about getting ready for the party. How long have we got?' Ben asked.

Ted looked at his phone.

'About an hour.'

'You don't have a signal on that thing, do you?' Steve asked.

'No, Uncle Steve. I'm just using it for the clock and the

camera. It's nearly dead now anyway, there aren't enough power sockets in this place.'

Mauricio had busied himself making Mr Aquino comfortable on the bed. He had removed his wet clothes and was beginning to dress him in dry clothing which he'd taken from his own suitcase.

'I only have a few clothes, but these should keep you warm. Mr Steve, please would you return to the main house and ask my wife for the other first aid box? It is stored in the kitchen.'

'Off you go, Henry,' Steve said. 'You'll be faster than me. And don't let Nan and Grandad see you wet through like that!'

Henry nodded and jogged off.

Mr Aquino, who'd been silent until now, began to mumble something.

'I don't understand him, he's not speaking in English—'

'Jesus, Steve. The man almost died. Give him a break. He's allowed to speak in his own language.'

'Yeah, sorry, I wasn't thinking,' Steve replied, looking sheepishly at Ben. 'What's he saying, Mauricio?'

'It's not clear, he seems to be very scared. Maybe he thinks he is still in the water.'

Ben moved forward to help Mauricio manoeuvre Mr Aquino into a resting position on the bed. He groaned as he twisted awkwardly.

'Still painful, bruv? Here, I'll help you.'

Ben sat down for a moment. He needed to recover from the pain.

'I'm going to go and get ready for the party, if that's okay,' said Ted.

'Not a word to your mum about this, Ted. It'll wreck the

evening if everybody gets into a panic. We'll tell them tomorrow.'

Ted acknowledged Ben's request, then left them. A few minutes later, Henry was back with the first aid box.

Mauricio set about cleaning and bandaging the wound on Mr Aquino's head. He seemed disturbed and agitated, but he was speaking in his native language and neither Steve nor Ben had a clue what was being said.

'You'd better head back to the house and get showered and changed, Henry,' Steve said. 'And don't tell your mum, either. Say you fell off the jetty or you went for a swim or something like that. I want to wait until after the party to let them know about Mr Aquino's accident. We've come all this way, we can't let something like this ruin the party.'

'What will ruin the party?'

It was Richard's voice.

'I just saw Henry, he said you were all over here. Jesus, what happened to Mr Aquino?'

'Bloody hell, Richard. Why don't we just relocate the party over here.' Steve snapped again. Ben looked up, surprised. Steve seemed to be very wound up. It was unusual for him.

'Hey, I just came to see what was up.'

'Look, sorry Richard, it's just a bit tense, that's all. Keep this to yourself, will you? Mr Aquino had an accident and we're just making him comfortable.'

Mauricio had finished dressing Mr Aquino's wounds and was waiting for a lull in the conversation to speak.

'Nimuel is comfortable now.'

'Who's Nimuel?' Richard asked.

'Mr Aquino!' Steve and Ben replied at the same time.

'Oh, right.'

'He is very – I don't know your word for it – he has lots of words ...'

'Delirious?' Steve suggested.

'Perhaps,' Mauricio continued. 'He has hurt his head. We must try to get him to the shore as soon as the storm dies down. But I am worried. He says someone came behind him and hit him on the head. He fell into the sea. He thought he would die.'

'Blimey,' Richard said. 'That's serious.'

'You're telling me it is!' said Steve.

Ben looked thoughtful. Mr Aquino's ramblings were worrying him.

'When Diana and I got cut off in the jungle, we found that abandoned hut. There were cigarette stubs in there. Does your son smoke, Mauricio?'

'My son never smokes.' Mauricio seemed quite adamant. 'None of my family smokes, it is too expensive for us. He uses that hut sometimes, but these days Jeremiah prefers the treehouse.'

'Somebody had been in that hut recently. The cigarette butt we found was still warm.'

'Where is it?' Richard asked.

'Through the jungle. Not far, but impossible to do in the dark.'

'Not impossible if we had flashlights. Do you know if there are any on the island, Mauricio?'

Steve looked fired up by the idea.

'You're kidding, aren't you? Are you suggesting we check out the hut before the meal starts? Is there time?'

Ben was thinking of Diana and the children – of Laura and Harper too. If there was somebody else on the island, he wanted to know. He felt a sickness in his stomach as he recalled the break-in at the house and the missing newspaper cutting. Both incidents had unsettled him in the same way.

'He's delirious, you said so yourself. He doesn't know what he's saying.'

Richard was clearly regretting what he'd just walked into.

'I have powerful flashlights in this cabin,' Mauricio said. 'They will be very good in the jungle. We have many such lights in case the generators become faulty.'

'Is it even safe?' Richard asked. He'd not ventured into the jungle yet, and it sounded particularly hazardous in the darkness.

'I've been there once already,' Ben said. 'It's much quicker when you know which way you're heading. If we have decent lights, we can make it. It would put my mind at rest. It could be anybody in that hut. Are there pirates in this part of the world? We should check it out, especially with all the kids here. I'd never forgive myself if something happened to them.'

They'd talked themselves into it. Mauricio fetched the flashlights and they got ready to head off to the jungle.

CHAPTER FORTY-EIGHT

The Island: The Day Of The Party

'Those torches are great!'

'Are you alright with your stick, Richard?'

'Yes, I'll be fine, although I wouldn't fancy my chances without one of these lights.'

Mauricio had handed out the industrial flashlights to the brothers and they were examining them carefully.

'I must return to the kitchen to finish off the preparations with my wife. I will check on Mr Aquino again when the meal is served. What should I tell your family?'

'Just say we sneaked off for a pre-party drink and to catch up on brotherly stuff,' said Steve.

'What about Gaby?' Richard asked.

'Gaby's accused us of excluding her for all of her life. Why disappoint her now? It'll give her something to feel wounded about.

'Whatever you do, Mauricio, keep quiet about Mr Aquino – Nimuel,' Steve continued. 'They'll be running around like headless chickens if they think there's a problem. I don't want Dad's party ruined because of it. We'll check the hut and if all goes to plan nobody needs to know we were even gone. Right, let's get to it!'

Steve was back in organisation mode.

For a moment Ben hesitated, checking out the level of pain in his groin. It was beginning to feel better. He'd have all evening to sit down and recover at the party and all the next day to sit out on the sun loungers. The hut wasn't far, he'd done the journey twice already. He was sure he'd be fine.

They had to pass the main house on their way to the jungle path. They switched off the flashlights and kept their voices down so as not to catch anybody's attention. Ben turned to look at his bedroom window – he could see Laura, already dressed for the party, holding Harper in her arms and dancing around the room. He wondered if they'd be happier without him. If he paid towards Harper's upkeep, and she came to stay with him and Diana from time to time, it could work, couldn't it?

'Guys, come on, we should be fine to turn the flashlights on now. No shining them towards the buildings, keep them pointed into the undergrowth.'

Steve was leading the way. Ben and Richard had to take more care of where they were placing their feet.

'That's spooky, can you see all those eyes looking at us when you move the beams?'

Ben was all for packing up and forgetting the exploratory trip. What type of creature could those tiny eyes be attached to?

'Don't be a coward,' Steve scolded. 'There are no nasty creatures in the jungle. We're safe enough out here, just don't trip over and you'll be fine.'

Richard started to laugh in the darkness.

'What?' Ben asked.

'It's like being kids again. Three incompetent explorers bungling their way through the jungle. Remember that walk in the woods we went on with Mum and Dad? The one when we all got lost because they let us wander off the path? Dad was livid – he was all but ready to send out a search party. God, that was funny when you look back on it.'

'If I remember rightly, we got a right telling off when they found us,' Ben replied. 'He thrashed you with a belt, didn't he? Because it was your idea?'

'Oh yeah, I'd forgotten that bit. Thanks for screwing up my memories, Ben. I was enjoying that until you came along and popped my balloon.'

'I take it you and Dad have made it up now?' Steve asked. 'Careful, there's a low branch just up here, you'll need to duck or move it out of the way.'

'Only because Mum made him,' Richard replied. 'You'd think now that he's 70 he'd have mellowed a bit. He doesn't need to be my best mate, but it would be nice if he could at least pretend to tolerate me. He is my dad, after all. It can't be that difficult. Do either of you guys hate any of your kids?'

'No!' they both echoed quickly and confidently.

'Dad always seemed to have it in for you, Richard, even before the ...'

There was silence.

'Sorry, we're supposed to be celebrating. I shouldn't have brought it up.'

'The crash is in the past. It took several years of therapy. I've let it go now, as best I can. It would have eaten me alive if I hadn't learned to deal with it.'

They walked on in silence, the occasional crack of a twig or a startled animal marking their progress.

'There's a tree trunk coming up soon,' Ben warned. 'You can go around it easily enough, no need to be Action Man and climb over it like I did.'

'You're quiet, Steve,' he said, after they'd successfully navigated the obstacle.

'I'm just sick and tired of the accident always coming up. For all the therapy you reckon you've had, you still talk about it a lot, Richard.'

They stopped and looked at each other. Steve was still on that short fuse.

'Woah, steady Steve!' Ben cautioned.

'No, Ben, this same thing comes up every time. You stole my car, Richard. You crashed it and you nearly died. You were pissed and high on drugs, end of story. Did your therapist talk to you about blaming mechanisms? You came up with that ridiculous story about me driving but it's a hallucination, Richard. It's a figment of your imagination. You need to accept your culpability.'

'Well, to hell with you, Steve, because it seems any amount of ridiculously priced therapy can't shake off that feeling that you stitched me up. You hung me out to dry and you've let the family deride me for all these years. You're a fucking case, Steve. You really are. There's only one of us who can't accept the truth—'

Ben heard an oomph as Steve threw down his flashlight and ran at his brother. They both crashed to the ground.

'Jesus Christ, guys. Stop. Stop it! Enough ...'

Richard was on the ground now, his stick beside him. Steve was astride him, his younger brother thrashing out with his fists. Ben placed his light on the ground, pointed it towards them, and went to pull Steve away. As he did so, he let out a cry of pain which stopped them both dead in their tracks.

'Oh, my poor bollocks!' he exclaimed, half-laughing, half-crying. 'They hurt so much, God they're so painful. Please stop, guys – my testicles can't take any more.'

There was silence. Then stifled laughter. A minute later they were all laughing out loud, finally realising the ridiculousness of their situation. Eventually the laughter subsided. Ben broke the silence.

'Look chaps, I know it's not all roses in the Harrington family garden, but can we please get through this holiday without a big bust-up? Please. For Mum and Dad's sake. Let's just check out this jungle hut and get back for the party. We're enough of a hazard walking through this jungle on our own without the threat of us killing each other. Let's just park it and have a nice evening, shall we?'

Steve held out his hand to Richard and helped him up. He picked up his stick and handed it over.

'I'm sorry,' he said. 'I need to move on too. I'm sorry, Ben ... Richard. You're right, Ben. We're all together, it's Dad's seventieth. Let's just get pissed and have a good time.'

'Agreed. Let's get to this hut, put our minds at rest then head back for the meal. I'm starving.'

They picked up their flashlights and continued through the jungle. Soon they could hear the waves.

'You were right, Ben. It really isn't a big island,' said Richard.

'No, I said it's not far, but it's impossible without a torch, mind you. That's why Diana and I decided to stay over.'

'Are you two getting back together?' Steve asked. 'Because if you ask me, the old spark is still there. You two are just like Mum and Dad, you belong with each other.'

'I always liked Diana,' Richard chipped in. 'She was always good to me.'

'I don't know what's going to happen,' Ben said. 'It's a difficult situation, what with Harper being born. There's no easy way out of it. However you look at it, it's a mess—'

'Look!'

'What, Steve?'

They all stopped dead. They'd reached the beach now and the hut was just ahead, they could see it in the flash-lights when they moved in that direction.

'Over there, look. There's a motorboat. Somebody else is on the island with us.'

CHAPTER FORTY-NINE

1992: The Fourth Lie

Kyle opened his eyes and took in the beauty of his garden. The rhododendrons looked spectacular as did the azaleas, radiating their beautiful colours in every direction. He'd gone for late-flowering varieties, he always considered it a bit of a waste having plants flower in spring when it was too cold to sit in the garden to admire them.

There was a long day ahead. Mick and Keith, Kyle's beloved red setters, bounded around on the grass, tussling with a rubber bone, their ears flapping as they larked around like young children.

'What time are you leaving the house?'

Kyle smiled up at Agnes.

'About five o' clock, no need to make me anything for tea. I'll grab something on the go.'

She walked over to her husband, kissed him on the forehead and ran her hand through his hair.

Kyle was very aware of what a lucky man he was. He

had a stunning home; his garden was his pride and joy and – even if he said it himself – he had the perfect wife. Agnes was happy to let him do his thing and he loved her for it. They'd had the two dogs, plenty of cash, life was perfect. He even loved his job – how many guys got to say that?

He took a sip of his G&T.

'Do you think we should go to Spain for a couple of weeks over the summer, after this contract is completed? We could do with a bit of a break.'

'Yes, let's do that. The dogs will enjoy running on the beaches too. I'll make sure the house is made ready for us.'

Kyle was a man who had it all. Granted, the evening work was a little disruptive to married life every now and then. But five or so jobs a year kept them living the high life. And besides, Kyle needed it. He wasn't entirely certain he would have managed to play the role of husband quite so well if he didn't have this other outlet.

'What time will you be back?' Agnes asked. She never wanted details. She understood that Kyle had unusual business interests, but it had delivered to her doorstep a life of luxury and privilege. She knew better than to push her luck. Kyle was a great husband. She had many friends who couldn't boast the same. She allowed him to do his thing because he left her to do hers. It was a marriage made in heaven.

Placing his gun in the waistband of his trousers was always the last thing Kyle did before he left the house. He didn't want to taint his home life with it. He would fuss the dogs, hug Agnes, then head to his study. There he would take a small key out of his pocket, unlock the top drawer of his desk, then take out his gun. He would then re-lock the door and leave the house, never putting Agnes in the position where she might see or feel the weapon. He liked to keep home and business separate, that's what worked best for him.

It always amused Kyle that he'd rarely had to use it. In his line of work, it went with the territory, but guns were such unexpected items in the UK, the mere sight of it would make most of his victims turn to jelly. His preferred method of killing was one that was bloodless. A broken neck was clean, quick and unfussy. Strangulation was good too, though if you got a struggler it could be quite a sweaty affair. He preferred no blood though, that was his abiding rule of killing.

As a younger man Kyle had practised neck-breaking on a plastic dummy. There was an art to it, completely unlike what he'd seen in films. The first time he'd killed a man, he had thought that's all there was to it. He'd gone to snap the neck, but it hadn't broken. His victim had fought back like a frightened cat – he'd had to knife him and it made a huge mess. He never did that again. He learned how to do the job properly. Although *The Sunday Times* never published a Top 100 of UK murderers, preferring instead to stick to the Rich List, Kyle really believed that he must have been one of the UK's most practised killers by hand. It's why he was so popular for contract work. The less mess, the less evidence. A quick kill, a properly disposed of body, the less chance of detection. It used to make him laugh watching *Crimewatch* on TV as they carefully reconstructed missing persons stories. He'd been proud of himself when his tally of televised crimes reached ten. Yet they never caught him because they never found a body, and that's why his services were in such high demand.

That night was a local kill. It would be easy, it always was when the victims weren't accustomed to violence. This was a vengeance attack, some local mobster's wife having an affair – with a lawyer, of all people. He was thankful that Agnes hadn't taken that course of action. Many wives grew out of the rough and ready husbands who'd brought them a life of ease and luxury, and they liked to move up the ranks and taste some sweeter honey. Well, these two were about to disappear into thin air. He'd done his research. They met at a local beauty spot and had sex in her car, which was big enough to put the seats down and move around in relative comfort. It had mirrored windows too. He'd open the boot, hold out the gun, then kill the woman first. She'd be noisier than he was, he'd just snivel and plead for his life. Kyle knew his sort. She'd be aggressive and violent, even though it was likely she might not be wearing many clothes at the time. He preferred not to have to strike anybody, it made his knuckles bloody and sore, and he could get really pissed off if a fleck of blood ever spattered a nice suit. When she lashed out at him, he'd snap her neck.

The kill would be quick and clean. His guys would be waiting in another car to pick up the bodies and take them to Harrington Meats for disposal. They never witnessed him killing – they'd park along the road at a designated spot and once they saw Kyle's car pass by they'd clean up the crime scene and retrieve the bodies. Kyle would drive directly to the meat-processing plant and get the kettle on. Shortly afterwards, the butcher would arrive, followed soon after by the bodies and the work would begin.

Kyle was always fascinated to see the butcher get down to business. His professionalism was impressive. Blood would be drained, then limbs removed, expertly and cleanly. He'd carve up a human being as if it were a farm-yard animal and then the carcass would be disposed of in the industrial processing machines. The reason that the arrangement with Tony Harrington had worked so well was that Kyle supervised every step of the process. The machines, floors and equipment had to be meticulously cleaned and disinfected. He would accept no corner-cutting and slacking – if the arrangement was to continue as well as it had done for all those years, he would never relinquish that control to anybody else. His personal freedom relied on never making a slip-up. Tony Harrington must never know that Kyle and his men had been in the factory, that's the only way it could work. And then Tony messed everything up.

When Kyle walked in on his two hired hands about to mince Tony Harrington alive, he was furious. He wanted everything in his business to be just like his well-manicured garden. Everything had a place and was perfect. Tony's arrival at the factory was like Mick and Keith taking a dump on his flower beds, it was simply unacceptable. So, it gave him a dilemma. Should he kill Tony there and then to make sure he never opened his big mouth and blew the lid on the entire operation? Or should he allow him to live, but in the process create a leverage that would mean he would never, ever talk about what he'd seen there that night?

Tony was dangerous to Kyle, because he was the kind of man who would jump off a cliff edge to end his financial problems. He was the kind of man who'd have an epiphany and suddenly decide to put things right. He had to be frightened off in some way. Kyle needed to make certain there and then that Tony would never open his mouth about what was going on in his own factory. So, that night, when he walked in on the disposal of two bodies and nearly ended up in the pigs' dinner himself, Kyle gave Tony a choice. Either he became fully complicit in their business arrangement, or it ended there and then. First he handed him the saw and told him he had to cut off the limbs of the mobster's wife. The moment the saw began to tear through the cooling flesh Tony was sick and almost passed out. With a gun to his head, Kyle made him saw right through that limb, then place it in the mincing machine himself.

'You're now fully aware of what's going on here, Tony, and you are an accomplice to it. If you ever breathe a word of it to anybody, I will take one of your children and feed them to the pigs. Even if the police get to me before, I can make it happen, I will arrange it from my prison cell. I'll tell the man whose wife you just cut up that you screwed her dead body before you got rid of her. He'll come for one of your children and do the same to them if you ever open your mouth. Understand?'

Sweating, sobbing, terrified, Tony nodded in agreement. It was immediately afterwards that his own thoughts turned to retirement. He could take it no longer, his Faustian pact with the devil had beaten him.

As for Kyle, at the moment he made the threat to Tony, he noticed a very pleasant blue in Tony's shirt and decided that his garden would benefit greatly from some delphiniums in the beds at the back of the garden, directly opposite his shed.

CHAPTER FIFTY

The Island: The Day Of The Party

The walk back through the jungle was quieter than it should have been, bearing in mind the special occasion that was about to follow.

'Is it something we need to worry about?' Richard asked. 'I mean, it could just be some Robinson Crusoe look-a-like. You know, one of these wilderness adventure guys who likes to live the way nature intended.'

'Did I tell you about the break-in at our house?' Ben said.

They were having to walk close together now; the wind was whistling through the trees and they were finding it difficult to hear each other.

'It was strange. They only took a newspaper cutting I was saving. It had a picture of a man that I'm certain I've seen before, when I was much younger. And I think I saw him again, at the factory late one night. I wanted to ask Dad about him.'

'What did you see at the factory?'

Steve was abrupt and aggressive again.

'Nothing, it was nothing. It was years ago when I was a teenager – I saw the same guy at the factory, late at night after closing. Dad said it was something to do with a game delivery. I thought nothing of it until I saw him again in the local paper. Some business event, I think it was. You know when you've seen someone before and you can't place them? I assumed he was Dad's game-hunting friend.'

'Yes, that's exactly who he must be,' Steve said, calmer now. 'That's weird about the cutting though. Are you sure Diana hasn't got it?'

'I'm completely clueless as to why our house was broken into, but I'm as sure as I can be that the newspaper clipping was taken.'

They carried on walking. They were nearly back at the houses.

'Not a word to anyone, okay?' Steve said. 'I'm sure it's just an adventurer – they probably don't even know we're all here. First thing tomorrow we'll get word to the mainland and check it out.'

Steve was always the man with the plan.

'I don't see that we have any other option,' Ben replied. 'I say Steve and Mauricio sort it out first thing tomorrow. You'll need to lay off the booze tonight, Steve.'

'Why me? You're the second oldest, Ben. Why can't you do it?'

'Because my balls are about to explode, that's why.'

'Damn, are they still sore?' Richard asked. 'I thought vasectomies weren't supposed to be painful.'

'They're not,' Steve answered. 'Only, Ben here thinks you can have your tubes snipped and keep it a secret from everybody. It's fine if you don't push your luck ... but I think you pushed your luck, didn't you, bruv?'

'You could say that. I'm going to have to take some paracetamol when we get back. Thank goodness there's no dancing at tonight's shindig. I've just got this nagging, dull pain all around my groin. It hasn't helped traipsing through the jungle like this. I'm going to need a day of rest tomorrow. If I can just make it through tonight, I'll be fine.'

'Okay, we're back, not a word to anybody – and that includes wives and partners,' said Steve. He paused and looked at his youngest brother. 'Sorry, Richard, I didn't mean to exclude you.'

Ben felt for Richard. He'd never found one special person in his life. He'd had girlfriends, but nothing that lasted. And there he was with family to spare. It was sad to him that Richard still seemed imprisoned by the past.

They headed off in different directions. Ben saw the light was still on in their room. He wanted to speak to Laura before they went to the celebration, it was important to smooth things over. They could talk properly once the party was out of the way. He slipped in through the side door to avoid having to walk through the central area in the main building. They were cutting it fine, the punctual members of the family would be gathering already, but he didn't want to walk in looking a mess.

'Where the hell have you been?' Laura asked. 'We're supposed to be downstairs now. I didn't know whether to wait for you or make a start without you.'

'I'm sorry, we got caught up in something—'

'Why didn't you let me know what was happening?'

'It's not like I could text you, Laura.'

'How is Mr Aquino?'

'He'll be fine. He had a small accident but he's okay.'

Ben didn't like lying but consoled himself that it was just a white lie, one that would be to the greater good. It would really set the cat among the pigeons if everybody thought Mr Aquino had been attacked. Even worse if they thought there was somebody else on the island with them.

'Anyway, get ready and let's go. Harper has been all unsettled this evening, we need a change of scene.'

Ben did as he was told, delighted that she hadn't pushed further to find out where they'd been or what had happened to Mr Aquino. He stepped out onto the veranda to take his shower, which he managed to successfully execute in the light thrown off from their room.

Within ten minutes he was cleaned up and ready to go. He took Harper from Laura's arms and she immediately settled with him.

'Typical, you push off for two hours then walk back in and she's all sweetness and light. Talk about a daddy's girl.'

'It's because she's not as used to me. I'm a novelty. Thanks for looking after her, Laura. I promise I'll help out more now.'

'Ben ...'

'Yes?'

'What we were speaking about earlier ...'

'I know, Laura. I've been thinking about it too. You're right about everything. We must talk. The way I feel at the moment, I'll be a completely captive audience tomorrow. I don't think I'll be able to move, I'm in so much pain.'

'Okay, tomorrow. We need to get away from your family and sort things out. We can't let things go on as they are.'

'Agreed. But first let's just enjoy tonight. I've got all my family together, it's my dad's seventieth and I want to have a good time. You too - whatever we decide to do, this is still Harper's family and you're a part of it. Get to know everybody a little better. I'm sure you'll find we're quite a likeable bunch when you get to know us.'

Ben walked over to her and gave her a kiss on the cheek.

'Okay, ready?' he asked.

Laura nodded and they walked along the long hallway and out into the central living area. Since Steve, Ben and Richard had left Mauricio and his wife to complete the final preparations, they had transformed the place. The lights were dimmed and there were candles on the long table. Bottles of wine and bubbly were positioned all along it and there were name cards at each neatly laid out place setting. There was a pile of presents on a circular table that had been moved to the side of the room and everyone was standing around chatting, drinks in hand. They were dressed smartly but casually, looking relaxed and happy. How right they'd been not to say anything about Mr Aquino or the mysterious and unannounced guest who was living on the other side of the island. There was just Richard and Steve to come, they were probably still getting changed after the impromptu excursion through the jungle.

Outside, Ben could hear the wind blowing, but inside it was warm, welcoming and convivial. This was his dad's seventieth birthday, it took an occasion like that to bring all the family together. And whatever might have happened in the past, it looked like everybody was on their best behaviour and looking forward to an evening of fun and celebration. Tony Harrington's special night showed all the signs of being a birthday party to remember.

CHAPTER FIFTY-ONE

The Island: The Day Of The Party

It wasn't long before Steve and Richard arrived – together. They looked flustered, as if they'd had words. That wouldn't be unusual, and Ben reckoned he wouldn't have been the only one to notice it. He sidled off to speak to Richard at the earliest opportunity.

'Wow, Dad's hitting the bubbly a bit hard, isn't he?' Richard observed.

'Yes, I suppose he is. But it is his birthday. What were you and Steve talking about on the way over here? You looked a bit out of sorts when you arrived?'

'Don't ask. You really don't want to know.'

'I do want to know. What was it? You're not going to be at each other's throats again this evening, are you?'

'I hope not. But you know that clipping you were talking about earlier?'

'Yes, what about it?'

'I just asked Steve if he knew who he was. Maybe you

didn't see his face when you mentioned that cutting, but he was rattled by it. He got all testosterone fuelled with me, told me not to stick my nose in where it's not welcome. You don't think he's connected with Dad in some way – with the business?'

'I wouldn't know. I never got involved with the business, just like you. Oh shit, Mina's going to do her musical interlude. Please don't let Gaby sing!'

Ben burst out laughing and it hurt. He made a sound that was half-joy, half-pain.

'I'd forgotten that. God, it was so funny.'

There was silence for a moment as they thought back to Gaby's wedding where she'd insisted on singing a solo of *I know him so well* while poor old Nigel had to sit there grimacing through bum notes and incorrectly rendered lyrics. Ben and Richard had nearly wet themselves, they'd been laughing so hard. As it turned out, Gaby didn't know Nigel so well, as he left her soon after Jaxon was born and was never seen again.

The room fell to a hush and Mina took out her violin. Ben noticed Mauricio slipping out of the kitchen. He was probably taking the opportunity to check on Mr Aquino while the family were occupied.

'So, Mum and Dad finally talked me round into doing a little performance for Grandad tonight. It's pretty embarrassing actually – so sorry Alice, Ted, Jaxon and Henry, but it's what the olds want ...'

'The little cow,' Steve muttered.

'So, in the light of my little announcement earlier, I thought I'd start with *Constant craving* by K.D. Lang.'

Steve lunged forward, but Kiki took his arm.

'Oh, we love this one!' Susan clapped. 'Thanks, Mina!'

Ben heard Kiki warning her husband.

'Leave her to it, Steve. Tony and Susan don't mind, just indulge her for one night.'

'She's trying to wind me up. I know she is.'

'So what? She's a teenager, that's what she does. It's your dad's birthday, just let it slip.'

'She's good,' Ben said to Kiki, once he sensed that the coast was clear and he was safe from entering any marital conflict.

He saw Alice at the edge of the room gently rocking Harper in her arms. Overcome by a feeling of love for her, he watched her for a few minutes, admiring the adult that she'd become.

There was a ripple of applause. Everyone was starting to move back into their huddles when Gaby stepped forward and stood by Mina.

'Just one moment, everybody. We've one more song for you.'

'Oh shit!' Richard whispered, taking care that he wouldn't be heard by Kiki.

Ben scrunched his forehead to signal to him to keep his voice down, but he was trying his best not to laugh.

'To show solidarity with the brave announcement that Mina made today, we're going to sing a surprise song for you this evening.'

'Oh no, she's really doing it!' Richard was trying desperately to stifle his laughter.

Gaby leaned over and hugged Mina as she perched on her chair, guitar on her knee.

'Well done, I'm proud of you, Mina!'

Mina began to play the first few bars of Adelle's *Hello* and Gaby was straight into the song, starting flat and not quite getting the lyrics right. She sang it with the passion and earnestness of a sixties protest song, but it sounded like a strangled cat.

Richard couldn't contain his laughter, and that set off Ben.

'More a case of *goodbye,* I'd say,' Ben laughed.

'Jesus, guys. Have some manners,' Kiki hissed.

Ben felt suddenly ashamed, but Richard couldn't help himself.

'I'm sorry, Kiki. It's not Mina, she sounds great, but just look at Gaby. You'd think she was on stage at Wembley stadium.'

Then Kiki started to laugh. Every wrong note Gaby hit, every incorrect lyric, made her laugh harder.

Having been granted permission to rejoin the jollity, Ben started to chuckle again. But Kiki had made the fatal error of taking her eye off Steve. He still looked livid with his daughter for making such a spectacle of her newly revealed sexuality.

'She does this every time,' he muttered. 'Trying to humiliate me in front of everybody. She needs to learn a lesson.'

The kids were all dancing at the front, oblivious to the tensions that a simple song could ignite. Alice was rocking Harper in time to the music and every time she changed direction Harper would give a scream of joy. Jaxon and Ted were doing a mock tango and Henry was dancing with Susan, being a complete gentleman with his grandmother. Laura and Tony looked comfortable with each other, chatting and laughing. And then Steve spoiled it all.

The moment the song finished, he lunged forward and took the instrument out of Mina's hand. She looked shocked, as if a spiteful child had just grabbed her favourite toy. Her face turned from a smile to a frown and Gaby turned around to face him, annoyed that he'd broken into the small applause that had been coming her way.

'That's quite enough for now,' he said. 'Thank you, Mina, for the performance, and thank you for so carefully selecting the songs.'

'I thought it was lovely,' Susan said, still holding on to Henry as if they were waiting for the next dance to begin.

'Steve,' Kiki warned from the far side of the room, now recovered from her laughing fit.

The dark cloud Steve had suddenly cast across them hung there for a moment as everybody figured out what to do or say next. It could have gone either way, but it was Laura, of all people, who saved them.

'I just want to say a few words,' she began.

Oh shit! Ben wondered what was coming next.

Susan glanced at him from over by the cake. What was she going to say?

'I just want to thank you all for making me so welcome at your family event. And for being so lovely with Harper.'

She beamed at Alice who kissed Harper on her forehead. She giggled and there was a collective 'Ah!'

'I appreciate your friendship and I realise it doesn't come easily for everybody. Diana, I want to thank you and the kids especially for being so gracious.'

Diana nodded and smiled but looked uncomfortable. Ben thought that if Laura wasn't careful, Tony would have a hard job to beat this with his own birthday speech. But then she turned it back to their host.

'Before we sit down and eat this splendid meal, I hope you don't mind if I raise this toast to Tony Harrington, his amazing business, his talented wife and his wonderful family. To the Harringtons!'

Those who had glasses raised them, those who didn't

just made the movement with their hands. Laura had successfully managed to take the heat out of the room and Ben was grateful to her. The conversations started once again and they began to move towards the long table, each person finding their place name and taking their seat.

Ben looked over to where Analyn Villanueva was standing by the door to the kitchen. She seemed distracted, as if she was missing her husband. And, for the first time, Ben wondered where Jeremiah was. He'd assumed their son would be playing some part in the event. He was like a cat, coming and going as he pleased.

He dismissed the idea and set about his prawn cocktail, hungry now after their earlier wander in the jungle. As the table settled down and the main courses arrived, Ben looked around and thought what a lovely scene it was, the entire family together like that, several generations of the Harrington family at a single table. Then the generator died and the room was plunged into darkness.

CHAPTER FIFTY-TWO

1998: The Fifth Lie

Steve Harrington was the kind of man that Kyle Hunter disliked. He was a little shit, a young man born into privilege and lacking the maturity and self-awareness to know how to handle it properly..

Drug use made Kyle nervous. Steve was into cocaine, the drug of choice for the affluent and the stupid. It made him think he was invincible, and coupled with a growing drink problem, Steve was fast becoming a liability. But Kyle did not want to kill the golden goose.

Steve's father was a coward, but that made him easier to manage. After his scare at the factory, it was only to be expected that Tony might want to distance himself from the business. But he'd gone all the way, effectively handing over the keys to his oldest son who was barely out of university.

Kyle had been using his contacts to monitor Steve for some time. At university he was popular, among his own kind. Although still a student, he'd liked to live the high life, surrounded by loud friends and always with a different girl. But he was running up debts, his lifestyle out-pacing his income. After graduating, he moved back home and was immediately put in charge of the family business. He would function at a high level by day, running and growing Harrington Meats with the cocky self-assurance of youth, but at night his dark side would emerge and the drink, drugs and women would dominate. Kyle thought Steve needed a wife – or at the very least, a steady girlfriend. He had nothing to anchor his behaviour and this made him danger-ous, a ticking bomb.

With Tony off the scene, the monthly cash deliveries continued, as did the night-time access to the factory facil-ity. Steve's behaviour was not impacting on Kyle's work, so he maintained a cautious distance, watching him from afar. Until Steve came to find him. It was the last thing Kyle had expected. It seemed that while he had been watching Steve, Steve had traced his father's mystery business partner.

'I'm Steve Harrington, but you know that already.'

Steve held out his hand.

Kyle had seen everything in his life and he was experi-enced enough not to show surprise when Steve greeted him one night in the darkness at the rear entrance to the factory. He was just about to open up and start the preparations for the arrival of a body. It was a councillor, a man who'd been particularly obstructive over some land deal or other. Kyle didn't particularly care about the details. The land deal was worth millions, so the disposal of the corpse brought in a good percentage of that for his services.

Kyle didn't take Steve's outstretched hand. This was an immediate disruption to social norms. He knew it would unnerve him, he wouldn't know how to react.

'You shouldn't be here. You know the terms of the agreement – your father will have explained. I would like you to leave.'

'It's my factory. You're using my premises. I have a right to know what you're doing here—'

Kyle's right hand shot out and grasped Steve's neck, tight.

'You're putting a very important business arrangement at risk here, you drugged-up prick. You need to think very carefully about what you say next.'

Steve could barely breathe, but his eyes were calm. Either it was the cocaine making him completely deluded about what was happening or he had another play to make, one in which he had a lot of confidence.

Kyle released his grip slightly.

'You've got one minute to convince me you have a good reason to be taking up my time. After that, things are going to become difficult for you.'

'I want to make a deal.'

Kyle's hand relaxed. This time he was the one who was taken by surprise.

'There's no deal you can offer me that would interest me.'

'I think there is. We can help each other. I have some unique information and I suspect that you have a network that can make things happen.'

'Half a minute left,' Kyle said menacingly. This boy was cocksure, but he certainly had the guts that his father lacked.

'The cocaine scene is run through the local chief constable,' Steve began. 'I have the evidence. I know most of their movements now. It must be worth a fortune. I propose that we compromise him and move in on his scene. What do you think?'

It wasn't the most conventional of business meetings, but it resulted in a very productive relationship between the three men. Granted, the chief constable was a not-so-willing partner, but photographs of his cocaine-fuelled orgies with two of the higher-class city rent boys and video footage of a meeting in Amsterdam with his main supplier soon convinced him to get on board. Steve and Kyle developed a nice sideline between them, never dealing with the drug-selling directly, but simply managing the supply chain. They were on first name terms – Kyle even had a spare key to Steve's bachelor flat. But, regardless of this new business relationship, Steve never knew how the factory was used at night – their connection was strictly drugs.

It took the crash for Kyle to finally convince Steve to come off his own product and get himself a family life. Kyle was with Agnes when the call came in. His wife was not unaccustomed to late-night calls so she knew the drill. Kyle would kiss her, excuse himself, then take refuge in his study. She'd hear his deep, muffled voice travelling along the downstairs hallway and, call completed, he would say a hasty goodbye and leave the house. When this call came in, it was later than usual, almost midnight. Kyle pulled on his dressing gown and went downstairs. It was Steve, in a state of panic. The idiot!

'Have you been drinking? Were you using drugs? What speed? There was someone else in the car? For fuck's sake, Steve! Your brother? You think he's dead. What junction? Right, you make sure that the car lights are turned off and you walk away from the scene. Yes, I'll go to your flat. I'll sort it out. When the police come to speak to you, you were at your flat all the time. You got that? Okay, I'm on my way.'

Kyle's wife had never heard her husband swear like that. She could hear him downstairs kicking his office furniture and cursing. He came back to the bedroom, curtly told her to go back to sleep and changed his clothes. He was away in no time and didn't return until mid-morning the next day.

Kyle was furious with Steve. If he'd had any reservations about going into business with him, they were based on his use of drugs and alcohol. He'd done the lucrative deal against his better judgement but for a couple of years it had worked well.

He went to Steve's flat first, wearing gloves and observing all the precautions. He placed a call to the police reporting Steve's car as missing, identifying himself as Steve Harrington. He tidied up any evidence of drinking and scoured the place for drugs. He then left the television on and headed for Junction 36, the location Steve had given him over the phone.

Richard was still, his leg badly cut by glass and twisted at an awkward angle. His face had been protected by the airbags. Kyle shifted him into the driver's seat. He made certain that Richard's prints were on the wheel and the gear stick, then he checked thoroughly for any giveaway signs, any tiny detail which might have placed Steve on the scene. At least it was his car, most things could be explained away, he had every reason to have his stuff in there. Kyle checked Richard once again. He couldn't feel a pulse, he was as certain as he could be that he was dead. The poor lad had eighteenth birthday cards stuffed in his pockets. And at that point he realised – was this the Harrington child who had forced the split with Susan? The child he'd once considered might be his son? There was no room for sentimentality, this was business.

Kyle started the engine of the crashed car and switched its lights back on. He ran down the embankment and quickly drove off before anybody could pass him on the quiet stretch of motorway. The car would be seen and reported, but it would be difficult for the cops to pin down a specific time for the accident. Now he had to create the wriggle room for Steve, an alibi was what was needed. It was time to call in a favour.

When Kyle got back to Steve's flat, he found him freshly showered and sober.

'This is the last night you take cocaine, do you understand?' he said.

'I understand.'

This was no negotiation.

'A woman is going to come around to the house shortly. Leave the door ajar when I go, don't make her knock and alert your neighbours. You spent the evening with her in your flat, you weren't aware that your car had been stolen until you went outside to see if you'd left your keys in the vehicle, as you were unable to locate them. Where's your phone? Give it to me. You lost it earlier this evening. First thing tomorrow, order a new one. Did Richard call the house? Right, you told him to take a taxi when he called, as he sounded drunk. The official story will be that he was pissed with you and found your car with the keys in it. To get his revenge on you, he stole your car. It's a good job your brother is dead because he's about to become a scapegoat for your family.'

CHAPTER FIFTY-THREE

The Island: The Day Of The Party

'What happened to the lights?'

'It's just the generator, it must have misfired.'

'What great timing that was.'

'Where is Mauricio? He'll know what to do.'

Harper began to cry. The candles on the table flickered, casting shadows on the walls.

'Woah, steady everybody, calm down!' Ben said, attempting to calm the flurry of voices. To his surprise, they listened to him. He wasn't quite sure how to respond.

'Look, stuff like this must happen all the time on the island. It's probably something to do with the storm. Let's eat our main courses before they go cold, and when Mauricio comes back we'll get the generator working again. Besides, all those candles on Dad's cake will look better with the lights off.'

There was laughter and they got back to their food.

Analyn Villanueva sidled up to Ben, as the self-appointed leader, and spoke quietly to him.

'I am worried about my husband – he has left me to serve the food by myself. That is unlike him. I am concerned that there might be a problem with Mr Aquino.'

'I'm sure everything is okay,' Ben replied quietly. 'Let's get the cake cut and then everybody will start chatting again. If Mauricio is not back by then, I'll go and find him myself.'

She nodded, clearly reluctant, but Ben didn't want to cause even more disruption. The main course was soon finished and it was time for Tony to cut the cake. Ben was distracted now. They needed to get the generator going. Where was Mauricio?

'Okay everybody, gather round. It's boring speech time!'

There were groans from the children and laughter from the adults. Ben looked for Harper and noticed she was now with Diana, which seemed quite a leap of acceptance for one evening. Perhaps there was a way out of all this without everybody killing each other. Something caught his eye. Alice was exiting the room. He knew better than to ask a teenage daughter where she was going, but it seemed odd that she'd chosen that moment to leave.

'You will check on Mauricio?' Analyn reminded him.

'I'll go as soon as Dad finishes, I promise. He's probably just got caught up with something. It'll be alright, Analyn. I'm sure.'

'Thank you so much for joining me and my beautiful wife on this wonderful paradise island for my fiftieth birthday.'

There were groans from the children.

'I beg your pardon, my sixtieth birthday.'

'Higher! Higher! Higher!' they all began to chant in unison.

'Okay, okay, my seventieth birthday. I can't believe that I'm really that old. But looking around at my sons – and daughter – I can see that I'm not the only one who's getting on a bit.'

There were mock protests and laughter. Everybody was focused on Tony, and Ben wondered if he should slip out. Alice hadn't reappeared yet and he was growing concerned about Mauricio. Mr Aquino's wounds weren't that bad - he'd been gone well over half an hour by Ben's reckoning.

'I can't tell you how proud it makes me to look around this room and see my grandchildren all growing up so nicely. And whatever the circumstances, little Harper over there is a delightful addition to any family. Welcome to the Harringtons, Laura.'

Even in the poor light Ben could see that Laura was embarrassed by that, but she smiled politely and thanked Tony.

'There was another reason for me gathering you all here like this. Things are about to change for our family. This has been a long time coming.'

There was silence in the room now. Tony had the undivided attention of his audience.

'I'm afraid to tell you that I'm quite seriously ill. It's dangerous enough to finish me off, I'm afraid.'

'Oh my God, Tony ...'

'Dad ...'

'Oh no ...'

Tony held up his right hand to silence them.

'I'm not going to die immediately, you'll be pleased to hear. I've received some very good treatment in Australia, and I'm managing it with drugs. But some of you mentioned my weight loss, and you're right, my illness has forced me to change my diet quiet radically. I've got a serious heart problem, eventually it'll kill me.'

Ben's eyes filled with tears. Diana had moved up close to him and was holding his hand. There was shock around the room. This was some seventieth birthday.

'I don't want you to get all gloomy. I've got some time left, thanks to those Australian doctors and I'm putting things straight in my life. But whatever happens with my health, I wanted to be with you all on this special day. I wanted to enjoy your company one last time. And I want to speak to you all individually over the next couple of days. But I'm not going to say any more about that now. I want you to get back to enjoying yourselves, let's carry on with the celebrations.'

'Mauricio still isn't back, please would you try to find him?' Analyn said to Ben. 'I am really worried.'

'Go Ben,' Diana whispered. 'You look like you could do with a couple of minutes on your own. Poor Tony, what terrible news. I always thought he was indestructible.'

'Me too. Okay, I'm going to slip out. Do you know where Alice went? She left before Dad started talking.'

Diana looked around, she hadn't even noticed that Alice had gone. Tony was encouraging them all to carry on chatting, Gaby was hugging him, Steve was hugging Susan. It was all too much for Ben. Diana was right, he needed some air.

'I'll be five minutes. Save me some cake.'

'Has anybody seen the kitchen knife?' Susan asked, as he left the room. 'We must have misplaced it. We'll have to cut the cake with something else.'

Ben walked out into the night. The wind was blowing fiercely now. It took him by surprise. He looked over towards Mauricio's accommodation – the lights were on and it was easy to identify where he was heading. Still sore and uncomfortable, Ben walked towards the house. The door was open, banging against the wall as it blew to and fro in the wind.

'Hello?' he called, knocking to warn them that he was coming in.

'Mauricio? Mr Aquino? Oh, Jesus Christ!'

Mr Aquino was lying on the bed motionless, a crimson gash across his throat. A pool of bright red blood had soaked through the bedding and was dripping onto the ground. Slumped in the corner of the room was Mauricio, his eyes barely open, the cake knife thrust into his chest. Ben ran over to him.

'Mauricio, what happened? Can you speak?'

Something caught his eye from outside, a flickering light. He ignored it.

'I don't know what to do. Mauricio, what do I do? Do I leave it in, do I pull it out? What do I do?'

Mauricio was trying to say something to him. Ben couldn't hear. Outside the window the flickering light was becoming brighter.

'I'm going to pull it out, Mauricio. I'm going to pull it out and stop the bleeding.'

The knife was lodged between Mauricio's ribs. Ben grasped its wooden handle and gave it a sharp tug. He looked on in horror as Mauricio slumped over.

Suddenly he heard a huge explosion. The lights he'd noticed were flames. Still clutching the kitchen knife, he ran outside. The whole of the main house he'd only just left was engulfed in flames, its wooden structure offering no resistance to the rampaging fire. Everybody that Ben cared about was in that building.

CHAPTER FIFTY-FOUR

The Island: The Day Of The Party

Ben began to run towards the burning house, the flames high and fierce, fanned by the wild wind. He felt a sudden, sharp pain in his groin, but worse was the sickness deep in his stomach.

As he hobbled closer to the inferno, he saw the silhouette of a man moving away to the rear of the building. Was it Steve? Had he got them all out? The house had taken no time at all to set alight – he'd barely been gone for ten minutes and now it was ablaze. He screamed out loud, both at his physical pain and the thought of his baby in there with the rest of his family. The roof was burning – surely the flimsy leaves and bamboo would be falling in on them by now?

The front door, which he'd left only moments previously, was surrounded by flames. There was no chance he could get in that way. Limping, Ben fought through the pain of his operation to move round the outside of the house.

He'd used the back door earlier – maybe they'd escaped that way, but if they were still in there, he could guide them out. The rear of the house was smoking but not yet on fire. He guessed the blaze had been caused by the generator exploding at the side.

Moving the kitchen knife to his left hand, he grabbed the back door handle. It was closed. He pulled it again, then saw what was holding it. It had been nailed shut – there was a nail at the top and a nail at the bottom. It was enough to stop the door from being opened from the inside.

Ben moved to one of the windows. He could see Steve slumped over by the far wall. The window frame had a single nail in it, enough to prevent it from being opened. He took the kitchen knife and began to dig it into the back door frame. He hacked around the nails, splintering the wood so he could flick them out.

He pulled open the door. Diana was resting against it with Harper still in her arms. Ben placed his hand over his mouth and tried to pinch his nose closed. He dragged her out onto the lawn, as far away from the house as he could. He was in excruciating pain now, but he fought through it. He had to get as many of them out alive as he could.

'Please God, let them be alive,' he prayed as he ran back to the house. Steve was coughing now, brought round by the fresh air rushing into the house.

'Jesus, Ben! They're all still in there.'

'Can you get up? I can't get them all on my own.'

'I'm so sorry I brought this on us.'

He was sobbing.

'Steve, we don't have time. Come on, we have to get everybody out of the house.'

Steve rallied and stood up. He had a shard of glass embedded in his leg. He winced as he moved. The two men stumbled towards the heart of the house. Tony was there, with Jaxon, they were exhausted, almost overcome by the smoke.

'Get Susan,' Tony said weakly. 'Make sure you get Susan. Don't let her die like this.'

Ben shook his shoulder.

'Dad, you need to stand up and get Jaxon out of here. Go that way and wait on the grass ... go!'

Steve had run into the house. It was full of smoke – it was almost impossible to see. Analyn had collapsed by the main window with Ted and Mina at her side. Again Ben saw that a single nail was preventing it from being opened. Somebody had done this; some evil bastard had locked them in and left them to burn. And what did Steve mean when he said he was the one who'd brought it on them? Was it the person in the hut on the far side of the island? The figure he'd seen running around the side of the house? There was no time to waste. Ben picked up a chair and rammed it against the window frame. Three blows and he had made a big enough gap to exit. Mina was still conscious.

'You have to help them out of that window!' he shouted against the roar of the flames.

'Mina! You have to do this. You get Ted and Analyn out, you understand?'

Steve emerged from the smoke, choking, his eyes streaming with tears.

'I got Kiki, Ben. She's safe. Who is left? Who don't we have?'

'Gaby. Gaby and Laura. Oh my God, Laura. And Alice, I don't know where Alice is.'

A large piece of wood fell from the ceiling sending a cascade of sparks across the room.

'Over there!' Ben shouted. 'Laura and Gaby are there. You take Gaby, I'll take Laura.'

They rushed over to the two women. Both were conscious – they'd kept low – but they were shocked and dazed.

'Where's Harper?' Laura screamed. 'I lost her. Where is she, Ben?'

'I got her, she's safe, Laura. Now get out of here, go! Go that way, the back door is clear.'

He looked around frantically.

'Where's Alice? I don't know where Alice is! She left the party when Tony started his speech, but I don't know where she went.'

Steve turned to look at him, tears streaming down his face.

'If she's in the bedrooms, Ben, she's gone. I'm so sorry. They're completely engulfed – we can't get near them.' Steve cried.

'This fucking island. We're completely shafted!' Ben yelled into the flames.

'This is my doing, Ben. You go outside, save yourself. Leave it to me.'

A ball of flames roared up in the centre of the room where only fifteen minutes before they'd been celebrating Tony's birthday.

'Henry, look, there's Henry! Get him out of here, Ben!'

'What about you, Steve? Your leg is in a right mess.'

'I'm coming, Ben, but first I've got to find Richard. He's the only one unaccounted for.'

'You make sure you do, Steve. Don't you dare die on me.'

He watched his brother disappear into the smoke.

Ben could barely move, but the adrenaline forced him to press on. He ran over to Henry who was out cold.

'Hang on in there, Henry!'

He stooped to carry him in his arms, but he was too heavy; the pain was just too much. Ben almost passed out with the exertion. Another section of ceiling crashed down behind him. He grabbed Henry's legs and dragged him out of the building. As he reached the back door, Tony came to help him and between them they carried him clear of the building.

On the grass, the family members were sobbing, coughing, comforting each other. Ben looked round in desperation.

'Alice, where's Alice?' he shouted, almost in tears. Mina rushed across the lawn towards him.

'Uncle Ben, she's okay. She's safe. She went for ... a walk. She wasn't in the building, honestly.'

There was a massive crash as the wooden frame of the house collapsed inward, the building now completely engulfed in flames. Whoever was inside would be dead. There was no way anyone could get out of there alive.

CHAPTER FIFTY-FIVE

The Island: The Day Of The Party

'Richard and Steve are still in there!' Ben shouted, unable to take in what he was seeing. He'd left the building only moments before it had burst into flames – what would they have done if he hadn't been able to break through the door? The entire family would have burned alive.

Tony came up to him, exhausted, barely able to stand.

'This is Kyle Hunter's work, Ben. I'm sure of it. He must be on this island somewhere. You can't let him get away with it. That bastard is not going to disappear into the night—'

'Who the hell is Kyle Hunter?'

'You know him already, Ben, but you don't realise it. You and Gaby are the only members of this bloody family with the integrity to keep clear of it. Remember that time you went back to the factory at night and I told you that what you saw was a friend processing game? I lied. It was Kyle

Hunter. He's nobody's friend, Ben. He did this. He's covering his tracks.'

'Jesus, Dad. I can't take this in.'

'Go after him, Ben. Take that knife over there – he's a dangerous bastard.'

Ben saw the kitchen knife discarded on the grass where he'd left it after breaking through the door. It was still splashed with blood. Ben wanted to stay with the others, he was desperate for rest, his entire body felt flushed of all life.

'Uncle Ben, I found Alice's stick!' Jaxon said.

'Where? Where did you find it?'

'By the path over there. Just at the beginning of the trees.'

'Okay, I'm going into the jungle. Dad, look out for Steve and Richard. I hope to God they made it out. And find out if there's any way we can get a message to the mainland to raise the alarm.'

'Where are you going, Ben?'

Laura and Diana asked the question at the same time. They were nursing Harper together, while still coughing themselves.

'Alice is out there somewhere.'

'And Jeremiah.' Analyn began to cry. 'Where are my Jeremiah and Mauricio?'

Gaby moved over to comfort her. Ben couldn't tell her yet – he slid the kitchen knife away from her view in case she figured it out.

'I'll find Jeremiah,' he said. 'I'll find Alice too.'

He set off into the jungle. He was in so much pain now but he had to fight through it. He had no choice. This time there was no flashlight, only the flares shooting up from the fire which lit his way up to the fallen tree. As he ducked around its side, putting his hand out in the darkness to feel for any undergrowth, he saw lights in the distance, way ahead. Two of them, roughly where the isolated hut would be.

He did his best to recall the details of the path through the jungle. If he kept to the track, he'd be okay, but if he wandered off he could be lost until daylight. He didn't have that luxury. Ben stumbled on. He was slowing now. He held the kitchen knife tight, not knowing what he would do with it if he found this man. What had Tony said? He knew him already? What did he mean by that? Then he remembered the newspaper clipping. Was that him, the man in the cutting? Is that why it had been taken? Was he clearing up some sort of mess?

Ben was almost upon the lights now, but he'd been wrong. This wasn't the hut, it was some place he didn't recognise further along the beach. In the distance he could see the hut and the boat was still there too. He watched as a man's form moved between the hut and the boat. Tony was right. If this was the person who'd started the fire, it looked like he was getting ready to disappear into the night.

Ben crept as close as he dared to the edge of the foliage. There was the crunch of a twig. The man turned around, alerted by the noise.

'Step out from the bushes!' he called. 'I have a gun trained on you. If I hear you move, I'll shoot.'

Ben cursed. Was the man bluffing?

'I see you over there!'

The man was moving directly towards Ben, his hand poised as if he was holding a weapon. Ben's hand tightened around the kitchen knife. Could he use it in a fight? Could he even fight at all in his state?

'Come out of the bushes!'

Ben knew the game was up. He moved forward, the

knife still in his hand, stepping out of the bushes onto the soft sand of the beach. There were worse places to die.

The man picked up a lamp and shone it in Ben's direction. He was dazzled, but as his eyes acclimatised he saw who he was looking at. The man must have been in his sixties or seventies, but still had a mane of dark hair. He was tall and sturdy. Even in that light, Ben could tell he was the man in the newspaper cutting.

'So, it's you, Ben. That makes sense.'

'Are you Kyle Hunter?' Ben replied angrily. 'Are you the man who broke into my house?'

Kyle laughed.

'That'll be me! You're the last member of the Harrington family I have to meet. Oh, and Gaby of course. I feel like I've known you all for a long time.'

'Who are you? Did you start that fire? You know I got them out, don't you? You know we got away?'

'Yes, I've figured that out. You Harringtons really are a pain in the arse. But not to worry, there's a Plan B. It's messier but it'll do the job.'

'Why would you want to destroy a whole family? You don't even know me, or Laura, Diana and the kids. What did we ever do to you? And why did you break into my house?'

'I was checking for evidence. I found a newspaper cutting of me after I was fined for speeding outside a local primary school – I was pleased I caught that. Your family are all collateral damage, Ben. It was too good an opportunity to miss, you all gathered here on this island. I've been monitoring your father's emails for many years now. It wasn't very nice of him to leave me out, but never mind, I just invited myself.'

Ben was inching closer to Kyle. He was making a bad

job of it – he couldn't conceal the pain as he winced with each tiny step. Just as he was about to make his move, Kyle planted his foot firmly in Ben's groin. Howling with pain, Ben dropped the knife and fell to the ground. Kyle kicked the knife out of his reach.

'I may as well make a start with you, Ben. I'm sorry it had to be this way. I'll finish off the rest of the family and be away from here before daylight. I do love these dodgy island jurisdictions. When I started out in the business it was only fingerprints a man had to worry about. All this DNA lark makes the job much harder. That's why I'm retiring from the business. And that's why Harrington Meats is closing down as from today.'

Kyle placed his gun in the waistband of his trousers, then walked over to Ben who was still writhing in agony on the sand. With the strength of a bull, he put his arm around Ben's neck, pulling him up off the ground and beginning to make the fatal twist.

CHAPTER FIFTY-SIX

The Island: Three Days After The Party

Ben thought it was the koel again at first, then he realised it was Alice's voice. He'd lost track of where he was. One minute it was the island, now ... somewhere completely different. Alice was talking to somebody outside, it was a voice he didn't recognise. Ben closed his eyes and drifted back off to sleep. Alice was alive, he'd heard her. Harper was out, Laura and Diana had escaped, Ted was safe. He was in a room now, not the hut. His family were there too. The people he cared about most were alive.

'You've been out cold for days, Dad.'

'Alice?'

Was he still in the same place? He thought not. The koel had gone. But he could still hear Alice. Ben forced his eyes open. A hospital. How had he survived? The last he remembered, that man was about to tear his head off.

'Welcome back, Ben!'

It was Diana. She was smiling. She had several dressings on her face, her skin looked raw in places, but she was alive.

'I feel like shit,' he said.

Then he thought back to the fire.

'Steve, what happened to Steve? And Richard?'

'Take a moment,' Diana calmed him. She sat at the side of the bed and took his hand. It felt familiar, the way the world was meant to be.

'It's all a bit of a mess,' she said, her eyes tearing up.

'Oh Jesus, who else died?'

Ben wanted to sleep again, he wanted the oblivion.

'Steve didn't make it, I'm sorry,' Diana said, tears now streaming down her face. 'I'm so sorry, Ben. Everything is such a huge mess.'

'What about Richard? Did Richard get out?'

'Uncle Steve saved his life,' Ted said from the other side of the room. Ben looked over, he was sitting in one of the two chairs that had been placed in the small room.

'He got him out of the side window, but the building collapsed before he could get out himself.'

'I can't take it in.'

His brother, dead. It was unbelievable.

'Steve wasn't who we thought he was,' Diana began cautiously. 'There are a lot of secrets in your family, Ben. That's why all this happened.'

'What secrets? What secrets could be so bad that a man would want to burn an entire family?'

'It's not a pretty story, Ben. I'm sorry. Your dad ... Tony—'

'They've arrested Grandad!' Alice broke in.

'He confessed everything,' Diana continued, uncertain whether Ben was ready to hear this.

'I want to know. Tell me.'

'Your dad and Steve were mixed up in some bad business, Ben. It's horrible. That man – Kyle Hunter – he was responsible for all of it. When your dad got the diagnosis for his heart problem, he was going to tell the police everything. After his seventieth birthday. He wanted us all together one last time. Then he was going to confess everything before he died and let Steve off the hook. A completely clean start for Harrington Meats. But Kyle Hunter had been monitoring his emails for years and decided to use it as an opportunity to cover his tracks. It seems he was looking forward to retirement too, but he wanted to make certain nothing could come back and bite him in the arse.'

'I can't take this in, Diana. Is it really true? Did Dad say this?'

'Yes, it's what he told the police, and then Susan told us. It turns out she had her own secrets with this man.'

'For Christ's sake, how have I missed all this stuff? It's been going on right under our noses.'

'Richard is Kyle Hunter's child. It's why Tony always hated him so much. And the crash – it was Steve. He set Richard up. He left his own brother for dead. Richard has always known it but none of us listened.'

Diana was crying now. Ben wanted to scream. It was an assault on his mind, the destruction of everything he thought he knew.

'How did I get away from that man? I thought I was dead.'

'It was me!' Alice said. 'I saved you. With Jeremiah.'

'How on earth could you have saved me, Alice?'

'Give me some credit, Dad. I'm an adult now. You treat me like I'm a three-year-old still, but I'm perfectly capable.'

Diana helpfully filled in the gaps.

'They were making out further along the beach when they heard Kyle preparing the motorboat—'

'I'm old enough!' Alice interrupted. 'I really like Jeremiah – he's hot!'

'I don't know if I can take any more,' Ben protested. 'I thought I knew my family but you're all like strangers to me.'

'We saved you from Kyle Hunter. We hid in the bushes, but when you came along, we had to get involved. We couldn't let him kill you.'

'Is that why your dress was on the floor when I woke up?'

'As I said Dad, Jeremiah is hot!'

'You didn't kill him, did you?'

'No, we hit him on the head with a chunk of driftwood. We tied him up, then left everything in a neat pile for the police. Jeremiah's dad is recovering in hospital, it's horrible what happened to him.'

'Mauricio survived that? Thank God! You're an amazing kid, Alice Harrington. Don't ever let me treat you like a baby again.'

'Speaking of babies, there's somebody here to see you.'

Diana got up off the bed and helped Laura as she came through the door, Harper in one arm and a large bunch of yellow and red flowers in the other. Alice was quick to take the baby from her and Laura gave Ben a long, deep hug.

Then she held Ben's hand and squeezed it. It was nice, but not the same as when Diana did it.

'Ben, Richard told me what Steve's last words were. I thought I should tell you straightaway. I reckon he was at least trying to put things right. He saved Richard, you know. They'd both be dead if it wasn't for what Steve did.'

'What did he say?'

'He said, "I owe you this one, bruv." Those were his last words to Richard. Richard says he can't think of another way that Steve could have ever made it up to him. He's resented him all his life, but he says he can start to forgive him now.'

'What about Kiki and the kids?'

'What do you think?' Laura said, her eyes full of sorrow.

Ben looked around the room, surveying the faces of the people who meant the most in the world to him. There was Diana, Alice and Ted, and his new family, Laura and Harper. He loved them all, but they had some serious talking to do.

'What a bloody family we are!' he said. 'We'll get through this together, we'll work all this out. Only this time, we'll do it without any lies.'

If you enjoyed this book, you'll love the Morecambe Bay series of psychological thrillers. Nine books and non-stop suspense. Available in paperback and e-book formats.

AUTHOR NOTES

So Many Lies is my eighth thriller and I can't believe I've written that many now. This is another psychological thriller which is based upon many real-life experiences and, although my dad's seventieth birthday was nothing like what happens in the book, I will tell you upfront that this story was inspired by the big family get-together we had to celebrate that event.

It's always struck me as fascinating how family gatherings are a hotchpotch of resentments, unspoken frustrations, old feuds and tensions between various family members or spouses. When you get extended family members crammed into the same room for one event, it can be a highly combustible situation. It's a combination of high expectations, historical issues, other people's children, elderly relatives who might be insensitive or just plain difficult – you name it, you're bound to have encountered it at a family get-together!

So this book is entirely about the complicated relationships and loyalties that make up family life and the events and deceptions that can tear it apart.

As with Pete Bailey in the *Don't Tell Meg* trilogy, I didn't want Ben to be an unsympathetic character. As a middle-aged guy myself I see men of my age in second relationships with younger women who often want to have children with their older partner – understandably so. With my family all grown up now I have to admit to a certain amount of horror at that prospect, particularly now I'm in my mid-fifties.

So Ben, just like Pete Bailey, has made a bad decision in a moment of weakness and it's messed up his life and his relationship with his wife. But he's not a bad man, he's just flawed, like so many of the characters in my stories. The older I get, the more empathy I have with the mistakes and missteps that people make in their lives. Most people, myself included, are just bungling their way through life, making screw-ups and experiencing some successes along the way. Most of us aren't bad, we're just human, and I love to explore that in my stories.

I really wanted to have a disabled character in this book and Alice Harrington is based on somebody that I follow online who has cerebral palsy and is quite simply an excellent ambassador for people who live with that disability. I'm not going to tell you who she is, but Alice was inspired by reading her excellent blog posts and learning about her experiences and difficulties in life.

Alice is a strong, capable and determined young woman and I wanted to involve her in one of the surprises at the end of the story to show how Ben's concerns for her future and welfare are unfounded. He demonstrates the concerns of a father, but Alice shows him that she is an impressive young woman who is perfectly capable of making her way through life on her own terms.

I mentioned characters who aren't necessarily bad, but

Kyle Hunter is just plain evil. I thought it was fun to have a scene in his garden where he is admiring his plants to contrast the barbarism he shows elsewhere the book. The funny thing is that even baddies have hobbies and can like the simple things in life, such as a lovely garden, an afternoon out in the sun and a nice, comfortable retirement.

Quite a lot of my books show people who have to make decisions based upon their precarious financial state. I like to ramp up the pressure on my characters and place them in a pot of water, then turn on the gas ring and see what happens. I think that relationship troubles and money pressures can make people do some silly things and you read a lot about this in my books. I do enjoy exploring human flaws and pass no judgement on my part – well, unless it's a black-and-white situation as with Kyle – I just like to show people muddling through and thrust into extraordinary situations to see what they'll do.

Much of this book was based on real-life experiences but, as ever, the details are changed, the characters are fictional, and it is all a figment of my imagination! However, Ben's unfortunate experiences with his vasectomy are entirely based on my dad's operation and the basics of the story are true. He ignored the advice of the doctor to take things easy, went into work, stayed late and ended up having to get one of the security guards to send him off in an ambulance because he pushed himself too hard and was in terrible pain.

So with Ben I was keen for the reader to feel that sense of a crisis building up throughout the story, confident in the knowledge that this was going to cause him some terrible problem most likely at a key point of conflict in the book.

When we celebrated my dad's seventieth birthday we didn't go to a desert island, but I was keen to place my characters in an environment where they can't escape. It's actually very difficult to isolate your characters in the 21st century. Think of Agatha Christie's *And Then There Were None*. She places her characters on an island, cut off by the sea, and at the time the story is set there's no such thing as a mobile phone – so all the characters are well and truly isolated.

In my psychological thriller *One Last Chance* I located my characters on a fort at sea to cut them off from all communication. Whenever I'm writing my books I try to put myself in the role of the reader and think 'Why doesn't he pick up his mobile phone and call the police?' When setting up a story you have to make sure that can't happen, so in *So Many Lies* I placed all my characters on a remote desert island where they're completely stuck.

The island on which this book is based actually exists in southeast Asia. You can find out more about it at docastaway.com and in fact those islands are not massively expensive to hire for a family event. It's the cost of the flights that would probably put the majority of people off.

Before writing the book I set up a Skype call with Alvaro Cerezo, the gentleman who operates those island holidays and got a lot of details about the jungle, the kind of beasts that might live there, the sea, night-time differences along the equator and how the accommodation would be set up, what the weather would be like and what it would be like to stay there. So again, if you thought it was a completely fictional concept, I tried to make the island location as accurate as I possibly could.

I must stress when talking about real-life influences that the people I have known and met have in no way been involved in anything like the kind of scenarios that I create in my stories – they simply provided an idea, a location or a character trait.

The meat business that is operated by the Harrington family is inspired once again by a real-life experience. When I was a teacher, many years ago now, I knew a family who ran a business which involved processing meat and I also had a student friend who worked in a meat-processing plant for the summer vacation and who recounted a tale of an accident involving one of the big meat-grinding machines.

I was also inspired by a very sinister scene in an excellent TV programme called *Gomorrah* which portrays Italian drug gangs, so I brought together all those ideas, firstly to create a business that the Harringtons could run and secondly to come up with something really horrible that could be done under cover of night in their factory unit.

I enjoyed playing with the release of information in this book, so that you read about the different lies which would eventually tear this family apart and each time I returned to that lie you learn something new about it that will colour your judgement about what had gone on.

I think the most shocking behaviour comes from Steve Harrington who, to all intents and purposes, is a respectable member of the community yet is quite happy to betray his brother to save his own reputation.

In many respects Steve is worse than Kyle – Kyle is just an evil man doing a job but Steve betrays a brother and lets down his family. I hope you agree with me that he gets what he deserves, but he does get a final moment to redeem himself.

I really enjoyed writing *So Many Lies* and I did ponder for some time about how Ben could resolve his family situation in the most honourable way, given that it was a bit of a mess for all concerned. I hope he managed to achieve that and everybody ended up getting what they deserved, some of it good and some of it bad.

If you liked this story and want to stay in touch, I'd be delighted if you registered for my email updates at https://paulteague.net/thrillers, as that's where I share news of what I'm writing and tell you about any reader discounts and freebies that are available.

Paul Teague

DEAD OF NIGHT PREVIEW

Sunday 00:23

There was a heavy thud against the bonnet of the car. Something – or someone – had emerged from the woodland, out of the fog and the darkness, onto the road in front of them.

Lucy cried out, abruptly woken from her doze.

'What the hell was that?'

It was late and, bored of chatting through the day's events with Jack, she'd been half asleep.

'Shit!' he cursed, slamming on the brakes. The car swerved onto the muddy verge. They veered too far to the left, running into a shallow ditch, the wing striking a tree. Whatever it was, it had shattered the glass of the windscreen and Jack had lost what little visibility he'd had.

'That must have been a deer. It was huge.'

Jack pulled on the handbrake and put the gear stick into neutral. As if it mattered, they weren't going anywhere.

'What lights have we got in this bloody thing?'

He scanned the control panel of the car looking for the

interior light. Damn hire cars, he could never find the right switch without fiddling around for five minutes. It was cheaper to hire than it was to get the clutch changed in theirs. When he found the light switch they gasped as they saw what was splashed across the windscreen. Blood. A lot of it.

Lucy began to panic.

'Look at the mess on the window. What would do that?'

'Keep calm, Luce. I'm going out to take a look. You coming?'

'No thanks, I'll stay here. Put the headlights on full beam, you won't be able to see a thing out there. Take your phone too, you can use the torch.'

'Good idea,' said Jack, retrieving his phone from the glove compartment and opening the door.

'Christ, it's cold! Pass me my top, will you?'

Lucy reached over to grab his tracksuit top from the back seat. It was still wet. She handed it to him and then felt her ankle to see if her sprain from earlier was any better. It had been some run. They'd both done well to finish. And now it was a long drive home in the dead of night. They wanted to get back for Hamish, to be there before he woke up

'Be careful out there. It's muddy.'

'No phone signal,' Jack said as he stepped out of the car and looked at his screen. 'The car is fucked. This thing is going on a tow truck. Who knows where the nearest phone box will be, if there even is one ...'

His voice trailed off as he moved to the front of the car.

'Don't you think you should close your door?' Lucy called after him, but he didn't hear her. She tried to lean over to close it herself, but she felt a twinge of pain in her leg. A half-marathon, the first in quite some time too. Of course she was aching all over.

Jack continued to inspect the damage to the car. Lucy lowered her window as he came round to update her.

'It was big and heavy, whatever it was. There's blood on the bumper and all over the bonnet. It's made a right mess of the front. You did remove the insurance excess when you booked the car, didn't you?'

'Yes, it's fine, there's no excess. We can blame the bump in the car park on this too. It'll be less embarrassing than admitting we didn't see that low wall.'

'There's something moving over there. Please don't tell me it's still alive. I don't want to have to finish it off.'

'Is there a wheel wrench in the boot?' Lucy suggested. 'You could kill it with that. Is it cruelty to animals if you put something out of its misery?'

'Press that button next to your knee and open up the boot. I'll see if there's anything heavy in there. I can't see a bloody thing in this fog.'

Jack walked off, holding his phone out for light, for what little good it did him. Lucy gently stretched her legs, testing for pain and strains. She was stiff, but everything was moving fine. Carefully she eased herself out of the car. It was on a slope and she was getting out into a low ditch. As she took her weight on her injured ankle she became more confident realising that nothing seemed to be too badly damaged. She leant back into the footwell, fumbled around for the boot switch and heard the click as it opened. Jack was cursing several feet away. They might be needing that wrench.

Jack appeared out of the gloom. She saw the light from his phone first, then the fluorescent strips on his top. He was pale with shock, she couldn't remember when she'd seen him look like that. She immediately knew it wasn't good.

'What happened? What is it?'

Jack lurched to the side and threw up onto the muddy verge.

'It's a man,' he said, wiping his mouth with a tissue. 'We hit a man.'

'Oh, my God. Is he alive?'

'He's alive. I don't know what to do. He's barely conscious. Can you get a phone signal? Is there a first aid kit in the car?'

'Damn it, Jack. Where did he come from? We're in the middle of nowhere. How can we hit a man out here?'

'Check your phone, Luce, see if we can get some help.'

'No signal. Nothing. My battery's almost gone too. Where is he? You haven't left him in the road, have you?'

'What else could I do?'

There was a feeble moan up ahead.

They turned and walked to the front of the car.

'Jesus Christ, Jack.'

Lucy surveyed the bloody mess on the road. It was a man, forties she thought, his dark hair was greying. He wasn't dressed for the outdoors, he looked like he'd just left the office. He was wearing a shirt, no tie, and dark trousers. His right eye was blackened and bruised, his face scratched and bleeding. His leg was bent back awkwardly, exactly as he'd fallen after being struck. Bone was sticking through his torn trouser leg. His thick glasses were damaged.

This time it was Lucy who threw up. She'd seen things like that on TV, but with a real person lying there, crying with pain, it got the better of her. She wiped her face, as Jack had done, and walked back over to him to try and figure out what to do next. She struck something with her foot and knelt down to inspect it. It hadn't felt like a stone or a stick. It was the man's wallet. She picked it up, they'd need it for identification when help came.

'What shall we do?' Jack asked. 'I don't know whether we should move him or leave him here. We might do more harm than good if we carry him to the car.'

'What's your name?' Lucy asked, finding the courage to bend down and get closer to the man. He was struggling not to pass out, muttering urgently. She put her hands on his head to try to make him more comfortable, but he flinched.

'Careful, Lucy, he might have broken his spine. We can't just move him, we'll need to get some help.

'What the fuck am I supposed to do? He's in pain, he could be dying. I wasn't the dickhead who hit him anyway!'

And there it was again. Her rage could surface at a moment's notice.

'Look, Luce, we're going to have to go for help. One of us will have to stay with him. We'll need to find the emergency triangle in the back of the car and set up some sort of cordon or warning in case another car comes along the road. There's nothing else we can do.'

She knew that he was right. And it made sense for her to stay with the man. Her ankle was not as bad as she'd thought it was, but who knew how far it was to the next village? Jack would have to go.

'You get off, try and find some help. I'll make it as safe as I can here. Put your running bib on, you'll light up better if any cars come. In fact, get mine out of the car too, it'll make us both more visible.'

In silence they put on the safety gear that they'd used during the race only hours before. Jack moved to kiss Lucy, but she was in no mood for it.

'Be as fast as you can, Jack. I don't want to be left alone here with him.'

He touched her arm and jogged off into the thickening fog. The man became agitated. At first Lucy thought it was the pain, but he was desperately trying to get her attention.

'What? What is it? What's the matter?'

She leant in closer, his voice was so weak.

'Run ...' he said, his hand reaching up to hold her arm, 'run ... for your life!'

From nowhere came headlights on full beam, a vehicle revving hard, speeding towards them. Lucy flung herself out of the way. It struck the man, spinning his body with the force of the blow. Lucy gasped.

'Jack!' she screamed, but he didn't hear her, he was too far along the road.

The vehicle stopped beyond their own car, and she heard the change of gears as it started to reverse. The passenger door opened. She saw a hand, it was holding something. It was a gun. She saw the light as it fired, the bullet hitting the injured man's head, its impact spattering her with blood.

Lucy watched as the shooter fired a second bullet into the body and then levelled up his weapon to aim at her. She'd seen all she needed to. Still clutching the wallet, she turned towards the trees and did exactly what the man had told her to do.

She was running for her life.

Dead of Night is available as a paperback or e-book.

ALSO BY PAUL J. TEAGUE

Morecambe Bay Trilogy 1

Book 1 - Left For Dead

Book 2 - Circle of Lies

Book 3 - Truth Be Told

Morecambe Bay Trilogy 2

Book 4 - Trust Me Once

Book 5 - Fall From Grace

Book 6 - Bound By Blood

Morecambe Bay Trilogy 3

Book 7 - First To Die

Book 8 - Nothing To Lose

Book 9 - Last To Tell

Note: The Morecambe Bay trilogies are best read in the order shown above.

Don't Tell Meg Trilogy

Features DCI Kate Summers and Steven Terry.

Book 1 - Don't Tell Meg

Book 2 - The Murder Place

Book 3 - The Forgotten Children

Standalone Thrillers

Dead of Night

One Last Chance

No More Secrets

Two Years After

Friends Who Lie

Now You See Her

ABOUT THE AUTHOR

Hi, I'm Paul Teague, the author of the Morecambe Bay series and the Don't Tell Meg trilogy, as well as several other standalone psychological thrillers such as One Last Chance, Dead of Night and No More Secrets.

I'm a former broadcaster and journalist with the BBC, but I have also worked as a primary school teacher, a disc jockey, a shopkeeper, a waiter and a sales rep.

I've read thrillers all my life, starting with Enid Blyton's Famous Five series as a child, then graduating to James Hadley Chase, Harlan Coben, Linwood Barclay and Mark Edwards.

Let's get connected!
https://paulteague.net